SHINERS

SHINERS

A Novel

JOHN T. BIGGS

Bestselling Author of *Sacred Alarm Clock*

ROGUE
RIVER

An Imprint of Roan & Weatherford Publishing Associates, LLC
Bentonville, Arkansas
www.roanweatherford.com

Library of Congress Cataloging-in-Publication Data
Names: Biggs, John T., author
Title: Shiners/John T. Biggs
Description: Second Edition | Bentonville: Rogue River, 2024
Identifiers: LCCN: 2024936382 | ISBN: 978-1-63373-877-5 (hardcover) |
ISBN: 978-1-63373-878-2 (trade paperback) | ISBN: 978-1-63373-879-9 (eBook)
BISAC: FICTION/Magical Realism | FICTION/Southern |
FICTION/Visionary & Metaphysical
LC record available at: https://lccn.loc.gov/2024936382

Rogue River trade paperback edition December, 2024

Cover Design by Casey W. Cowan
Interior Design by George "Clay" Mitchell
Editing by Staci Troilo

I dedicate this novel to my friend, Glenna Gilstrap, who let me use her first name with no strings attached, and to my wife, Margaret Biggs, who took my last name when she had no idea how complicated it would make her life.

Acknowledgements

I'D LIKE TO give a special thank you to Bill Bernhardt, who has had an influence in almost all literature that has come out of the Sooner State in the last twenty years. I'd also like to thank Casey Cowan, the beating heart behind the original Oghma Creative Media and the steward of its conversion to Roan & Weatherford Publishing Associates. Casey has more brilliant ideas than belong in a single mind.

Prologue
A Miracle Girl For Sure

WHEN OLIVIA ANOLI opened her eyes, the only thing she knew for certain was that she had to make a bathroom trip really soon. She rubbed her belly, giving her unborn baby an indirect massage, hoping to stop its tap dance on her bladder.

She'd try to hold out a tiny bit longer because there were so many people in the room. Her minister, Reverend Cheetwood, stood on one side of her bed—which wasn't really her bed at all. This one had bars on the sides to keep her from rolling out. How would she climb over those things when she finally decided she couldn't put the bathroom off a second longer?

The man on the other side of the bed was a minister too. He favored her with a broad smile that would have looked more sincere if he didn't have a shiny gold cross inlaid in his left central incisor. Olivia recognized that smile from posters advertising charismatic tent revivals her significant other liked to attend.

A slightly overweight woman who seemed to be in charge crowded in. She wore a green scrub suit with a Choctaw Nation Health Care Center nametag that said, *HI MY NAME IS SYLVIA.*

"Y'all move aside and give my patient a chance to catch her breath. Comin' back from the dead is exhausting work."

Reverend Cheetwood took that as a sign to hold Olivia's hand. The fire-and-brimstone minister grabbed the other one. It looked like a tug-of-war was about to start, but the two men suddenly let go. They stepped back and looked at their fingers.

"Goddammit," the charismatic one said. "Pardon my French, but this girl's still full of electricity."

Olivia crossed her legs, looked at Sylvia, and asked, "*¿Dónde está el cuarto de baño?*" That was something new. She shook her head and repeated herself, hoping her question would come out in English the second time because she couldn't understand much Spanish, even if she was the one speaking it at the moment. *Baño* maybe, but that was about as far as her south-of-the-border vocabulary reached.

Sylvia shooed the preachers away from Olivia's bed and told her not to worry. "Weird things happen when a girl gets struck by lightning."

Lightning? That might explain the holes in her memory and why her arms and legs tingled like they were waking up from the world's biggest shot of Novocain. But when she tried to ask about it, her lips and tongue wouldn't follow orders. "*¿Qué sucedió? Relámpago?*"

No chance of her understanding any of that.

Reverend Cheetwood held his hands toward the heavens like God had just hit a fly ball and he meant to catch it. "And when Paul had laid his hands on them, the Holy Spirit came on them, and they began speaking in tongues and prophesying." He looked around the room. "Acts 19:6," he said, daring anyone to disagree.

Disappointment colored the charismatic minister's face when a regular preacher beat him to the punch. He rattled off a string of made-up words that sounded more like baby jabber than real language then finished with plain English and a big gold-cross smile.

"Pleased to meet you. My name's Reverend Junior Johnson."

His reputation—rousing sermons, prophesies, and faith healings lasting long enough to pack up the tent and get it to the next town—preceded him.

Sylvia escorted the two preachers as far as the door with some unladylike shoves and threats to call security.

Reverend Cheetwood protested but let her wrangle him into the hallway. He was a gentleman, but the other one... Olivia wasn't sure about Junior Johnson.

Her baby jumped against her rib cage, like a somersault, the kind of thing her grandmother said could wrap an umbilical cord around a baby's neck and choke it to death. That was probably one of those urban myths people were always going on about, but it was a mother's responsibility to worry. She pulled herself up in the bed and asked, *"¿Cómo está mi bebé?"* The thought was pure Oklahoma English—*How is my baby?*—but it twisted into Spanish as it rolled off her tongue. She tried again. Repeated herself slowly, folded her hands over her baby bump. The words stayed Spanish, but any woman could figure out the body language. Sylvia did.

The nurse threw a panoramic threatening look at the ministers then shut the door.

"Are you pregnant, sweetheart? Who's your doctor? Talk real slow and maybe I can understand."

Olivia hadn't broken the news to anybody yet. Not even Shorty, and he had a right to know. Maybe he'd make an honest woman of her this time. He hadn't married her after Jonathan was born. Promised he would, but Olivia didn't pressure him because she wasn't sure she was ready for that much honesty quite yet.

"No tengo doctor." Lucky for her the languages overlapped quite a bit.

"You're a miracle girl for sure. Struck by lightning. No heartbeat—not that anyone could find, anyway—for most of fifteen minutes." She counted off the inexplicable facts on her fingers. "Pronounced dead before you got to the hospital. Probably a mistake, but you never know."

Olivia didn't remember anything except waking up in a Choctaw Nation hospital bed speaking Spanish she couldn't understand to two ministers and a nurse.

Sylvia's face bore a permanent expression of understanding. She reached for Olivia's hand but pulled back when a spark of electricity snapped between them. "That long without oxygen. A million volts of electricity. That's more miracle than most would get." She tapped only her fingers on Olivia's belly and received another shock that made her recoil.

"You've got a decision to make if you're not too far along." After a deep breath, she patted Olivia's belly again. This time, despite the sparks, she didn't pull away. "Something you need to figure out for yourself before all these high and mighty men get into the act."

Sylvia talked a little longer. Olivia followed some of it: dementia, hypoxia, cerebral palsy. "No one knows what happens to an unborn child." She stopped and thought about a better way to make her point. "Nobody knows what happens to a fetus that's been electrocuted."

"Shorty." That word came out of Olivia's mouth in English, perhaps because it was a nickname. She didn't think Shorty would feel good about raising a child God had seen fit to strike with lightning.

So many bad things happened when men made decisions for a woman. She definitely had a lot to think about, but her baby reminded her about another important matter by pushing an insistent foot against her bladder.

"Got to pee," she told the nurse in Mexican flavored English. Maybe the miracle was beginning to wear off. She'd be able to think much more clearly after she'd paid a visit to the *baño*.

THE DOCTOR AND Shorty agreed the baby had to go. They explained it to Olivia. "You don't really have much choice." Didn't matter which man spoke because the two men were of a single mind and were in agreement on that matter.

Shorty clutched a *Book of Mormon* to his heart so he could absorb all its religious power. Not that he was Mormon. The book was a kind of religious rabbit's foot, something to make him feel like God was on his side while he talked Olivia into doing the convenient thing.

The doctor looked at his watch and pretended he didn't care one way or the other. "Your decision in the end of course, miss." He gave Shorty a look that told a totally different story. He'd already gone over the ins and outs of getting rid of Olivia's baby. "The procedure's totally safe. Hardly any complications. Nothing to worry about."

Unless she decided to keep this baby, and then there'd be plenty to worry about. Olivia thought she saw the doctor wink at Shorty before stepping out of the room. Nurse Sylvia was there, tapping her foot, crossing and uncrossing her arms, looking at Shorty like she had a pretty unflattering idea where he got his nickname.

The two preachers wanted to put in God's two cents worth, but Sylvia told them, "Wait in the lobby." She would have chased Shorty out too if he hadn't been the father.

"How come I didn't know nothin' about all this?" He complained like he had no idea where babies came from.

"Couldn't be helped." Olivia's English had come back and that made her situation seem a lot less miraculous. She still had an accent, like someone who grew up speaking Spanish and couldn't convince her tongue to forget the old days. "Just figured it out myself a little while ago."

That was a lie, and not the first she'd told Shorty, but it was more believable than most. He'd been doing his long-haul trucking thing, so he wasn't around when the morning sickness started, and she was over that part now. Her breasts had been sore for a few weeks. She'd been emotional. Things that used to smell good smelled rotten now. Her Clearblue digital pregnancy test device had told her the undeniable, one-word truth— *PREGNANT*—in easy-to-read letters, for only $24.99 plus tax. Shorty didn't know about any of those things, and he didn't need to know.

She cupped her hands over her baby bump and felt the life inside her do its best to make her uncomfortable with the doctor's recommendation. That probably meant her so-called fetus was a boy, getting an early start on causing women pain.

"Aren't there tests? You know, to tell us if the baby is all right?"

She wanted Sylvia to answer her question, but Shorty clutched his *Book of Mormon* a little tighter and said, "Reckon we should pray on it." He did that a lot, mostly when he and Olivia were likely to disagree. God spoke in tones only Shorty was able to hear and divine inspiration always seemed to go his way.

"Why don't you go out and get some coffee?" Sylvia bumped a hip against Shorty, daring him to resist her. She invaded his personal space with a pair of super-sized breasts he was clearly afraid of. She walked him to the door then shoved him hard enough to make him stumble into the hall. "We girls need to talk this thing over by ourselves." She raised her voice so the preachers could hear her all the way in the lobby.

Olivia waited to hear something that would make her feel better, but Sylvia's face told her that wasn't very likely.

"A pregnant girl's already got enough baggage to carry without some man adding the weight of a pair of testicles, but—unfortunately—everything the doctor said is true." The nurse crossed her arms and didn't say anything more for almost a minute. "There's a lot more to consider here than facts." There weren't any tests to prove the baby's brain was going to be in apple-pie order. When all was said and done, mother's intuition was as good as anything else. What Olivia had to ask herself was whether she was willing to take a chance that everything would be all right and how she would feel if the worst happened.

The baby turned somersaults again, much more than it had before the lightning strike. That could mean something bad, but was it bad enough to end the life she felt inside her? The doctor would forget about the baby seconds after the procedure was done. It might take a week or two for Shorty.

It would stay with Olivia forever.

The door pushed open and the doctor walked in. He gave the nurse a hard look. Shorty and the two ministers followed him.

"Looks like the girls are outnumbered again," Sylvia said.

The doctor tapped his watch and told Olivia it was time for a decision. "We can take care of your little problem, or you can put things off and take a big problem home with you."

"*No entiendo.*" She didn't have a clue what she told him, but it had the desired effect. The doctor blushed. He turned and left the room without another word.

"What did I say?" Olivia's English came back, dripping with Mexican charm.

"He went to school in Guadalajara," Sylvia said. "Any time he hears Spanish, he thinks people are insulting him."

"EVERY DAY YOU put this off makes the decision harder." The doctor assumed he knew how the decision was going to go in the end. Shorty was on his side, but he had never married Olivia and that legally put her in *no man's land.*

In Oklahoma, a man could come forward and assert his rights, but those rights had to be recorded first on a document registered by the County Clerk. Sylvia reminded the doctor that Olivia was still a single girl. She wrote it down on a clipboard and shoved it in front of his face.

"A clinic note a day keeps the doctor away," she said after the man with the white coat and the superior attitude marched out of the room. Shorty followed him down the hall, full of questions about paternal rights he might not have after all.

"I'm one-eighth Choctaw blood," Sylvia said. That was more than Olivia. More than most Choctaw these days. "The doctor doesn't have a drop. No need to worry about me getting fired even if the doc is right—and he probably is."

The two ministers came in while she explained to her patient one more time all the terrible things that could happen to a short-circuited, oxygen-deprived unborn baby.

Reverend Johnson said, "Abortion is murder."

Reverend Cheetwood frowned. "More like manslaughter I'd say."

The two men took up their usual positions beside the hospital bed and slipped into a stereophonic prayer about the sanctity of life. They had totally different praying styles but eventually came to the same conclusion—God might have struck Olivia's baby with lightning, but that didn't mean he wanted it to die.

"Not by your hand, anyway," Junior Johnson told her.

It seemed the almighty had some complicated rules that only applied to women.

"A child is a special blessing," he added. "One my dear Elizabeth never got to experience before the Lord called her home." He closed his eyes and mumbled a prayer that ended with "Sorry, darlin'," instead of "Amen."

"God had plans for every child," Reverend Cheetwood said. "Must have a real special plan for one He's marked with lightning."

Olivia's baby couldn't speak for itself, but it rolled around inside her and kicked and pushed and did everything possible to tell her it was alive. "I'm going to sleep on it," she told them with only the slightest hint of Mexico in her voice. "Come back tomorrow morning." The preachers wanted to pray over her some more, but Sylvia wouldn't allow it. She chased the men out of Olivia's room and showed her how to work the remote control for the TV mounted on the wall.

"Let me turn on some TV, sweetheart," the nurse said. "It always takes my mind off life-and-death decisions."

That didn't make a bit of sense to Olivia, but it didn't matter. Her life and death decision was already made. She just had to figure out the best way to break the news.

Olivia would never get used to waking up surrounded by people. The moment she opened her eyes, the doctor held his watch so she could see the second-hand jerking across the numbers. The jittery movement meant it wasn't a *real* Rolex, but it was a very convincing knock off.

He didn't bother repeating all the many reasons why she couldn't keep the baby.

The preachers mumbled nearly unintelligible prayers. Reverend Cheetwood's theme was being submissive to God's will, and Junior Johnson's dealt with what happened to people who weren't.

Shorty stood at the foot of Olivia's bed fanning himself with a copy of *Watchtower* with "The End of The World" printed across the top in giant black letters and "Good News" printed across the bottom in smaller ones. Ordinarily he'd offer an opinion, but the preachers had more pull with God and the doctor was a scientist. He reached into his pocket with his free hand and jingled his keys.

Olivia knew what he was thinking. He could be in his truck in a matter of minutes, and out of the state in a matter of hours. She might have the right to keep her baby, but good luck getting child support if things turned into a mess.

"I had a dream." She misquoted Dr. Martin Luther King, but the hint of a Spanish accent made it sound brand new.

The doctor looked at his counterfeit Rolex. He watched the second-hand tick away his valuable time.

The preachers stopped praying. Dreams were right up their alley. A dream from a woman who was struck by lightning and returned from the dead was solid gold. Shorty fanned himself so fast the cover of his *Watchtower* became a blur.

Nurse Sylvia said, "Tell us about it, sweetheart."

Olivia told a mixed-up Spanglish story featuring skeletons and luminous ghosts. There was a tall man with a missing hand and a long list of things that had been on God's to-do list for a thousand years.

"This baby boy is going to be born." She ended her story without a trace of Spanish accent. "The Good Lord has plans for him, like Reverend Cheetwood says."

"Well then," the doctor crossed his arms as if that might be the only way he could prevent himself from beating some sense into Olivia. "I wish you luck with your mentally-challenged messiah."

Sylvia scribbled something in the chart and followed the doctor out of the room.

The preachers took their places at the sides of Olivia's bed and pretended they would be around to help when things got tough. Shorty jingled his keys some more and pretended to be happy.

Olivia remembered some of the dream she described, but couldn't tell which parts were totally made up and which parts were mostly true.

She asked, "Do miracles always start with a lightning strike?"

Junior Johnson jumped in before Reverend Cheetwood could come up with a Bible verse. "When God wants to get your attention, He doesn't mess around."

A PROPHETIC DREAM wasn't enough for the doctor. He wanted a sonogram. Shorty could have been there, but he was on his way to Austin, Texas, delivering canned goods to a Walmart and picking up flat screen TVs from a Buy for Less warehouse.

"You can still change your mind about keeping the baby," Nurse Sylvia said. "Say all that religious talk was just hormones running wild. Men believe everything a woman does comes from hormone craziness." She advised Olivia to think about it one more time before she looked at the sonogram images.

Olivia had been thinking of little else since she woke up in a room full of people who all had opinions about her baby. Hard not to think about the little foot that pushed against her ribs and the little hand that pushed against her bladder. She had an image of her baby fixed in her mind already, maybe not as detailed as a sonogram, but everything important was there. Maybe the way she felt was hormonal madness, but that didn't change a thing.

———

PRACTICALLY EVERYTHING IN the room was paper covered. Olivia had on a paper apron. Sylvia wore a paper gown. The vinyl upholstered exam table was covered with a sheet of paper. All of it was an unpleasant blue turquoise color that reminded her of the luminous ghosts that paraded through her dreams. Would they go away when all of this was finished? Would she lose the electrical charge that made people afraid to touch her?

She hated the coarse feeling of the paper on her skin and the crinkling sound when she made the slightest movement. It would all be discarded at the end of the procedure. Thrown into a plastic bag and carted off to a landfill. What did the hospital do with discarded babies? Olivia didn't want to know.

As Sylvia applied a lubricant to her baby bump, Olivia felt electric current pass between them. The nurse clenched her teeth but didn't pull away—offering support, even if her patient made the wrong decision.

"*Muchas gracias.*" Olivia lapsed into Spanish again—an emotional language for an emotional moment. She watched images on the screen Sylvia turned her way after a final warning.

"Can't unsee a picture."

Olivia's mind had to put the pieces together—an arm, a leg, a head—as Sylvia moved the probe across her belly. There was her baby, incomplete but recognizable. Not a handful of cells that could be washed away without leaving a stain on her conscience. The nurse was right about not being able to unsee the image.

"These are digital measurements." Sylvia explained the lines that jumped along the baby's limbs and across its skull. "The program does it automatically."

New lines and new numbers appeared every time the baby turned or kicked, and there was a lot of turning and kicking.

The screen jumped. Jagged streaks of light flashed across the image like the lightning that had brought Olivia to the Choctaw hospital.

"Unusual," the nurse said. "Impossible. No way mother and baby could still be full of electricity. It should have discharged long ago."

Even the doctor said so. But there was no denying the sparks.

"Maybe that's why this baby girl moves around so much." Sylvia froze the image and stepped over to the screen. She pointed to the spot where the baby's penis would have been if she were a boy.

"*Mi hija,*" Olivia said. "My daughter."

Sylvia said, "I guess the dream was wrong, at least about that. Still not too late to change your mind."

But Olivia knew it was far too late for that.

"Do you suppose...?" Heavy Spanish emotion colored her bland English question as jagged flashes of electricity danced across the frozen image on the television screen. Caught in a lie she couldn't untell, watching a picture she couldn't unsee.

"I can delete this image." Sylvia answered the question Olivia hadn't been able to ask. "It doesn't fix anything, but it will give you a little more time."

"Yes, please." In the end, a little more time was the most anyone could hope for.

1

Storm's Comin'

MOMMA AND MRS. DOREEN Cheetwood stood face to face in the middle of the empty classroom, like fighters in the boxing matches Daddy watched on cable television. The discussion was about Glenna, as usual. How much trouble she'd always been. How much more trouble she'd become since she reached her teenage years.

"Pretty as a model," Momma said. "With about as much common sense as a cat."

Mrs. Cheetwood found a pencil and piece of paper and walked Glenna to one of the student desks.

"Here, sweetheart. Entertain yourself with this." The backside of the paper was plain and empty, but the front was covered with printing and a picture of a smiling man. The teacher laid the paper face down. "Draw me something pretty."

Glenna drew a jagged lightning bolt, but when the teacher went back to arguing with her mother she turned the pamphlet over to the interesting side. The man had dreamy eyes and a smile that would have looked normal except for the gold cross on one of his front teeth.

Printing filled up most of the spaces around the picture. Lots of words Glenna had never seen before, but she could sound them out.

"Junior Johnson." Her lips moved when she read the smiling man's name. According to the advertisement, he knew all about the Rapture and the Second Coming and just about everything that would happen when the world came to an end.

"Junior Johnson." She managed a whisper, with a little whistling noise when she said the letter S. Mrs. Cheetwood looked her way. The teacher tipped her head like a dog that's heard a sound it doesn't quite understand.

Glenna's hair crackled with static electricity. She held her pointing finger close to the metal frame of the student desk until a spark snapped across the gap. The teacher shook her head and turned her attention back to Glenna's mother.

"Always understood my girl was special," Momma said. "Even before she was born." She was taller than the teacher, a little thicker through the middle too, but Mrs. Cheetwood shifted her weight back and forth and looked like she'd be hard to hit if it came to that.

Glenna wrote *Special Education* in perfect cursive on the back of the Junior Johnson pamphlet. She thought about showing it to Momma, but the wind blew against the classroom window and sounded like a voice advising her to let things be.

Voices usually gave good advice. Whether they came from spirits or from short circuits in her lightning-struck brain, Glenna followed their instructions when she could.

Today was a good day for writing. She wrote her name, Momma's name, Mrs. Doreen Cheetwood's name. She printed SHORTY in big block letters. That was Daddy's name, but she never called him that.

She spelled out Jon and Billy—her brother and her uncle. She wrote Glenna bigger than any of the other names and surrounded it with jagged lightning bolts. Then she was done with writing names and drawing. Done pretending she couldn't hear her mother and Mrs.

Cheetwood talk about how hard it was to have a special child who was getting more special every day.

"It's bad enough she talks to people who aren't there, when she bothers to talk at all." Momma didn't look Glenna's way when she ran through her list of mother miseries. "Bad enough my girl's full of sparks that jump out and shock anybody who gets close."

Things with Glenna had always been difficult, but now, at least according to Momma, they'd gotten a whole lot worse. Now boys took an interest in Glenna and wouldn't leave her alone. "They hang around, bump into her—you know what I mean."

"Before long...." Momma looked like she was going to tell Mrs. Cheetwood what everybody expected to happen next, but then thought better of it.

The special needs school in Idabel could deal with a lot of things, but not a girl who attracted boys like bees around an A&W Root Beer stand. Somebody was bound to get stung sooner or later, and the special school didn't want to be responsible.

"Won't be responsible," Momma said, "Even after the Choctaw Nation wrote checks and asked them pretty please."

So now it was up to the Sacred Lamb Academy to take her in, and tuition fees were out of the question.

"I wouldn't have her if it wasn't for Reverend Cheetwood," Momma told the teacher, who just happened to be the preacher's wife. "So...."

Glenna watched her mother edge closer and closer to Doreen Cheetwood, close enough for a static spark to jump the gap if Momma stored electricity. The teacher held her ground but leaned away, as if Momma's breath was bad.

"Abortion doesn't look like such a sin when they kick your special needs child out of school because boys think she's pretty."

Glenna knew all about abortion, when mothers decide their babies are too much trouble to bring into the world. The problem is, mothers have to decide before they really know.

She felt static electricity building up in her hair again the way it always did when Momma talked this way. It crackled as the sparks jumped back and forth. Sounded like a nest of rattlesnakes warning sensible people to stay away.

The voices came next. Dead people mumbling in a dead language Glenna could almost—but not quite—understand. That usually meant a storm was on the way.

Momma and the teacher were too busy staring each other down to notice when Glenna got out of her chair and drifted closer. She followed an indirect path like a cat that isn't sure whether it's feeding time or time to find a new place to live. The two angry adults didn't pay her any mind until she reached out with her hand and got close enough to Doreen Cheetwood for a spark to jump the gap.

My, how that teacher could scream. Way louder than anyone Glenna had shocked in a long time.

Panicked noises erupted from the children in the classroom next door—jittery monkey house screeches followed by anxious whispers that sounded like leaves turning over just before a rain.

"Storm's comin'," Glenna said. Those words came out clear as day. Easy to understand. She could see how proud Momma was, so she repeated herself—kept repeating herself until her mother smoothed down her poofed-up hair and kissed her on the forehead.

Momma disguised her love as complaints. She kept it hidden under the trials and tribulations of raising a special needs child who had become a lot more special since she became a simpleminded young woman.

"It'll be okay, Glenna." Momma kissed her again, and electricity crackled between them.

Momma didn't mind the sparks.

Ms. Cheetwood pulled her hands against her chest like she might have to fight for her life against a teenage girl who had more electricity in her head than words.

"Praise the Lord." The teacher kept talking, but she slipped into the mumble language Pentecostal ministers speak when they run out of sensible things to say.

Glenna imitated her. "Lubba dubba lacramubba." She spoke tongues a lot better than Doreen Cheetwood, which must have been embarrassing because the teacher's face turned bright red.

"Storm's comin'." Glenna pointed to the door that was easing open. She cupped her hand behind her ear, as if she needed to do that to hear the two men arguing about who was going to enter the room first. The men's voices rumbled while the children's voices from the other room lowered to a twitter.

"Well, there he is." Momma turned her hands into fists and put them on her hips. Mrs. Cheetwood backed away, shrinking as she did, so she was practically invisible by the time Daddy and Reverend Cheetwood were close enough to take charge.

Men always took it personal when Momma used the word, "he," even when it wasn't clear exactly who she meant.

"Storm's comin'." Glenna spoke barely louder than a whisper. She thought about trying some *ubba* talk on Reverend Cheetwood, but it looked like Daddy might be about ready to give someone a smack.

"Ain't nobody in my family ever been like her." Daddy ignored Glenna—and everybody else in the room—while he talked to Doreen Cheetwood.

The teacher crossed her arms, shivered like she was cold for a second or two, and then looked at her feet. If Momma or the preacher noticed anything funny about that, Glenna couldn't tell.

"Howdy, Missus...." Reverend Cheetwood trailed off, probably because he remembered Daddy had never made her an honest woman like he promised he would about a hundred times.

"Miss Olivia." The preacher looked like he wasn't ready to be on a first name basis, but he couldn't think of any other way to talk to the adulterous woman in the presence of her daughter and still come off like a good Christian man. Like all preachers who need to stall for time, he suggested they take a moment for a prayer. He crossed his arms, uncrossed them, then let his hands dangle at his sides for a few seconds while he ran through a list of Bible verses in his mind.

"We can pray after this is settled," Momma said.

The preacher crossed his arms again, which probably meant everything was already settled as far as he was concerned.

Daddy shuffled away from Momma and the preacher, closer to Mrs. Cheetwood. The two looked at each other like a pair of children watching their parents argue. Glenna figured they'd be close enough to hold hands in a second or two. If Momma and the preacher noticed, they gave no sign.

Momma lifted her right fist off of her hip, flipped up her pointing finger. She waved it in front of Rev. Cheetwood like she might be about to poke out one of his eyes. "Goddamn it, Preacher!" A touch of Spanish accent sweetened her swear words. That was something that happened sometimes when Momma was excited. She pointed at Glenna. "That girl wouldn't be here but for you."

Glenna felt a pair of tears race each other down her cheeks and drip off her chin. She didn't speak much, but she understood everything. Her hair filled with electricity again, and voices chattered in the background. They were louder and clearer than they usually were when it wasn't raining.

She looked out the window and watched the day turn dark, as if God had twisted a dimmer switch.

"Ubba dibubba...." She hardly noticed when the *ubba* talk started but was in a regular tongues before she was able to get it under control.

A pair of Shiners hovered in the shadows in the darkest corner of the room. Sometimes they looked like glowing balls of foxfire. Sometimes they took on human shapes. Men, mostly, but sometimes women and children too, pointing fingers, jabbering advice. Usually their words were no more useful than *ubba* talk, but this time they spoke

English. They pointed to Daddy and Mrs. Cheetwood, who were standing so close they were bumping into each other.

"Storm's comin'," the Shiners said.

The words came from them, but they sounded like Glenna's voice. She didn't remember moving close to Momma and Reverend Cheetwood, but there she was. Reaching distance, touching distance, and the preacher stared at her as if he was looking at a ghost.

She held up a fist and flicked her pointing finger up the way Momma had. She moved the finger toward Rev. Cheetwood in a shrinking circular path like water running down the drain. When the finger was two inches from the preacher's nose, a bright blue spark jumped the gap. At that exact moment, the first drops of rain began to fall.

"Doreen," the preacher said. "Get this girl enrolled. We'll figure out the details later on.'

Glenna, Reverend Cheetwood, and Momma turned toward the preacher's wife. She looked surprised to find herself holding hands with Daddy. Both of them shook themselves free and stepped apart.

The lights in the room flickered then went dark enough so Glenna could see the Shiners clearly—two men, Native American men, without a drop of white blood as far as she could tell.

"Maybe we should get to the basement," Reverend Cheetwood said. It sounded like the sensible thing to do, but Glenna and the Shiners knew it wasn't that kind of storm.

2

Weird Old Man

ON GLENNA'S FIRST real day of school, she stood in front of the class beside Mrs. Doreen Cheetwood. Her hair crackled with static electricity the way it always did when people stared at her.

She kept her eyes forward, slightly out of focus, searching shadows for glowing circles of light that meant Shiner friends were near. In the corner, at the back of the room, one danced into view. It didn't disappear until she nodded her head in acknowledgement.

Sometimes they'd tell her to smile, to make eye contact. Sometimes they'd put words into her mouth and for a few minutes everyone would think she was an ordinary girl instead of a "special child" whose brain had been fried by lightning before she was born. Today, the Shiners were quiet.

Mrs. Cheetwood led the classroom in a welcome song. Glenna felt her lips moving in time to the music and for a moment thought she might be singing along, as if she'd accidentally landed in a place where she belonged. But her lips kept moving when the singing stopped and her brand-new classmates laughed at her the way children had done as long as she could remember. They did it all together, the way laugh tracks follow pratfalls in silly comedies on television. They kept on laughing until the teacher clapped her hands and made them stop.

Less than a second—that's how long it took Mrs. Doreen Cheetwood to get her students under control. They shut their mouths and pulled their lips against their teeth so no signs of ridicule could slip out.

"Whuppins," Glenna said, apropos of nothing. She heard that word a lot at home, from Daddy mostly, and from Uncle Billy when Daddy wasn't around. Every student in that classroom knew the concept. She could tell by how quickly they snapped in line when Mrs. Cheetwood clapped her hands. Daddy, Uncle Billy, and the Sacred Lamb Academy shared a common educational philosophy—no sense wasting minutes with persuasion when whuppins could do the trick in seconds.

The school was not equipped for special students—not that anyone was equipped for girls as special as Glenna. Twenty teenage faces blended into a single expression of righteous judgment as they introduced themselves at their teacher's direction and dared the new girl to memorize their names.

She let her eyes skim over the students seated in neat lines like rows of corn. She gazed out the window, beyond the parking lot, across the street to a copse of cottonwood trees shading a non-descript grey car with the driver's side window rolled down.

Behind the steering wheel sat a white-haired man holding a pair of binoculars. He scanned the school playground, adjusted the focus, then peered through the windows at Glenna.

She waved at him.

He put down the binoculars, stepped out of the car, then walked around it, putting the vehicle between himself and the school.

Afraid. Glenna knew as surely as if a Shiner whispered it in her ear.

Behind the white-haired man was an untidy little graveyard with weeds growing between tipped granite stones. Misshapen, dimly glowing spheres drifted above the graves—Shiners, tethered by invisible cords to buried bones, bobbed like helium balloons struggling toward heaven.

"Take your seat, Glenna," Mrs. Cheetwood said.

Too much information had come too quickly for Glenna's brain to process—new faces, new names, a stranger lurking by the school. She couldn't remember whether Mrs. Cheetwood had told her which seat was hers. The Shiners were no help and, until she figured it out, her legs refused to move.

The teacher gave her a little shove toward an empty desk in the middle of the classroom, not five steps away. But when Glenna reached her destination she did something totally unexpected. She pushed the desk to the rear of the class, behind the very last row, near a shadow in the corner where a dancing circle of light waited for her.

Students moved their desks out of her way, like clumps of arctic freeze yielding to the prow of an ice breaker. The closest ones reached out their hands and touched Glenna as she passed. Each touch was rewarded with a spark of static electricity.

The room smelled of ozone. Students stared at their shocked fingers as if they'd touched a miracle. Rumors would spread quickly once they got home. How Mrs. Cheetwood brought a special girl into class, as pretty as an actress but too feeble minded to speak more than a single word.

"Whuppins." Glenna reminded them how things would go unless they turned their heads back to the front of the class and watched the teacher dash off a series of fractions separated by multiplication and equal signs. Students at the Sacred Lamb Academy kept their eyes on Mrs. Cheetwood, but their minds were held prisoner by the electrified girl sitting in the back of the class.

No one expected Glenna to learn anything. She was present. If she could be silent, too, that would be enough. She reached into her desk and found a stack of Junior Johnson pamphlets and a pencil. They expected her to amuse herself drawing mustaches and spectacles on the

charismatic preacher whose crew was outside at that moment leaf-
leting the cars of the faculty of the Sacred Lamb Academy, providing
paper for a simple-minded girl to doodle on while smarter students
learned fractions.

———————

MATHEMATICS, HISTORY, READING, spelling, and lunch used
up most of the school day, but the final hour belonged to Reverend
Cheetwood. He picked up a piece of chalk, held it in his hand as if it
were a cigarette, then stared at each student in turn until the room
was supersaturated with silence.

The respiration rate of Glenna's classmates increased too fast for
her to count. At first, the jumbled breath sounds blended into a steady
hiss like a slow leak from an overinflated tire, but gradually the inspi-
rations and expirations found a common rhythm.

"Life support." Glenna didn't mean to speak, but the words floated to the surface along with the memory of her Grandmother on a
ventilator in a Pittsburg County Hospital. The Choctaw Nation paid
to keep her alive long enough for her family to gather around her
bed and cry. A priest gave Grandma last rites even though she wasn't
Catholic—wasn't religious at all, as far as the family knew.

Glenna played the scene out in her head—magic water, a strip of
cloth the priest kissed and placed around his neck, the circular wa-
fer he touched against Grandma's lips beside the tube that kept her
breathing. There was a prayer then a silent wait while everyone pretended she made her peace with God. The priest nodded to a nurse,
who flipped a switch that broke the connection between Grandma's
body and her soul.

Glenna did a reasonably good imitation of Grandma's last seconds
of life. Three deep breaths through a plastic tube and then a sound like
the dial tone on a telephone. How long ago had it been? One year, two—

just before she shot up three inches and filled out in ways that made the boys want to watch her. About the time her thoughts got tangled in complicated knots and started coming unraveled at the ends.

Reverend Cheetwood quoted a Bible verse that didn't have a thing to do with Grandma as far as Glenna could tell, but it turned the class's attention back to him.

There would have been trouble if anyone but Glenna had broken the preacher's spell. For the first time in her life, she was happy to be special. She wanted to say, "I'm sorry," but the more she struggled with the words, the more impossible it was.

Her lips had it all worked out, but no sound followed, and she looked a lot like a fish that had been out of water too long.

"Well...." The preacher turned his back to the class and drew a circle on the board. He said it represented faith. This was the part of the day they studied religion so the students would go home with Jesus on their minds.

Reverend Cheetwood looked out the classroom window into the parking lot where two men argued loud enough for words to make it through the triple-pane glass. He walked over to the window and wrapped it with his knuckles hard enough to get the men's attention.

"Jon and Uncle Billy." Glenna hadn't meant to claim the two parking lot combatants, but she couldn't take it back. Her brother, Jon— big and strong with a man's body and a boy's emotions—and Uncle Billy, who always seemed to be around when Glenna's father wasn't. They'd come to the school to pick up Glenna because Momma was doing something else.

"Jon." Glenna shrugged and hoped everyone understood she could explain no more than that. She couldn't tell the class Uncle Billy was interested in her the same way the boys at the Idabel Special School had been. Touching when he could, staring when he couldn't. His nasty thoughts left her with a taste like milk starting to go bad. She thought Jon could taste it, too. Only Momma never seemed to notice.

"Uncle Billy." Glenna made a face and smoothed down her hair as best she could. It was already puffing up with electricity. She rifled through her desk until she found a Junior Johnson pamphlet and printed the clearest, loudest words that made it through the classroom windows.

"Goddamned pervert." Jon said those words just before he shook his fist under Uncle Billy's nose.

Reverend Cheetwood looked at his watch. The shouting match in the parking lot looked like it would turn into a fistfight soon, but the preacher tried to ignore it. He tapped his piece of chalk in the center of the misshapen circle on the board and said, "Faith!" much louder than necessary to get the class's attention.

"How much faith can a person have before it becomes a mental illness?" He drew lines from the center of his circle to its perimeter so it looked like a cut pie with imperfectly proportioned servings.

The students' breathing rates picked up again—faster, perfectly synchronized. All spell-struck, except for Glenna, by a minister who was telling them to temper their faith with reason.

He wrote JUNIOR JOHNSON on the board in sloppy block letters that Glenna probably couldn't have read if she didn't already know about the traveling evangelist faith healer with the gold cross on his front tooth.

She held her Junior Johnson pamphlet up so everyone could see and read, "Goddamned pervert," on the back right after Jon screamed it on the parking lot again.

Embarrassment was something she usually didn't feel, but now she did. Her uncle and her brother shouted strings of curse words and traded a couple of ineffective slaps. Glenna tried to ignore them. She folded the Junior Johnson pamphlet into a perfect square then put it into the back pocket of her jeans.

"Charismatic!" The preacher shouted loud enough to pull the class's attention away from the parking lot disturbance. He wrote that word beside Junior Johnson and underlined it twice. He swallowed hard and bent his knees the way Glenna did when she was about to jump off of the diving board at the Durant public swimming pool.

"False prophets." Reverend Cheetwood looked at the ceiling so everyone would know he was getting his message directly from the source. "They come to you in sheep's clothing, but inwardly they are ferocious wolves. By their fruit you will recognize them. Do people pick grapes from thorn bushes or figs from thistles?"

Glenna looked for Shiners in the shadow under the desk at the front of the classroom.

Nothing.

The preacher ranted about the age of miracles, raved how magical things used to happen all the time. "But that was long ago, and anyone who thinks those things still happen is a fool."

He circled Junior Johnson's name and wrote "fool" beside it in cursive as sloppy as a doctor's signature.

The students shifted in their chairs. They ground their teeth and chewed their fingernails to the quick. Everything turned quiet, the way things get before a tornado sweeps through Choctaw country.

Glenna wasn't worried. That wasn't going to happen—the Shiners were nowhere to be seen. Couldn't even hear them speaking in tongue-twister languages.

If it hadn't been so quiet, no one in the class would have heard the argument that had shifted into a lower, much more threatening volume. Even in the silence, their words barely made it through triple pane windows.

"Son of a bitch." That was Jon.

"Fart knocker." Uncle Billy's special name for Jon.

The two squared off like a couple of overgrown little boys pretending to be Kung Fu fighters. Jon stood on one leg dangling the other for a killer kick. Billy moved his hands in lazy crooked circles like a handicapped mime.

"Goddammit." Reverend Cheetwood looked like he'd try to take those words back if he didn't have something more important to do at the moment.

He knocked on the window again. When that didn't work, he unlocked and raised it and raised it until it wouldn't go any farther.

"You boys cut that out." He leaned out the window as if he might actually climb out and jump into the fight.

Jon dropped his hands and looked at the preacher. Billy turned toward the preacher, too, but when he noticed Jon's defenses were gone, he took a swing. Only landed a glancing blow, but it started the fight all over again. This time, neither did pretend Kung Fu.

While the preacher climbed out the window, Glenna headed for the front door of the classroom. Maybe there'd be Shiners in the basement.

Shiners didn't breathe. At least, Glenna never heard them breathing. They laughed. They cried. The talked. They screamed. Sometimes the sounds they made came through her ears and sometimes they went right into Glenna's electrified brain like the sound track of a dream.

Shiners didn't make promises or declare undying love. They didn't grunt or say, "Oh, God."

Those things were what Glenna heard as she walked down the stairs. The dirtiest, dimmest light she had ever seen spilled out the open cellar door into the hallway in front of her. Shadows moved like sharks swimming just beneath the surface of polluted water, but Shiners danced along the walls and slipped through the doorway where it sounded like a life and death struggle was underway.

"Oh, God. Oh, God!" That was Mrs. Cheetwood, calling on the Heavenly Father in a very unreligious tone.

"Shorty." A barely controlled scream from the preacher's wife was followed by a string of curses from Glenna's dad. Most were variations of "whore." It seemed to be exactly what Doreen Cheetwood wanted to hear.

Glenna followed the Shiners into the cellar and watched them move beside her father, who was pushing the preacher's wife against the wall. Her legs were wrapped around him, his pants pulled down, her panties lying on the dirty floor.

Glenna knew things like this happened, but the motivation was a mystery to her and the Shiners weren't bothering to explain.

"Disgusting," was the word that came to mind. Perhaps she said it out loud because Mrs. Cheetwood looked at her.

"Oh, God!" The teacher's tone was more religious this time around.

Glenna's hair puffed out and sparked like a Fourth of July display. The Shiners drew her closer, even though what she really wanted to do was run.

"Please, God!" Doreen Cheetwood's jaws clenched, and her legs must have clenched, too, because Shorty cried out in pain and his knees buckled.

Glenna hardly noticed she was backing away until she reached the stairs. She bolted toward daylight and ran to the parking lot where Reverend Cheetwood was arguing with Uncle Billy and Jon.

She ambled without a plan between cars, moving away from the school toward a lightly-used older car parked on the street, at least twenty yards off of school property.

The white-haired man she had seen before sat behind the steering wheel, scanning the parking lot with a pair of binoculars. He trained his surveillance on Glenna as soon as she stepped into his field of vision, adjusting the focus as she drew nearer.

He smiled when she opened the passenger door and climbed in. "Away." She pointed at the ignition key. "Away now."

"My, you are a pretty girl." He breathed fog onto his binocular lenses and polished them with his shirttail.

While Glenna fumbled with the seatbelt, he reached out to touch her, slowly, the way a monkey reaches for a piece of fruit he suspects may be bait in a trap.

"You look too young to be a cop." He pulled his hand back when a spark jumped the gap between his fingers and her hair. He clutched his chest, took a few deep breaths.

The Shiners talked to Glenna in their *ubba* language. They didn't sound worried about the weird old man who looked like he was thinking about trying for another touch. Their words would make more sense if a thunderstorm moved in.

She rolled the passenger side window down, leaned out, and scanned the sky for clouds. Some dark ones gathered in the southwest, but they were a long way off, and she needed some advice right now.

"Not part of some kind of sting operation, are you sweetheart?" He lifted his binoculars again and checked the cars in the parking lot. "No unmarked vehicles as far as I can tell."

The electricity gradually leaked out of Glenna's hair. She touched the car door and waited for a spark, but none came. She could speak more clearly when her electrical charge was gone. Words lined up in a row rather than trying to come out backwards or sideways.

"Go." She stuck to the simplest language possible. "Go now." Two and three letter words instead of the story racing through her mind about her father and Doreen Cheetwood. About her mother and Uncle Billy and her brother Jon. About how the Sacred Lamb Academy would make things worse in her family. And things were already pretty bad.

Explanations were too complicated even when her mind wasn't cluttered with electricity.

"*Ubba didubba skimubbadi.*" That didn't explain anything, but maybe it would get the old man's mind off the police and on to driving her away from the school, where things were getting very complicated.

"So much like a grown-up woman." The old man looked disappointed. He reached her way again, more slowly than he did the last time. His fingers trembled as they approached her breasts. Before they reached their destination, he made a fist and buried it in his lap. "How old are you, sweetheart?" He picked up his binoculars again and pointed them at the three-way argument still going on between the preacher, Jon, and Uncle Billy.

Mrs. Cheetwood and Glenna's dad walked out the front door of the school, holding hands and bumping hips. When they saw the preacher, they separated. Mrs. Cheetwood wiped the hand that had been holding Shorty's on her slacks and pushed her way through the crowd that had gathered around the loud words.

"Go now!" Glenna touched the old man's shoulder. He winced as if she were still full of electricity and clutched his chest again.

"Guess you're right. An opportunity like this doesn't come along very often." He smiled and brushed his fingers through her hair. No shock this time.

Glenna couldn't help but smile. This was the first time in a very long while that she'd felt wanted.

3

The Equinox Revival

REVEREND JUNIOR JOHNSON kept his hand on the bone handle of the chrome-plated six-shooter strapped around his waist. He put a gunfighter's swagger into his walk and sucked in his belly. If he'd known he was going to get into a pissing contest with a scientist, he would have worn two guns.

"Who died and made you king?" The preacher tried to stare into the anthropologist's eyes, but his gaze kept shifting to the double hooks at the end of the man's left arm where a hand should be. The metal didn't look like a handicap from the preacher's point of view.

Fred Bennett raised his prosthesis and evaluated it the way an ordinary man might examine his fingernails. He twisted his arm and the hooks sprang open like a mechanical lobster claw.

When he snapped them shut, Junior flinched. He tugged at his revolver to remind Dr. Fred Bennett which one of them had the power of life and death. He spat on the ground, missing the scientist's boots by inches.

Junior's head throbbed from leftover drugs he hoped would be out of his system by the time the faithful arrived for the Equinox Revival.

He turned toward the crew—overzealous workmen pounding metal stakes into the ground that would hold his tent steady in the Oklahoma wind—and almost told them to cut out all the racket, but that would be a sign of weakness. And it didn't pay to show weakness to a hook-handed man of science.

"Fall equinox draws big crowds." Junior released the pistol grip and wiped his palm on his shirt. It took a lot of effort to keep his eyes locked in a staring match with the anthropologist while the man worked his hook hand open and closed.

"Big as Easter. Big as Christmas." The preacher forced a smile so Fred Bennett would have to look at the gold cross on his front tooth. Dental ornamentation always made the educated class uneasy.

"Couldn't call it off if I wanted to." He spat on the ground again. If he wasn't mistaken, a drop or two might have hit the scientist's pant leg.

"Equinoxes, solstices, cross quarter days. They're important to the Indians." Junior shrugged, demonstrating there was really nothing he could do to stop the local Choctaw from flocking to his tent when the sun went through its acrobatic routines. That much of the old times was still in them—worship of the sun and looking for magic on special days when light and darkness divided time equally.

"Be careful. That's all I ask." Fred Bennett scratched his chin for a good thirty seconds with his prosthesis before waving it at a ragged little hill behind where Junior's crew pitched the revival tent. "Excavation's already underway. Artifacts removed and sorted." He snapped his hooks again and looked pleased when the preacher jumped. "That brush-covered pile of dirt might be the greatest archeological discovery of the twenty-first century. Culture that built this mound goes back nine thousand years at least. Be a shame if something disappeared."

Junior looked around for the ugly pair of Indian assistants who usually followed him around like a pair of well-trained pit bulls. There they were, twenty feet back, spread out at four o'clock and eight o'clock so the hook handed man couldn't curse both of them with a single look. He motioned them closer, but they were stuck in place, torn between loyalty and fear. If he ever got them moving, there was no telling which way they'd go.

"Nine thousand years." Junior tried to work some skepticism into his tone, but his headache jumped to a higher pain level. The pulsations in his temples synchronized with the rhythm of the tent crew sledge-hammering metal stakes. "About the time God kicked Adam and Eve out of the Garden of Eden."

He crossed his arms and dared the anthropologist to contradict him. The sturdy pair of Guarani Indians shuffled closer, still afraid of Hook Hand, but less afraid now that Junior was talking back. He pushed through the pain of his throbbing head and let his right hand fall onto his pistol butt again. A clear threat for anyone with the intelligence to pay attention.

"Heard all about you," Junior said. The anthropologist had been all over Leflore County, talking to high school science classes about evolution and all manner of blasphemy. "None of it good." He lapsed into silence for a few seconds, the way he did in sermons when he wanted to draw the crowd into his spell. But he couldn't be sure religious magic would work on an atheist, so he didn't stretch it out as long as usual. "Not good at all."

There were rumors all over the county about Fred Bennett. The preacher started the best one himself. How the scientist grew up in the hills of Tennessee among a sect of serpent handlers. How he lost his hand when he was sixteen years old and tried to hold a rattlesnake to prove his faith. How his soul traveled all the way to hell where he made a pact with Satan. No truth to it, naturally. Like many stories the preacher told, this one was a parable. Or maybe it was an allegory. Junior always got the two terms confused, in spite of having spent considerable time memorizing words on his vocabulary calendar.

"I abjure everything you stand for," Junior said.

The scientist scratched his head with his hook and looked confused.

"Who's the smart one now?" A preacher needed to have a way with words. Holy men had known that since humans walked the earth side by side with dinosaurs. Words were the simplest kind of magic. They could make people angry, make them cry, make them reach into their pockets and fill an offering plate with money.

"Your calumny will not detract from God's teachings." That was a really good one. Totally incomprehensible, even to a man with a Ph.D.

The anthropologist broke the spell by opening his double hook and popping it shut.

Junior resisted the urge to turn around and watch his Indian assistants run off to hide in the trees.

"This is a burial mound." Fred Bennett continued as if the words Junior threw at him had no effect. He talked about ground penetrating X-ray machines and sealed pots full of bones. "Won't know how important they are until we open one."

"Burial pots." Junior didn't like the sound of that. It probably meant nothing. Non-Christian savages fell into the same pagan practices the world over. Human sacrifice, idol worship, and—of course—there were the vision drugs. He massaged his aching temples and said a silent prayer that the pain would go away so he could concentrate on getting rid of the pesky anthropologist.

"Indians around here might not like white men poking around in their burial grounds." Junior had no problem telling that lie. The Choctaw in Leflore County, Oklahoma wouldn't put up a fuss when a white scientist dug through a bunch of old bones. They wouldn't protest or file lawsuits when Fred Bennett pulled skeletons out of graves and put them on display in a museum. They were way too civilized to give a damn about burial pots that Junior preferred were left alone.

"You okay?" The anthropologist reached out with his human hand and put it on Junior's shoulder. An act that could be interpreted as either concern or superiority.

"Burial pots." The preacher whispered the word, which called attention to it almost as much as if he'd shouted.

"Unheard of in this region," Fred Bennett said.

"South America." Junior thought about the dozen cemetery pots that stood in rows in the middle of the Paraguayan Mission Compound he and Elizabeth set up before she—

"That's right," Fred Bennett said. "How did you know?"

It wouldn't do to tell the scientist about his Paraguayan mission. Wouldn't do to get him started snooping around down there looking for some kind of connection that probably didn't exist.

"I'll keep my flock away from your little hill," he told the scientist. "You be careful with those pots. No end of trouble when you open up something like that."

Junior turned and walked back to his trailer. A little nap before the evening meeting would do him a world of good. As long as he didn't have bad dreams about Elizabeth.

GLENNA COULDN'T GIVE the old man directions to her house, but that probably didn't matter because it was pretty clear he already had a destination in mind.

His name was Carl. She thought that must be right because there was no one else in the car but every few minutes he said, "Old Carl thinks you're really pretty."

He kept his eyes on the road, except for a few occasional sideways glances, and his hands stayed on the steering wheel, except for a couple of times when his right one let go and drifted her way. When that happened, he must have thought about the spark he got when he touched her earlier because he'd pull that hand away and hold it over his heart as if he was about to say the pledge of allegiance.

Old Carl was fragile man with a nervous disposition.

"Chihuahua," Glenna said. He reminded her of the pups Momma's best friend raised to buy things her disability check wouldn't cover. Shaky little animals with bad tempers they kept hidden until someone got close enough for them to bite.

"Smile for Old Carl, sweetheart." He massaged his breast bone as if he was trying to rub out a cramp. "Show me those pretty, white teeth."

He looked disappointed when Glenna smiled. Not surprising. Forced smiles always felt like snarls. Probably looked that way too.

"Still," he said. "You're pretty enough to turn a man's heart to mush. Even prettier than my fresh, young things."

His hand right hand fell into his lap and did things Glenna didn't want to consider. Her brother Jon did things like that when he thought no one was looking. Uncle Billy did them too and didn't seem to care who saw him, as long as it wasn't Daddy. Old Carl was a lot like Uncle Billy.

"You know my name, sweetheart. Tell me yours." He put both hands on the steering wheel, in the ten o'clock and two o'clock positions, the way Daddy showed her back when he tried to teach her how to drive.

"Hopeless." She repeated what Daddy said after their third lesson when he decided she would never learn.

After a few seconds she added, "Never had nothin' like that in my family." That was about all Daddy ever said to her except for threats, and she didn't think she should mention those quite yet.

Glenna was talking much more than usual—clearer, too. She leaned forward and watched the sky through the windshield. Clouds were moving in from the west. That accounted for it. Lightning flashed deep inside the darkest cloud. Thunder rumbled a few seconds later.

"Storm's comin'." She smiled at the old man. He tried to smile back, but it turned into a twitch when his right front wheel ran off the road.

"Eye teeth are the thing." Old Carl turned down a dirt road bordered by shoulders so overgrown with trees that branches scraped along both sides of the car. "Once those eye teeth come in, a girl's life begins to change."

He tried to smile again. Almost made it.

"They lose that fresh, young attitude about the time they turn eleven." He took a deep breath and held it, the way Jon and his friends did when they smoked marijuana behind the house.

"Old Carl's been sick for a good long time. Sick in the heart. Sick in the soul. Know what I mean?" His voice turned thick, his eyes turned red, and it looked like tears would fall in a matter of minutes.

Glenna tried to think of something to say, but nothing came to mind. She lapsed into *ubba*-language. People usually stopped asking questions when she did that.

Carl unbuttoned his shirt and made her look at the scar that ran down the middle of his chest. "Bypass."

It was a keloid an inch wide, the color of a ripe tomato with little dots along the sides. A big, golden locket rested in the center of the raised ribbon of a scar, the kind of locket mothers wear to hold strands of hair—memories of children who had grown up and moved away. A hazy glow surrounded the locket, not as bright as Shiner light, but like something a Shiner had touched.

When Glenna reached for it, he pulled his arm across his chest and almost ran off the road.

The old man's anger flared for a moment, then he apologized.

"Old Carl's a sick man." His expression was a mixture of worry and shame. "A real sick man." The worried look vanished, but the shame remained. He told her about his heart attack, his quadruple bypass, and the three cardiac arrests he had. "All that was before they fitted me with a defibrillator."

They both knew Carl's sickness was much more complicated, but neither one of them was ready to talk about it.

"Defibrillators are wicked scary." He told her he had to watch out for things like microwave ovens and airport metal detectors. "Can't even have my teeth worked on by one of those all-electric drills."

The rest of Carl's sickness was wicked scary too. The old man had a sickness that couldn't be fixed with vaccinations and antibiotics. It had something to do with the way boys had been looking at Glenna for the last year or so. Something to do with where babies came from but in a dark way that made her nauseous to think about.

"You might be the cure," Old Carl said. "So I won't be thinkin' of fresh, young things all the time."

He told her how people didn't always want the same thing, and when what a person wanted was different enough to be considered strange, the police came and locked them in prison.

"Even criminals think they're better than you. The thieves, the kidnappers, the murderers...."

His sentence lost all of its energy in the end until nothing was left but the hissing sound of the letter S. Old Carl didn't want to talk about kidnappers and murderers any longer.

Glenna didn't either. Voices whispered messages. If more storm clouds moved in, their meaning would get clearer. Still, she knew for sure it was a warning.

She tried to repeat the words. They got twisted up behind her lips and came out in a jumble, but they were enough to scare the old man into bumping off the road again. He struggled to pull the car under control and went into a skid that nearly got them stuck for good.

"Close one." He put the car in park and tried to slow his breathing. His golden locket fell forward. It tapped against the steering wheel.

The Shiner glow was stronger. Glenna thought that was partly because the old man was afraid and partly because clouds covered the sky and piled on top of each other. The voices moved closer—still too jumbled to understand, but they were children's voices. Children crying, pleading, promising to be good. Children who wanted to go home.

"You can help me." Carl tucked the locket back into his shirt and struggled with the buttons. "Always been drawn to things ordinary men don't want, but you're so pretty, maybe you can change all that. Will you help me?"

He gave her a half minute to answer.

She didn't because her vocabulary was temporarily out of reach.

Old Carl smiled and put the car in gear.

4

Fresh, Young Things

OLD CARL'S HOUSE was the kind of place a girl would never go unless a man like Old Carl brought her. It was a prefabricated ruin, trucked in from far away, assembled on the site by minimum-wage workers with a simple plan and a total lack of enthusiasm. Carl's home was dressed in dented aluminum siding and covered by a roof that looked one hailstorm away from disaster. Trees crowded around it. Limbs raked against the walls as if they were trying to erase the structure from the world.

Unfortunately, there was nowhere to run and no place to go but inside. Rain floated down from the sky in tiny droplets hardly larger than a mist. Lightning danced in a thick layer of dark clouds that hid all signs of the sun except for a faint green luminescence at the southwest horizon, hardly brighter than a Shiner glow.

Glenna's family would be turning on their radios and moving to the cellar. Daddy would open his Bible to a random page and read as if he'd been personally appointed by God.

For the first time ever, Glenna wished she were down in that dreary basement.

She wanted to argue with Old Carl. Raise her voice. Tell him to take her home right now before he got into so much trouble the best lawyers in Oklahoma couldn't get him out. But her body tingled from the top of her head to the tips of her toes like a lightning rod just before an electrical storm, and her lips and tongue refused to follow orders.

Accusations swirled in her mind—kidnapping, child abduction, worse crimes she didn't want to think about. Her internal vocabulary was large, her mental arguments were persuasive, but everything was stuck inside her head by static electric superglue. If she had a pencil, she could write them on the back of the Junior Johnson pamphlet in her back pocket.

"Storm's comin'." A jagged strand of lightning connected the clouds with a tall tree deep within the forest. Thunder cracked so loud, it sounded like the world breaking in two. Glenna's hair collected so much static charge, it snapped and popped when the wind stirred it.

Old Carl had looked harmless in the school parking lot, watching children through binoculars, too shy to venture close. He'd seemed timid and vulnerable, willing to cooperate, but that all changed as he led Glenna through the front door of his house.

Naked, low-watt bulbs in uncovered ceiling fixtures were barely enough to light the interior. Mismatched chairs were arranged on the pine floor without a plan. A full-length mirror hung on the wall opposite the door, so she could watch Carl twist the deadbolt into place.

"Safe," he said.

But Glenna didn't think her safety was what he had in mind. He removed a sheet from a broken-down couch, uncovering holes in the upholstery large enough to expose rusted springs. He hung the sheet over the mirror then tucked it around the wooden frame as if he were making a bed.

"Mirrors turn the world backward. Make things look worse than they really are." The lack of reflected light dimmed the room and made the interior look even shabbier. The old man's face looked harder and more angular. His smile—if that's what it was—more threatening.

Most Oklahoma houses were built on cement slabs, but Old Carl's had a crawl space. Glenna knew this because Shiners talked and bumped underneath the floor. Spirits with children's voices, still afraid of the old man even though they were well beyond his reach. Their glows shone between the floorboards as they moved about beneath her.

Carl stood in front of the door, an immovable obstacle between Glenna and the only exit. His lips ran through a complicated list of soundless words—the same ones over and over—too quick to lip read easily, but the repetition made it possible.

Suzy, Christi, Donna, Ada.

He unbuttoned his shirt—slowly, one button for each repetition of the names. His hands trembled, but his fingers moved as if they had a lot of practice.

Suzy, Christi, Donna, Ada.

He removed his shirt and dropped it on the floor—the sight pathetic and terrifying at the same time.

Carl's body was a scarred map of medical procedures.

"Gall bladder." He pointed them out as he took her on the tour. "This one here's appendix. You know about the bypass." His locket bumped against the keloid scar. Old Carl took a step toward her. He reached out to touch her hair, slowly, carefully, the way a cat prods at a rat that might still have some fight left in it. He pulled his hand back from the sparks, gave his defibrillator a moment to betray him, and when it didn't, he said, "Thank you, Jesus."

Why did the worst men always think God is secretly rooting for them? Daddy came to mind, riding through Texas, Arkansas, and Oklahoma in a big truck with a bulldog hood ornament and a plastic Jesus mounted on the dashboard. He was a bully of a man who carried a Bible while he intimidated children and slept with every woman who would have him. He drove from one tent revival to another, buying salvation for five dollar bills the way he bought smiles from pole dancers in gentlemen's clubs.

"A man can't help it if he wants the wrong things." Carl looked at the ceiling, so Glenna couldn't tell if he was talking to her or to God. The lights flickered for a few seconds then finally failed completely.

"Damn."

She could feel the air move as the old man reached for her. She could see the faint glow of his locket as he stalked her around the room. She could see him moving like a shadow in the faint Shiner light leaking between the pine planks of the floor.

Ducking under the old man's grasp was easy while the lights were out, but as they flashed on and off again, Carl disappeared in one place then reappeared in another, reaching for her, whispering the names of the four fresh, young things buried underneath the house.

How long ago.

She'd kick him if it came to that. She'd scratch and punch, attack him in ways his eleven-year-old girls had never thought of.

"Help me be a better man," he said.

Not what she expected to hear from an old murderer chasing her through a dark, ugly room.

She pulled the sheet off the mirror so Carl would have to look at his reflection when the light flashed on—so he'd have to see the scars, watch his lips reciting the names of the girls who'd come to this house before Glenna.

The wind slapped leaves and rain against the windows. The house shook. Thunder drowned out the sound of the Shiners giving Glenna advice.

Run, hide, beg for mercy.

Bad advice from fresh, young things who had never stood a chance against a man like Carl.

Glenna stood before the mirror, watching the reflection of the old man's glowing locket closing in. Behind him, four Shiners slid between the pine planks in the floor and lit the room—for her, at least. Carl stumbled like a blind man, completely unaware of the spirit lights.

They weren't spheres or discs this time. These Shiners were shaped like young girls, slender children. This one had the hint of a nose. That one the suggestion of eyes. They drifted toward Carl. Reached for him but didn't touch. Could she still see them if she turned away from the mirror and looked at them directly?

"It'll be so much easier in the dark," Carl said.

Easier to pretend Glenna was what he actually wanted.

"Pretty as you are." He said it like he knew it might not be enough. She was past her prime as far as the old man was concerned. Still too young according to the law, but a giant step toward being normal. "People might understand why a man would want a pretty girl like you."

The Shiners moved around the room in a panic. They didn't tell her how they'd come to be under the old man's house, but they didn't have to.

"What's your name, sweetheart?" Carl spread his arms like a monster in a 3-D movie.

No way she could get around him. No way she could get to the front door, turn the dead bolt, run out into the rain. The old man clenched and unclenched his hands as if they could already feel her neck locked in his grip.

She watched him in the Shiner light, getting stronger as he thought about what he meant to do. He wouldn't be able to wait if she were younger. If she were a slender little girl like the spirits in the room who were warning her away.

"Real important that I know your name, sweetheart." Carl tilted his head, focusing in on Glenna as his eyes adjusted to the dark. "It won't feel right unless I know your name." He took a step closer. "Suzy, Christi, Donna, Ada. Got to add yours to the list."

His face changed in the Shiner light. Glenna understood it changed the same way every time. Harder, stronger, meaner. His eyes emptied out completely. This is what a killer looked like up close and personal, something only a victim sees right before she says the last thing in the world she's ever going to say.

Glenna felt the last words of the fresh, young things Carl had killed bubbling up inside her.

"I can't breathe." It came out exactly the same as it did when Carl's first victim said it to him.

Some emotion found its way back into the old man's eyes. Not sympathy, but perhaps a little shame. An understanding that what he wanted from his fresh, young things was wrong.

"Those were Suzy's words." His hands quit clenching. He slumped a bit, looking more resigned than aroused. "Girls say the damnedest things right before…."

Glenna wanted to promise him she wouldn't tell. Explain her mental challenges, swear she'd never be able to lead police to his little ruined prefabricated house in the middle of the woods. She'd forget what he looked like and go back home. He could go out again another time searching for his fresh, young things.

For once, Glenna was glad she couldn't say what was on her mind.

"Tabasco." She repeated the last thing Christi said exactly as she said it.

Carl dropped his hands a little lower. He still meant to kill her, but he didn't feel excited about it anymore.

"That was pretty strange," he said. "Who'd think that would be the last thing on a little girl's mind? But one was stranger yet."

"Filmore." The little girl's last words came easier as Glenna's time grew short.

"How could you know that?" Carl still had the eyes of a killer, but they weren't empty eyes. They were full of doubt, full of regret.

The wind outside the house died down. The rain stopped.

"Jesus." Glenna repeated Ada's last word. Whispered it the way the ten-year-old had right before Carl choked the life out of her. Exactly the same tone. Exactly the same volume.

The lights came on in a flash. Carl could see again, leaving Glenna with only two advantages—youth and the will to survive. She stood with her back to the full-length mirror, full of fear and static electricity. Carl stood in front of her watching his reflection—an old man ready to grab a young woman and choke the life out of her.

"Never wanted it to work out this way, sweetheart. I'll make it real quick, but I still need to know your name." The one remnant of his fantasy he couldn't let go. "You look like a Stephanie to me. That's who you'll be if you don't tell me your real name."

Lightning flashed, spearing light through the windows. Cracks of thunder followed. The dirty bulbs flickered but didn't go out. The Shiners gathered at her side, ready to stand beside her while Carl ended her life. Ready to welcome her to her new home in the crawl space. They didn't touch her, but she could feel their power seeping into her body. From the tips of her toes to the tips of her fingers to the top of her head. Glenna was as full of power as a freshly charged battery.

"What will *your* last words be, Stephanie? Go on, now. You can tell Old Carl."

Glenna stepped into his embrace. She put her hand on the center of his bypass scar and watched his face change as his defibrillator fired. The old man made a satisfying thud when he hit the floor. His arms and legs did an interesting little dance. Foam collected at the corners of his mouth.

5

It's a Tupa Thing

THE REVEREND JUNIOR Johnson stood in front of his revival tent and whispered a prayer that sounded like a complaint. He listed all his sacrifices, counting them on his fingers, and when he got to ten started counting all over again. He reminded God how Elizabeth was taken from him at the moment he needed her most and rubbed his eyes until he summoned some tears.

"I didn't complain." He knew it was a lie. God understood that, of course, but Junior had repeated this prayer so often the Heavenly Father knew better than to argue.

"We have a dangerous situation here, Lord. Just sayin'." God had brought storm clouds from the west along with gusts of wind that put his revival tent rigging to the test. Junior sent a silent request for assistance toward the clouds with an intense psychic push—straight to God with copies to Jesus and the Holy Spirit. He crossed his arms and waited for results.

When a storm-warning siren blew in the distance, he thought it was a sign, but like so many signs Junior had encountered, this one had what he liked to call, "a depressingly natural explanation."

Miracles never seemed to happen anywhere near a dependable witness. The preacher adjusted the holstered six-shooter on his hip and fished his Tupa bottle out of his pocket.

He showed it to his identical-twin Indian assistants so they could come to his aid if something bad happened—like it did with Elizabeth. The bottle had a screw-on eye dropper for a top, and Junior loaded it and let a tiny bit of jungle drug dribble into each nostril.

"Just enough to get the Holy Spirit rising," he told the Indians.

His fingers were the first to tingle, but his toes weren't far behind. Before a minute passed, he heard mumbling from the spirit world. No point in getting his hopes up. Ghosts hardly ever told him anything useful. They rarely told him anything he could understand—except Elizabeth, and she mostly told him things he didn't want to hear.

"Stay away from the excavation," she whispered. "Stay away from the excavation." She repeated it over and over. The words buzzed like a mosquito inside his head.

"You're not the boss of me," Junior said. No risk of looking childish. The only human witnesses were his ugly Guarani assistants. He didn't think they understood a word of English, but they stepped away from him, on opposite sides so if he drew his pistol and started shooting, he'd probably only get one of them.

"Stop looking at me that way, Pedro."

The Indians had names, but they were hard to pronounce, and he couldn't tell them apart, so he lumped them together in one homogenous Spanish blend of humanity.

"Sorry about the tone, boys." He held his hands away from his pistol and tried to look like a politician telling the news media, "mistakes were made," without admitting guilt. He worked his apology over in his mind. When he had the tone exactly right, he repeated it. "Sorry, boys." Coupled it with a shrug—the kind of universal gesture that worked when you cut a driver off in traffic or let an accidental fart slip out in a wedding reception line. "It's the Tupa talking."

And the Tupa was telling his assistants he was sorry because they were the ones who put an endless supply of it into his hands.

"Creo and Conozco." Junior repeated the Indian's names, though for the life of him he couldn't remember when he learned them.

They backed away a little further, turned their attention to Fred Bennett's dig, then edged in that direction, slowly, as if the world had tipped and gravity pulled them against their will.

The tornado siren drowned out the spirit noises and made Junior's ears ring, but he could still make out muffled voices coming from the excavation.

"Wait up, Pedro." Junior followed his assistants, ignoring his promise to Fred Bennett. What did pledges to an atheist mean?

"I'm doing God's will here," he said in case the Heavenly Father was eavesdropping.

"Lying bastard." Elizabeth's voice blended perfectly with the shrill drone of the storm warning siren.

Having a dead wife who followed him around like a supernatural stalker might be considered a miracle by some.

"There are miracles you like and miracles you don't."

He looked toward the sky again so God would know he was registering another complaint, but instead of the sky, he saw the canvas tarp covering the anthropologist's dig. The storm warning siren's volume diminished to an annoying hum, like the tinnitus he would have for days after a venture this deep into Tupa land.

Junior applied another drop or two to each nostril even though the effect of the first dose hadn't reached its peak. He looked reverently at the canvas and crossed himself. Catholics had it all over evangelical Christians when it came to drama.

"See me, God." He crossed himself again, in case the Heavenly Father missed it the first time. It was a well-known fact that God had X-ray vision, a short attention span, and a long-term memory cluttered with grudges.

"This is your old pal Junior Johnson being humble." At that moment, the siren faded into silence. Rain began to fall, the drops tapping a coded message on the canvas that was just on the edge of making sense to the preacher.

"Perhaps another drop of Tupa." He reached for the bottle, but one of the Pedros grabbed his wrist and shook his head so vigorously his face turned into an indigenous blur.

Creo, or maybe it was Conozco, pointed to the burial jars Fred Bennett had removed from the cemetery mound. They stood beside a rectangular hole strung over with jute ropes. It looked like a three-dimensional graph. Screen sifters were stacked beside the jars and, on a primitive wooden table, small artifacts recovered from the dig were organized in labeled plastic bags.

A few of the artifacts were gold—lost wax castings of heathen gods and goddesses. Did the prohibition against other gods and graven images give him license to steal? He decided it did, as long as he used the profits for the greater good.

His Paraguayan mission was the greater good he had in mind. Things were going pretty well, but they'd go a lot better if he had money enough for more publicity and substantial bribes.

"Hell yes." Junior stuffed his pockets with everything that looked like it might have value.

"And not atheist scientific value, either." That was a rationalization God could get behind. Junior would blame the theft on his Choctaw congregation. It would be easy for a white man to believe... even a white man with a string of letters after his name.

Junior's pulse rate edged gradually into the danger zone, ready to break right through hysteria into tachycardia—a sure sign he'd either taken too much Tupa or misinterpreted the will of God.

"I told you so," Elizabeth whispered again. She was about to start one of her arguments from the bully pulpit of the spirit world when his Indian assistants started chanting.

"Damn Injuns." As far as Junior was concerned, indigenous people from the Western Hemisphere were the worst singers in the world. They had one all-purpose tune and a string of words that didn't fit the music.

The Pedros sat cross-legged on the ground in front of a pair of burial jars, singing monotone in the barbershop style. They reached forward, as synchronized as a case of double vision, and stroked the pair of jars like a mother soothing her baby.

The pots weren't exactly like the ones in Paraguay but were too similar to be totally unrelated. The lids were sealed with a compound perfected nine thousand years ago—if Fred Bennett was right—and protected by Oklahoma clay until yesterday. A spirit glow surrounded the seal, magic escaping through the gaps. Tiny cracks in the ceramic glowed, too.

The jars were decorated with twisted lines that looked like a primitive counting system, similar to the Paraguayan jars, but these lines and curves seemed like they would fit together to compose every picture ever drawn. Energized by Tupa, they danced over the surface in time to the Pedros' song and illustrated the important people in Junior Johnson's life—his mother, his father, Elizabeth—before settling on a face he didn't recognize. A girl so pretty, it hurt his head to think of her.

"Don't touch that that one," Elizabeth told him. "She'll use you up and throw you away."

It might be worth it to be used up by such a girl. Her face was not perfectly symmetrical. Not an interchangeable mask that could be distorted into anything with the aid of makeup. This girl had her own face, one that stuck in his mind and would never let go.

But then it did let go. The lines separated and returned to their places, and try as he might, Junior couldn't recapture the image.

He walked between the Pedros to one of the jars. He grabbed it and prepared to pop off the lid.

"*No, señor,*" one of the Pedros said. It made no difference which. "*No es tiempo.*"

They never spoke, so he knew this was an important moment.

"Don't do it," Elizabeth said.

The storm-warning siren blared. The wind shook the protective canvas tarp. Rain fell in torrents, mixed with marble-size hail, all but assuring no one would come to his equinox service.

He walked out from under the canvas tarp, flanked by the Pedros. Oblivious to the rain and hail, he waded onto the parking area, already ankle deep in water.

Not empty as he had expected. Two dozen pickup trucks were parked in front of the tent, Choctaw Nation tags on every vehicle. Headlights came on as he walked in front of them. Engines started.

Showing up to a tent revival while the storm warning sirens blew was an act of faith. The Choctaw understood that God kept score on things like this. The Heavenly Father would write their names in the book of good works. An act of faith like this could offset a theft, a visit to a strip club, maybe even a foray or two into adultery.

Now that God and the preacher had taken notice, they could leave. Junior couldn't let that happen. He drew his pistol, pointed it at the sky, and fired six shots with no thought of where the bullets would come down. Afterward, he holstered his weapon then held up his arms in an imitation of the capital letter Y.

"Now's the time, God." Lightning struck near the anthropologist's excavation. Some of the pickup trucks shifted into gear, but they could no more stop watching the preacher than they could look away from a train wreck.

"The power of Christ commands you." He borrowed that line from The Exorcist, the scariest movie he had ever seen.

There was no rushing God when asking for favors. Junior filled time by reciting words from his vocabulary calendar. "Labyrinthine. Obdurate. Abstemious."

The Tupa and the excitement made him forget the meanings of the words, but that didn't matter. They'd sound like magic to the Choctaw Christians, especially if something happened that looked like a miracle.

And it did.

The rain stopped suddenly, as if God turned off a faucet. The storm-warning siren faded into silence. Clouds in the west blew over Junior's head toward the Arkansas line, taking the rain and lightning with them.

Cell phone lights came on in pickup cabs as brothers texted sisters and cousins. Junior's fame grew with every tweet and Facebook post. Photographic flashes temporarily blinded him as he turned and walked into the tent. Truck doors opened then slammed as his congregation followed.

There wouldn't be any need to enhance the crowd with Tupa spiked Kool-Aid for this service. God had done the dirty work for him. But he snorted a couple more drops himself to calm his nerves and put him on a proper frequency to channel the Lord.

6

Foreseen

THE OLD MAN'S chest rose and fell. Glenna reached her hand toward his bypass scar again, but her electricity was gone. Her hair lay over her shoulders, and her hands and feet had no tingling sensations. She lifted Carl's locket over his head and popped it open.

Locks of hair inside, just as she knew there would be. She walked to the front door, opened it, and let the hair float into the wind. After losing sight of the individual tresses, she tossed the locket into the trees. Its glow faded—a smoldering ember with nothing left to burn.

Thunder rumbled in the east like a great machine rolling from Oklahoma into Arkansas. The last sunlight of the day lit the western horizon as clouds followed the thunder. In an hour, stars would fill the sky, clear and crisp, the way they always were after rain cleaned the air.

The old man's danger had vanished for the time being, banished by the power of electricity. The Shiners retreated to the crawlspace, and Glenna considered how she could find her way back home.

"Jesus." Carl coughed and wheezed. He regained consciousness like a used-up drunk who has to push his way through a hangover, sputtering a prayer that couldn't possibly make up for the things he'd done. "Jesus, help me!"

As if Glenna could fetch Jesus to his side. As if she would after all the things he'd done. He thrashed on the floor, struggled to his knees—weak, but his strength would return and, when it did, his contrition would vanish without a trace.

"It's like I've been in a prison, Stephanie," the old man whined. His eyes filled with tears, but he wasn't crying for the four dead girls in his crawlspace. "Like a demon's had a hold of me and only just now let me go. Like you were sent here by God to turn my life around."

Men like Carl believed their own lies. Men like Daddy too, and Uncle Billy. Maybe all men.

Glenna believed Carl—for the moment, at least. As long as he was sick and wobbly. As long as he needed her help.

His hand moved across his chest, looking for his locket. When he didn't find it his face turned to a mask of anger, but only for a second.

"That part of my life is done." Sitting in one of his mismatched chairs that faced the door, he rubbed his hands together as if he could wipe away all the evil in his past. The last rays of the setting sun fell on him and turned him the color of clotted blood.

"Help me, Stephanie." He'd settled on her name. "Help me be a better man."

Already he was repeating himself. When men like Carl slipped and fell, their old ways were always there to catch them. How long would it take for his strength to return? For him to remember how sweet it was to squeeze the life out of a fresh, young thing? To collect her dying words and add her name to his list?

"Show me what to do, sweetheart." His smile was genuine, but there was trickery at the edges. "Show me, angel." He put his hand on his chest where she had touched him and driven out his demons for a while.

Glenna stood facing Carl, her back to the setting sun so all he saw was a silhouette, requiring him to fill in her features with his imagination. She reached into her back pocket for the Junior Johnson pamphlet she'd taken from Sacred Lamb Academy, unfolded it, and placed it in his hands. She gave Carl a few seconds to read it before turning and walking to his car, knowing he would follow.

———————————

THERE'S NOTHING IN the scriptures that tells an evangelist how to act after delivering a full-fledged miracle like stopping the rain with a six-shooter. Junior considered taking a bow but guessed the Heavenly Father might take offense at that. A righteous man gave credit where credit was due, so he settled on a couple of head bobs and the most sincerely humble look he could summon up.

The Holy Spirit moment was tainted by the fact that all six portable restrooms Junior rented from Johnnie On The Spot Inc. had been blown onto their sides. The turquoise blue boxes were a reminder of the frailties of the flesh and would become much more of a reminder if his equinox sermon went on as long as he expected.

He'd get the Pedros working on that right away. Nothing spoiled an act of God like a parishioner with no place to relieve himself. That was one condition Junior found totally resistant to the laying on of hands.

He tried to look unconcerned—above human worries and necessities—as he tapped the nearest disabled toilet with his knuckles. "Don't worry, folks. Jesus is a journeyman plumber." He knocked on the plastic a little harder and stared at his Guarani assistants.

Standing water in the parking lot had been ankle deep, but by the time the Pedros got the first Porta Potty more or less upright, it was barely over the preacher's shoes. The polish on his wingtips was ruined for sure, but that was a small price to pay for the public relations bonanza sure to come his way.

People climbed out of their vehicles. They gathered in small knots, using their cell phones to spread the world of Junior's show-down with the storm. The story would grow like a game of gossip by the time the service was over and everybody had texted everyone they knew. If he was lucky, someone would post a video of him stopping the rain on YouTube. If he was really lucky, he'd look like a thoughtful man of God working magic with his pistol and not a drug-crazed fanatic having a gunfight with cumulus clouds.

Setting Porta Potties upright was a lot more work than he imagined. The ugly twins collected rocks to serve as a foundation. Understandable. If Jesus built his church on a rock, Junior would do the same for his rented toilets. He almost announced that unorthodox thought to the crowd but at the last second saved himself with a couple of sentences in tongues. Too much talk about bodily functions—natural though they may be—is a sure way to get a congregation out of the revival mood.

A miracle can throw a man right off his game. Junior preferred to be inside the tent when the congregation entered. He liked to stand beside the podium looking like God's special deputy, sent from heaven to get things straightened out in this little backwater corner of Oklahoma. He didn't have a badge, but he had the lawman's thousand-yard stare and his trusty six-shooter holstered at his side.

As soon as he started his walk down the center aisle toward the stage, he thought about the spent cartridges in his pistol. Nothing more dangerous than an unloaded gun. Any expert worth their salt would testify to that.

Especially if there was a gunfight.

The extra bullets he carried in his pockets were usually easy to reach, but they were hard to sort from the stolen anthropologist's trinkets. And of course, there was the dropper bottle full of Tupa that clinked against the graven images and made a wind chime sound.

Junior favored .38 special bullets with a few .357 magnums mixed in for variety. A few days back he'd seen an ad for a company that would custom-make ammunition at a reasonable price and had pretty much decided on a box or two of silver bullets.

"Not that I believe in werewolves or vampires." He mumbled that but could see the people close by took in every word. He went on mumbling but mixed in some vocabulary calendar words and complicated names from the Old Testament and, before long, nobody thought it was strange at all. Funny what people considered normal on an Equinox Revival night.

He dropped spent cartridges on the ground and replaced them as he walked. He could hear parishioners scrambling for the brass—a little something to keep as a souvenir of the night Junior Johnson stopped the rain.

"Hey, Preacher." A Choctaw man with strong Native American features and a grey ponytail grabbed Junior by the shoulder before he could mount the stage. Not a smart thing to do to a man with a freshly-loaded pistol and a brain full of jungle drug. "Okay if I pass these out?" He shoved a pamphlet into Junior's hands. "Little Glenna Anoli's gone missin'."

"Pretty girl," he said before he could stop himself. He traced her image with the index finger of his right hand. A crooked smile he'd seen somewhere before, Native American eyes filled with secrets and a touch of sadness, black glossy hair with blue sparks scattered through it like sequins.

"What's this?" He pointed to an irregular luminous circle that backlit the girl's head like a halo.

"Kind of makes her look like an angel, don't it?" The Choctaw pamphleteer handed a few copies to passers-by while he waited for the preacher's official okay.

"Glenna Anoli." Memories swam just below the turbulent surface of Junior's mind. "Lightning bolts, abortion, lines on a cemetery pot...." He recited pieces of the memories and just about had them put together.

"That mean I can pass them out?" The Choctaw man waved his papers in front of the preacher's face.

Junior fished the bottle of Tupa out of his pocket and applied a drop to the tip of his tongue. Memories pulled themselves together the way they always did after a few drops of Jungle drug. God only knew what would happen when the latest drop of Tupa reached its full potential. Already, he could see the face drawn on the cemetery pots every time he closed his eyes, like a contract made between God and the preacher back when time began.

Junior knew a lot about pretty girls. Attractive young ladies from most of the little towns in Choctaw country were busy passing out information and escorting parishioners to their chairs. There were lots of pretty girls in this part of the world. Something to do, he supposed, with the way Indian genes mixed with European ones. There were lots of pretty girls, all right, but this one was something special.

"Foreseen," Junior said. That's what Glenna Anoli was. Foreseen in ancient days by a clever artisan who took time to draw her picture on a burial pot, the way civilized folks put their missing girls on milk cartons. No way that old potter could have known when Glenna Anoli's time would come. He folded the pamphlet with more delicacy than he intended, tucked it into his shirt pocket over his heart and patted it as he would a long-lost dog that had just come home.

"So that's a yes?" The Choctaw man held the stack of papers up so Junior could see them again. "Quicker we find her, the better. Right, Preacher?"

Junior couldn't argue with the man's logic. Nine thousand years and, apparently, the search was still going on. His last drop of Tupa kicked in and left him momentarily speechless. He nodded his head like one of the crazy bobble-head dolls some locals mounted on the dashboards of their cars.

He walked through the circle of men and women who had gathered around him. Some of them whispered prayers. Some held his discarded brass shell casings over their heads like banners—spell struck, every one. Junior climbed onto the stage and prepared to start his sermon.

This was going to be a special night, no question about it.

"You be careful," Elizabeth told him. "That's all I'm gonna say."

It wouldn't be all, of course. Wives, dead or living, always had a little something on their minds.

Junior talked right over her—the way he had when she was alive. He talked about a lightning-struck woman, a pregnant woman, looking for guidance from a man of God. It didn't really matter what he said because the energy radiating from him was so full of the Holy Spirit, it penetrated all the way to the bones of every member of the congregation.

Cell phone cameras flashed as the audience documented this miraculous Equinox Revival. They danced and sang and waved their hands in the air as more and more people filled the tent. Way more than the fire marshal would approve of.

Junior pitched his voice the way old time Holy Roller ministers always have. Before long, he had a chorus of "amens" and "halleluiahs" going so strong, he probably couldn't stop them if he tried.

People moved toward the stage, ready for some laying on of hands. Cripples who wanted to walk again. Blind people who wanted to see. There was no way Junior Johnson could fail. Nothing could spoil the moment when the holy word combined with the power of a nine thousand-year-old prophesy coming to pass. Until he looked into a central row of the congregation and saw Glenna Anoli's no good bastard of a father, hand-in-hand with Doreen Cheetwood.

"Be quiet!" Junior shouted at the top of his already booming voice. The crowd hushed the way it always did when the preacher drew his pistol and held it over his head.

Not something they hadn't seen before. Gunplay had been part of his oratory style for quite some time, but it made them nervous. It seemed to especially make Shorty nervous. Junior fixed his eyes on the disreputable little man, considered firing a couple of shots in the air, and only refrained because of the cost of patching his tent.

"Look there, folks."

Everybody turned toward Shorty and Doreen. If they hadn't noticed Reverend Cheetwood's wife with the father of the missing girl before, they certainly couldn't ignore them now.

Junior focused on the woman, the way preachers always seem to do when they talk about adultery. He described the special kind of relaxed smile on a woman's face after she's made love to a man whose clothes she doesn't have to wash and whose meals she doesn't have to cook. He slipped the pistol back into its holster after reminding his audience it was a sin to kill.

The preacher shook the tension out of his shoulders. Most probably thought he was about to drop the matter and move on to other things. Instead, he jumped off the stage, shoved parishioners aside as he plowed through folding chairs, stepped on the legs of people who didn't get out of the way quickly enough. He shouted a fire and brimstone sermon about the consequences of adultery as he closed in on Shorty and Doreen, who—like everyone else—stared wide-eyed like they had no idea what he might do when he reached them.

Doreen Cheetwood stayed in her seat, but Shorty popped up like a jack-in-the-box and disappeared into the chaotic crowd.

"Run, you cowardly little bastard!" A glowing blob of light roughly the shape of Elizabeth hovered in front of Junior, blurring his vision like a cataract.

"You've done it again," she said.

And she was right. Phone cameras flashed, documenting his rant that he had to admit didn't sound as much like a sermon as he intended.

"No healings. No souls saved. The collection plate didn't even make the rounds." Elizabeth had an endless list of missteps.

He had to admit she had a point, but it might not be too late to save the day.

"The Lord works in mysterious ways," he said, as if that explained everything. Then he turned and walked back toward the stage.

7

You Look Like a
Stephanie To Me

O LD CARL PULLED into a marshy spot across the road from the Equinox Revival tent. He leaned over the back seat, found a sealed-beam flashlight, and began searching the parking area.

"Policemen ain't friends with people like Old Carl," he told Glenna. "Pays to be careful." He kissed her on the forehead, held her hair in his flashlight-free hand, then rubbed it between his fingers.

No sparks now that the storm had passed.

"You sure are a pretty girl." Since his defibrillator began functioning properly again, the old man seemed to be having second thoughts about exactly how Glenna was meant to lead him down the road to salvation. She pulled the Equinox Revival pamphlet out of her back pocket, unfolded it, and held it where he could shine his light on "The Good News."

He chewed his lower lip while he read the message on the paper and stroked Glenna's hair. When it looked like his decision might go the wrong way, she opened the passenger side door and stepped out onto the muddy shoulder.

"Come on." Her language skills were in a sweet spot. The storm had blown over but the scent of ozone was still in the air. She could have said anything she wanted, but she knew Old Carl was much more likely to follow a simpleminded child who couldn't possibly tell on him than a young woman with a vocabulary and a plan. She considered running for the safety of the crowd of Choctaw Christians who would take her side against the twisted old man, but if she did, he'd drive away and go back to adding to his collection of crawlspace Shiners.

"Storm's passed." Glenna walked toward the revival tent and motioned for him to follow.

She watched his face change as he pictured a future Old Carl in his mind, an Old Carl not driven to snatch unattended girls and kill them for his pleasure.

"Ain't had sex with none of them," he called to her, "even though I could have. Only touches, and that hardly counts." He slid across the seat and followed her out the passenger door, all the while explaining how what he'd done wasn't really his fault. "If only they'd been sensible." He held his hands out so Glenna could see how harmless his touches would have been. "If they'd just been sensible."

She wouldn't take the old man's hand, so he laid it on her shoulder, pulling her into an envelope of funk she hadn't noticed in the car. Glenna turned her head so her face was as far away from him as she could manage and found enough clean air to keep nausea away.

The tent was filled with light and noise, the disorganized rumble of people on the edge of frenzy. Glenna had heard that kind of noise many times before when Daddy took the whole family to hear evangelical ministers who traveled with caravans of trucks like the Ringling Brothers and Barnum & Bailey Circus. Preachers laid hands on her, cried out for the Lord to fix her, then hustled her off the stage promising God would complete the process in his own good time unless he had other plans.

She had a pretty good idea what Junior Johnson would do if he ever laid hands on Carl. Glenna took a deep breath, turned to look at the old man's face, and smiled at him as if she were too mentally challenged to know exactly how evil he was.

Chaos is a word preachers like to use, and that's exactly what Glenna found as they entered the tent. People kneeled in the aisles. They stood on chairs. They milled around the stage shouting made up words that sounded like prayers said backwards.

The Reverend Junior Johnson walked among the crowd as if he'd forgotten he was supposed to be in charge. A silver-haired woman played a gospel song on a miniature organ. She pounded the keys with so much energy, the instrument sounded like a calliope.

The preacher climbed onto the stage followed by a blurry glowing light that Glenna knew must be his own personal Shiner. He wore a pistol strapped to his side and put his hand on it as if he might control the crowd with violence if they didn't settle down.

"This ain't the right time nor place to change my ways." Old Carl's hand slid off her shoulder. He found a pamphlet on an empty chair with the words *MISSING GIRL* printed in bold letters over a picture of Glenna.

She moved away from him and blended with the milling crowd that was coming out of religious hysteria and turning its attention to the preacher.

"Take your seats, *please.*" Junior Johnson yelled above the noise. The glowing mist that followed him onto the stage hovered in front of his face. Talking to him, Glenna knew, because that's how Shiners looked when they had messages.

The preacher slid his hand off his pistol and pulled a bottle out of his pocket—a brown glass bottle with an eye-dropper top. He carried the dropper to his nose and deposited a drop into each nostril.

Glenna moved close enough to see his pupils expand to swallow his eye color completely.

He walked to the podium, picked up a microphone, and spewed

out a series of complicated words that got the crowd's attention. His Shiner pulsated, disapproving, predicting disaster.

"Take your seats, ladies and gentlemen. Take your *seats!*" He tried to remind the Choctaw how civilized they were, how compliant with the word of God. His eyes moved in different orbits as if he were trying to see things in two worlds at the same time.

Glenna had seen chameleons' eyes do that on TV documentaries, right before their tongues lashed out and caught flying insects. There were no insects for the preacher to snatch out of the air, but his tongue stumbled over words and a stream of drool dribbled from the corner of his mouth as he called for peace and order.

The congregation's full attention turned his way, cell phones raised above their heads, ready to document whatever was about to happen—the end of a famous evangelist's career or the beginning of a new era. Things could have gone either way until the moment Junior Johnson locked his roving eyes on Glenna.

"Halleluiah!" He aimed his index finger like a weapon. The congregation followed it to its intended target—Glenna and Old Carl.

"Time to go, Glenna." Old Carl knew her name now that he had seen it on the MISSING GIRL pamphlet. "Glenna." He put one hand inside his shirt and massaged the scar from his bypass surgery, as if repeating the name might trigger another defibrillator misfire.

"Glenna!" the preacher shouted into the microphone before he stumbled off the stage and lurched toward her.

"Glenna?" Her father called out from behind a knot of worshipers who had dropped to their knees in prayer.

"Glenna…." Doreen Cheetwood rose from her folding chair and scrambled toward the girl, who now had no direction she could turn without seeing an adult who was calling her name.

Old Carl, Shorty, Junior Johnson, and Doreen Cheetwood smashed into each other as she stepped aside. The preacher landed a punch on Old Carl's nose. Shorty got the preacher in a headlock.

Doreen Cheetwood tried to break them apart and was caught up in a tumbling ball of four people that rolled through the folding chairs and the seated faithful. A trail of golden trinkets in numbered plastic bags lay behind them in the path of destruction. The nine-thousand-year-old treasures from an ancient culture disappeared into the pockets of congregants as the fight lost energy.

Old Carl was first to break away. He took a final look at Glenna, rubbed his chest, then shifted his gaze to an eight-year-old girl who'd drifted away from her parents.

"What's your name, sweetheart?" In three quick steps he scooped her into his arms. "You look like a Stephanie to me." He tried to cover her mouth but wasn't quick enough to keep her from screaming.

Glenna lost track of Old Carl but followed the girl's muffled screeches as he carried her outside the tent toward a worksite covered by a canvas tarp. She pointed the direction Old Carl had run as the preacher, Shorty, and Doreen Cheetwood joined her. It was too dark to see where he had gone, but everyone heard the little girl shriek again.

Junior Johnson drew his pistol and aimed in the direction of the scream. He called on the power of the Lord to make his aim true and emptied his pistol into the darkness.

Flashes from the gunshots made yellow spots dance in Glenna's eyes but an even brighter pair of luminous spheres floated through the canvas tarp covering the worksite. They hovered in the air.

An identical pair of ugly men dressed in clothing that looked like it had been borrowed from the pages of a history book moved out of the crowd to stand beside the preacher.

Everyone watched a white man with a hook for a hand carry a little girl out of the darkness below the hovering Shiners. He handed her to an anxious couple then turned his attention to Junior Johnson. "Your bullets just destroyed a pristine pair of burial pots." The white man held his hook in front of the preacher as if he might be planning an attack. "No telling how much damage you've done."

Glenna watched the floating Shiners move over the forest like ball lightning. If other people noticed, they said nothing.

Daddy took her hand and pulled her toward his pickup truck. Mrs. Cheetwood tried to follow, but he held up a hand the way crossing guards stop cars at crosswalks on the way to the Sacred Lamb Academy. "Olivia wouldn't understand, Doreen."

Glenna thought Momma would understand perfectly.

"Some things are best left unsaid." Daddy fastened the shoulder strap of his pickup truck across Glenna's chest and checked to see if it was snug. One of those Daddy things he never did unless he wanted something from her.

"Keeping quiet's not the same as telling lies." A Bible lay in the front seat between them. He opened it and pretended to read a complicated passage about how children shouldn't tell their mothers about their fathers' girlfriends. The verse was peppered with throat clearings and nervous coughs. He snapped the Bible shut and put it in her lap.

"See for yourself, sweetheart. Old Testament. The most tried and true half of the Good Book."

Glenna felt electricity building in her body, not enough to make a defibrillator misfire, perhaps, but enough to remind her father she was not like other girls. She reached out and made a spark jump between them.

"I came here lookin' for you."

At least he wasn't pretending to read from the Bible any longer.

"Me and Missus... well, you know."

He didn't want to say Doreen Cheetwood's name in case it might be one of those rare things that stuck in his simpleminded daughter's head until it popped out at an inconvenient moment.

"I found you, didn't I?" Daddy said it as if he were answering an argument. He started his pickup truck and revved the engine but didn't put it in gear. "Things like this are hard for a girl your age to understand, darlin'."

"Old Carl," Glenna said, as if Daddy would know who she was talking about. As if he would care. He was busy putting a complicated explanation together out of bits and pieces of excuses that had worked over the years. He didn't see the pair of Shiners hovering in front of his truck. She pointed at them.

He looked, but only for a second. Daddy's eyes weren't open to Shiner things. Glenna thought the Reverend Junior Johnson's might be, but she couldn't be sure. Perhaps she was the only one. The pair of luminous spheres floated through the windshield of the truck, filling the cab with light and warmth and puffing Glenna's hair with electricity.

Daddy couldn't see the light but saw her hair spark. It made him angry for reasons she couldn't understand.

"Where the hell did you go?" His voice took on the sharp edge that usually came before a slap. "Who was that old man that brought you to the revival?" He drew back a hand, preparing to strike her across the face, not hard enough to leave a mark, but enough to put her in her place.

She reached out and snapped a spark from her hand to his, reminding him they had a secret.

"Doreen Cheetwood." She zipped her lips shut with a gesture she'd seen other children use when they promised not to tell.

Glenna could see Daddy's face clearly in the Shiner light. Anger and guilt were in a battle, each trying to take control of his expression. She knew something about him that her mother only suspected, and he couldn't decide whether threats or bribery would be the best way to keep her quiet. For the first time she could remember, he was happy she seldom spoke more than a word or two and never bothered to explain anything.

The Shiners passed back through the windshield then moved to the side of the truck. Glenna watched them bounce around the parking area, stopping at major characters in the drama that played out around the revival tent. They paused over Doreen Cheetwood for a moment before shifting to Reverend Junior Johnson, who was holding her hand. They illuminated the hook-handed man, who was busy accepting pats on the back from the parents of the child he'd carried out of the darkness.

The Shiner light danced over assorted Choctaw Christians, capturing them in candid moments like a ghostly photographer. It settled on a frightened old white man standing just beyond the reach of the headlights on Daddy's truck. He rubbed his chest and hunched over like a frightened animal preparing to run away from hunters.

"Old Carl." Glenna pointed to him, repeated his name so Daddy couldn't mistake her meaning.

"What the...?" Daddy flashed his high beams and froze the old man like a deer. He shifted the truck into drive and fishtailed through the mud, twisting the wheel to keep Carl lined up with his bumper.

"Old bastard." The truck went into a slide, but Daddy managed to slam Old Carl with the passenger door.

His face pushed up against the glass. His lips shaped her name, Glenna. His gaze locked onto hers, and she understood this would not be the last time she'd see Old Carl. The old man slid off the door and crawled through the parking lot on all fours. The Shiner light followed him until he disappeared in the woods.

"Old pervert." Daddy drove out of the parking area and onto the road, a smile on his face, his need to discipline satisfied.

"Taught that old bastard to mess around with my daughter." He looked at Glenna as if a thought had just occurred to him. "He didn't, did he?"

"Doreen Cheetwood." She opened Daddy's Bible and put it on the seat between them. It was too dark for either of them to read after the Shiner lights were gone, but she'd have bet anything the verses had something to do with keeping secrets.

8

Doreen Cheetwood

STORMS THAT BACKED into Oklahoma over the Arkansas border were the strongest kind. Clouds loaded up with water and electricity from the Gulf of Mexico, dragged it across Mississippi and Louisiana, then dumped everything on the western side of the Ouachita Mountains.

"This rain is like homeschool," Momma said. "It keeps going even when the bell has rung."

Glenna watched a pair of Shiners bob up and down outside the living room picture window. It was practically as good as television.

These two had followed her ever since she got away from Old Carl. They started off like all the rest—balls of light without much shape and no sign of personality. Now they had real faces. Their eyes darted back and forth, stopping for a few seconds on Momma before moving on to her brother Jonathan then settling on Daddy. She didn't like the way they looked at him and didn't think he'd like it either if he knew.

The Shiners had Native American cheekbones and Native American eyes, but they weren't like the Choctaw who lived in Glenna's corner of Oklahoma. They looked like the ugly pair of Indians who guarded Reverend Junior Johnson.

Most people would have thought they were scary, but not Glenna. Shiners weren't pretty, but at least they were interested in her. They bobbed and floated wherever she went, usually out of sight or almost out of sight. They were the closest things to friends she had, and Glenna supposed it would always be that way, especially since Reverend Cheetwood said she couldn't come back to the Sacred Lamb Academy.

"Not that she isn't welcome," he told Momma with a smile. "But you can't bring her here anymore." He used words like liability and responsibility, and some complicated words with lots of shameful syllables. Glenna was pretty sure they had something to do with what happened between her and Old Carl.

Momma said, "Not knowin' is the worst part."

Everybody had an idea what went on between Glenna and the old man. She could have told them if she wanted to. Electrical storms loosened up her vocabulary, and there'd been one after another since revival night. Two solid weeks of thunder and lightning. Trees were struck, and houses. Even a person or two.

Daddy said it was the wrath of God, but that was all he'd say because he and Glenna had a secret.

Her brother Jonathan didn't try to hide his curiosity.

"What did that asshole do to you, Glenna?" He flexed his muscles and punched at shadows, pretending he was calling out Old Carl. Only he didn't know anything about Old Carl. Only she and Daddy knew his name, and Daddy wouldn't talk about revival night.

Glenna pointed at the pair of Shiners bumping against the living room window. Her parents didn't notice. They were too busy trying to think of something that would take their minds off the simple-minded girl who'd made their lives so complicated. It didn't matter if Glenna was a mentally-challenged child of God, the Sacred Lamb Academy wouldn't pretend to educate her any longer.

Reverend Cheetwood put the blame on Momma. He said the Lord

still held a grudge from when she'd considered abortion and had just now got around to giving her a time out.

"Mothers always carry the burden." She hardened her look and put her hands on her hips so everybody would know she thought Glenna was to blame.

"Hush, Olivia," Daddy said. He wasn't taking his daughter's side. He didn't really care how things went between them when he was off on a long haul, but while he was home....

"Peace and quiet's what we need. Bible-reading time. Prayer. Repentance for our sins." He crossed himself Catholic style, which he knew drove Momma crazy, and looked at the ceiling as if he was looking into the eyes of God.

"Amen," he said, as if that settled things.

As far as Glenna was concerned, it was time to do something interesting. She scooted her bare feet across the carpet, collecting the electricity that rode in with the storm. She imagined flashes jumping in her puffed-up hair like lightning in clouds that gathered over the rising moon. She timed her breathing so it matched the gusts of wind and moved toward her older brother, Jonathan.

A bright spark jumped from her fingertips when she reached for him. She scooted around the room again gathering another charge.

"Make her stop." Jonathan looked to his parents for support as he backed away.

Glenna followed him with dragging, lurching steps, one hand held in front of her like a partially paralyzed sleepwalker. No matter how fast he moved or how many pieces of furniture he ducked behind, she kept coming.

"Stop it, Glenna. Please!"

A lightning bolt struck in the forest behind their back yard, and the flash shined through the picture window like a spotlight. For just a second, Glenna saw the silhouette of a man standing in the trees.

She'd try to figure out who he was later on. At that moment, she had Jonathan boxed in between the sofa and the wall. She stung his ear with another spark then celebrated her victory with a string of whisper-words full of glottal stops and consonants. It sounded like a language, but nothing anybody in the room understood.

Daddy turned on the radio so he and Momma could hear about the storm. He held his Bible over his heart and told Glenna, "Quit jabberin', girl. It ain't Christian."

She whispered another string of funny words. Her Shiners whispered back. Their voices harmonized perfectly with the thunder and the wind.

Daddy let the Good Book fall open of its own accord and read a passage that ended with a warning against girls talking to no-see-'em friends. "Ain't natural. The Heavenly Father's likely to give you a good smack."

Lightning struck close by, followed by a thunderclap that made everybody but Glenna jump. She scooted around the room and kept on whispering.

Daddy opened the Good Book again and read quietly for a couple of seconds. He looked like he was coming to some conclusion, held up his right hand with his pointing finger aimed at heaven and opened his mouth to speak. Before he made a sound, the lights went out.

"Shit," he said, but left off talking when the wind blew leaves against the picture window where the Shiners were.

Jonathan took advantage of the dark. He ducked away from Glenna, but the voices told her how to find him the way they sometimes led her to Momma's lost car keys or Uncle Billy's spare change that had fallen between the sofa cushions. Jonathan didn't stand a chance. By the time she reached her big brother, she had built up enough static electricity to jump a spark across the three inches that separated her fingers from his nose. A miniature copy of the lightning strikes outside.

Thunder shook the house. Warm Gulf air swept past the Ouachita Mountains and sent people scampering to their cellars all over southeastern Oklahoma. The weatherman on the radio read off the names of towns from Idabel to Heavener. He talked about tornados cloaked in rain that nobody could see until it was too late.

Daddy fished a book of matches out of his pocket and told Momma, "Get out the candles. The radio man says there's power failures all over the county." He held his Bible up so the Heavenly Father could see it, and recited bits and pieces of the Lord's Prayer.

Momma put a dozen half-used candles in saucers and set them up around the room. A thunderclap jarred the house and made her drop the matches just after she lit the last one.

Voices whispered, "Trouble's comin'."

"Let's see what Jesus has to say." Daddy moved to the kitchen table, put his Bible between two candles, then let it flop open so the Lord would select a passage.

"This here's the book of Exodus." He stumbled over a list of shalts and shalt nots, but stopped after reading Thou shalt not commit adultery. "Well, this part's way before Jesus. Probably don't mean nothin'."

The lights flickered on for a second and then went out again. The storm turned quiet, the way they do sometimes when things are about to get really wild. Chain lightning filled the world with flashes, like a thousand cameras going off at once.

Glenna's big toe touched the matchbook Momma had dropped. Easy to recognize because the striker felt like sandpaper on her skin.

A voice told her, "Pick it up."

Another told her, "Read it."

A name and telephone number were written inside the cover with a red sharpie. It was hard to read in the dark, but a brilliant lightning strike burned a blue afterimage into her eyes, as bright and clear as a neon sign. "She recited "Doreen Cheetwood" and the number as clear as the weatherman calling out the names of towns where people should take cover. Her voice was deep and rough, the way her Uncle Billy sounded when he had enough money for whiskey.

Daddy got up from the table so fast he knocked a chair over.

"Doreen Cheetwood." Glenna said the name again as the afterimage faded. Her voice was so rough it gave her a sore throat. She tried to talk some more but everything came out in mixed up words.

"Think I'll go check out the cellar," Daddy said. "Just in case the storm takes a turn for the worse."

As soon as he was out the door, the lights came on. Momma said the storm had passed.

Glenna supposed she must be right because the wind stopped blowing and the lightning stopped flashing. She scooted her feet across the carpet again, but all the electricity was gone.

9

Asshole Cousin

U NCLE BILLY SAT Glenna on his lap and pretended she was a cute little ten-year-old instead of a pretty teenage girl. His breath smelled like bourbon and cigarettes, and the skin on his forehead glistened with hair gel he used to make his cowlicks lie down.

Voices buzzed around Glenna like a pair of angry hornets. They didn't like Uncle Billy. Neither did her Daddy, but Momma did. And when Daddy was on a long haul, Uncle Billy always came around.

He wasn't Daddy's brother or Momma's. Just somebody who came to family gatherings without being invited and didn't leave until someone chased him away.

"Asshole cousin," is what Daddy called him when Momma couldn't hear.

Uncle Billy's hands found places on Glenna where she didn't want to be touched, and Momma always seemed to be looking the other way.

Glenna squirmed on Uncle Billy's lap, trying to slide off, but he was too determined. His whiskey breath stung her eyes, and she had to turn away when she needed to breathe. She drew in as much air as she could hold and faced him again because Uncle Billy needed watching even if he was hard to look at.

Static electricity began building up the way it always did when she got angry. It poofed out her hair and covered Billy's whiskey smell with ozone. She held her pointing finger up where he could see it. She moved her fingertip in a circle so his eyes would follow.

"Like hypnotizing a cat," the voices told her. "Like hypnotizing a fat, lazy cat." The words came through Glenna's lips, slow and squeaky, like a recording playing on the wrong speed.

"Signs and wonders." Billy smiled big enough so she could see where his real teeth ended and his plastic ones began.

The circles she drew went into a spiral, like water going down a drain, closer and closer to Billy's nose until her fingertip was close enough for a spark to bridge the gap.

"Goddammit!" He jumped off of the couch, spilling her onto the floor. "Goddammit, Sparky. You built up quite a charge in that little finger."

Jonathan came out of his room long enough to be a witness if Billy did something Dad should know about.

"Don't curse inside the house, Uncle Billy," he said. "Daddy don't allow it."

Billy looked at Jonathan like he might strangle him if Momma wasn't in the room.

"You've got to be careful, Billy," Momma said. "My girl's got enough problems without being all crippled up." She dusted Glenna off—maybe a little harder than necessary—and told Jonathan, "Everything is under control."

"Sorry." Uncle Billy rubbed at a little red spot on his nose where Glenna's spark had stung him. "Took me by surprise is all." He tried to walk toward the kitchen, but Glenna dropped down on all fours and crawled into the exact spot he meant his foot to go.

"Goddamn—" He balanced on one leg for a second then tumbled backward and landed on the couch again. His weight collapsed the springs against the wooden frame with a loud crack that promised to leave the sofa with a permanent sag. "What the hell's she up to?"

Glenna hated it when people talked about her like she wasn't in the room. With Billy, she supposed it didn't really matter because when he was around even she pretended she wasn't in the room.

She crawled on all fours to the edge of the couch, pushed Uncle Billy's feet aside, and picked up a small, brightly-colored plastic package that had fallen from his pocket—circular, almost exactly the same size as a silver dollar. But there was no coin inside—not even a chocolate coin like Momma put in Christmas stockings sometimes. The weight was wrong, and whatever was inside the package was soft and squishy.

"Glenna's good at finding things," Jonathan said. "What you got there, sis?"

She held it up for him to see.

"One-Eyed Jack," Jonathan read the label printed in big, black, loopy letters beside the profile drawing of the Jack of Hearts like the ones in a deck of Bicycle playing cards. "Pleasure Plus Condom?"

Jonny was a good reader, so Glenna knew he got the words right, even if he didn't know exactly what they meant.

"What the heck is this?" Jonny pinched the edge of the little circle and wiggled it back and forth, just out of Uncle Billy's reach. "It's some kind of rubber, ain't it?"

"Not mine," Billy said, but he followed the little package with his eyes, sweating like a pony that's been ridden way too hard. Perspiration mixed with the hair gel on his forehead and dribbled off his chin in greasy droplets. "Let me have that, Jonny. I'll dispose of it proper."

Momma didn't look like she had any doubt who the condom belonged to. She tried to look somewhere else but her gaze kept coming back to the colored circle Jonathan dangled in front of Uncle William.

"Prevention of disease." Jonathan kept all of his attention on Uncle Billy so Glenna knew he only pretended to read the small print on the package. "What disease is that, Uncle Billy? Maybe I'll ask Daddy."

Billy lurched at Jonny, but Glenna stepped into his path and sent him sprawling on the floor. The house shook when he hit. It kept on shaking while he crawled around on all fours yelling, "Give me that rubber, you little fart knocker!"

Momma stepped in front of him, stood with her arms crossed, and put a foot on Billy's shoulder. She told Jonathan, "Give it to him. This instant!"

Uncle Billy held out his hand and took the condom, but he'd lost interest now that he could look up Momma's skirt.

She saw what Uncle Billy was doing, but instead of taking her foot down, she twisted the sole of her shoe back and forth on his shoulder as if she was crushing a cigarette butt. It looked to Glenna like something more was about to happen. Something she and Jonathan might not want to know about. Something Daddy would definitely want to know about.

The breeze picked up the way it did when someone opened the front door. Momma's skirt fluttered like the flag at the top of the pole in front of the Idabel post office. Billy craned his neck so his face moved a little closer to her hem.

"What the hell is going on here?" Daddy stepped into the room.

Momma uncrossed her arms and turned them into a shrug. "Ain't what it looks like."

Billy didn't say anything. He crawled past Daddy on all fours and headed for the open door like a dog that just had a number-two accident. Daddy kicked him in the butt as he went by then turned back toward Momma. His eyes never made it high enough for him to look at her face. His attention was stuck on the One-Eyed Jack condom at her feet.

"That ain't what it looks like, neither." Mom put one foot over the condom and asked Daddy, "Why didn't you call and let me know you were coming back?"

"WHORE," WAS THE only word that made it all the way through Glenna's parent's bedroom walls. Daddy said that word as loud and clear as a radio minister predicting the end of the world. He wasn't talking about the *Whore of Babylon,* either.

He was talking about Momma.

Glenna covered her ears too late to do any good. Her hair swelled with electricity. Static sparks jumped between her and everything she touched. Daddy started shouting early in the morning, after he caught sight of a man lurking in the forest who he thought was Uncle Billy.

"Not close enough for a good look. By the time I found my shotgun, he was gone." Shouts came and went all day. Ugly words. Slaps too, and tears. Something was about to happen. Glenna knew that for sure, even though there hadn't been a storm since Uncle Billy left.

Daddy moved through the house like a whirlwind. He knocked things over, never stopping anyplace long enough to say, "Hello, Glenna. How're you doing?"

He looked at her the way an owl looks at a mouse that's wandered too far from cover.

Glenna kept chairs and tables between them when she could, and she kept a good supply of tears close to the surface. She wasn't sure they'd be enough to calm him down.

"You don't look nothin' like me." Daddy closed one eye and then the other, evaluating her from different points of view.

"Jonny looks like me!" He shouted at his and Momma's bedroom door. "But this one don't look like me one bit." He clenched his hands into fists and waited for an argument.

The few seconds of silence that followed was more threatening than Daddy's shouting. Glenna wanted to run, but the door squeaked on its hinges as it opened, freezing her in place.

Momma stepped out of the darkness of the bedroom and stood perfectly framed in the doorway. Her eyes were swollen from tears. A bruise the size of Daddy's palm colored one of her cheeks. "Billy ain't nothing to me. Never was nothing to me." She stepped into the living room, walking carefully as if she was afraid the floor would swallow her up if she put her feet in the wrong place. "Just a friend is all." She stood in front of Daddy so he had to look at her while she talked to him. "Glenna's your blood. And blood is the most important Choctaw thing."

She never seemed to remember Daddy didn't care about Indian ways. Barely had enough tribal blood to get his teeth fixed at the Hugo dental clinic.

He turned away from Momma, back to Glenna, his face still full of anger. She tried to hide behind a table, but his gaze settled on her with no trouble. "Ain't nobody in my family ever spirit-jabbered like she does." He ground his right fist into the palm of his left hand.

"Your blood," Momma said. "Glenna's your blood."

But Daddy was remembering that she was Momma's blood, too. Cheating blood. Unfaithful blood. Uncle Billy-tainted blood.

Glenna stood up straight as he walked toward her. She stepped out from behind the table and held her arms out to him the way she did when she was three years old and wanted to be picked up.

He stopped in front of her, frozen like he was trapped inside a block of ice.

"Daddy." Glenna used her little girl voice. She touched his arm and mouthed the words again, silently.

He pushed his face closer to hers, deciding whether to bite or kiss. When his lips were a quarter inch from her forehead, a spark jumped the gap.

He jerked back. Stood. "Nobody in my family ever—" He wheeled around, strode to the door, then left.

10

Temptation Sorts the Apostles from the Perverts

"BLOW OUT THE candles, darlin'." Uncle Billy cleared his throat, spat into a birthday napkin, then smiled. "Can't be sixteen 'til the fire's put out."

He made sure Momma wasn't looking while his hand drifted in Glenna's direction, slow and steady, as if it had a mind of its own. Closer and closer until her brother said, "Best not touch her, Billy." Jonathan showed him one of the scary looks he'd learned from the hoodlum friends he'd taken up with.

"No harm done, Jonny." Uncle Billy stepped behind Momma. "Tell him, Olivia. I didn't mean no harm."

"It's Daddy's way, is all." She rubbed her hands together as if she were washing away a stubborn stain and looked at Jonathan to see if he'd pretend not to notice what she said.

When Jonathan's right hand turned into a fist, she tried again. "Uncle Billy, I mean. Hard to keep my men straight since Shorty left."

She leaned over Glenna's cake and blew the candles out. "Now it's done. We can all relax."

They fidgeted in silence while the paraffin-scented smoke rose to eye level and spread across the kitchen.

Finally, Momma thought of something more to say. "Birthdays are family time." She crossed her arms and lowered her voice the way she always did right before she talked about Choctaw ways. "Spirits come around on birthdays." She waved her hands around like a show-girl on a TV gameshow, as if ghosts were prizes her family might win if they answered the questions right.

She looked from Uncle Billy to Jonathan and then settled on her daughter. "You feel them. Don't you sweetheart? That's one of the ways you're special."

Glenna nodded her head instead of trying to explain. She felt Shiners, all right. Felt them really strong since Daddy had gone away and Uncle Billy came and took his place. They floated outside her bedroom windows, pulling her attention like a magnet. Waiting for her to invite them inside, like vampires on late-night horror shows.

Glenna didn't think Shiners were the same as spirits. More like the fingerprints spirits left on this world when they went on to the next—hints at what they used to be a long time ago before everything changed and swept their world away. Most of the time their voices sounded like a radio with its dial between two stations—squawks, chirps, foreign phrases, and half-words that didn't come in through her ears.

A cold spot settled in the kitchen and made the candle smoke sink closer to the floor.

Momma said, "Family is the most important thing." She didn't care if family was alive or dead. Brothers, sisters, great-aunts, half-cousins twice removed. Even nasty old uncles who wanted you to call them Daddy.

"Family." Momma touched her fingers to her lips and blew Glenna a kiss. Her way of saying she loved her daughter no matter what. Even if Daddy never came back. Even if Glenna couldn't go to school anymore and kept her trapped in the house pretending to be a home-school teacher.

"What's wrong, sweetheart?" Momma asked.

So many answers to that question, but the words wouldn't take hold. Glenna put her back against a wall and edged out of the room so Uncle Billy couldn't watch her from behind. She moved as if she were on a ledge that ran around the top floor of the tallest building in the world. After a few careful steps, the image was too real to break the spell. The pretend-ledge narrowed as she got closer to her room then disappeared as she reached the door, so she jumped.

A thunderclap shook the house as her feet hit the floor. Scattered raindrops tapped a pattern on the roof like a coded message—the way Choctaw soldiers talked to each other in World War II, when Indians saved America by speaking languages nobody else could understand.

"Things are changing fast," is what Glenna thought the coded message said.

She tried to say, "I already know," but the words turned backward before they made it to her lips. Like they did when she tried to tell Uncle Billy, "Don't look at me that way. Don't smell my hair. Don't bump into me by *accident.*"

Thoughts twisted into circles. They stuck in her throat so she couldn't get enough air until she opened a window.

A spring storm had blown into the Choctaw corner of Oklahoma, full of lightning and wind. Sparks jumped between the clouds. Thunder rumbled. Rain fell from the sky in marble-sized drops, round and perfect, each one a lens that held an upside-down image of the world.

Lightning flashed in the forest a hundred paces from Glenna's bedroom window. The trees stood out in sharp relief. A small herd of deer stared at her. Behind them stood two men, twenty feet apart, hunched over in the rain. Both turned toward her window, unaware of each other, unaware of the deer, unaware of the pair of dimly glowing discs hovering between them like a double swarm of fireflies.

The Shiners pulled at Glenna with a force as irresistible as gravity.

She climbed out her bedroom window and let the storm wash away the grime from Uncle Billy's secret thoughts. The wind blew her hair into dark, wet tangles. Voices followed her as she walked toward the forest, jumbled spirit-thoughts from everywhere at once.

The Shiners told her things she could almost understand, even though she didn't want to. About Uncle Billy and Momma. About Daddy. About Jonathan. About natural things that nobody could stop and unnatural things that might happen if she wasn't careful. And being careful was the opposite of walking toward the forest in a storm where two men watched her for reasons she didn't understand.

Lightning struck a tree behind the deer herd and sent it running. The two men turned toward the noise and noticed each other for the first time. The flash printed their faces in Glenna's mind as clear and detailed as drawings in India ink.

Old Carl and Reverend Junior Johnson.

The preacher drew his cowboy pistol. Holding it in a double-handed grip, he aimed it at Old Carl, pulled back the hammer, and prepared to violate Commandment Number Six.

The old man's full attention was already back on Glenna. He ignored the rain and the thunder and the pistol pointed at him and moved toward her, stumbling through the underbrush until he stood beside the lightning-struck tree that smoldered in spite of the rain.

Glenna's Shiners moved between her and Old Carl. Their foxfire glow highlighted every line and angle in his face. He held out his arms like a long-lost uncle meeting a favorite niece after a long separation. He motioned for her to come closer, and she might have if his eyes hadn't reminded her so much of Uncle Billy's.

Reverend Junior Johnson moved closer to Old Carl. His lips formed words, but rolling thunder drowned out his message. He shut one eye and sighted down his pistol barrel even though he was so close he could hardly miss.

Glenna watched the preacher's finger tighten on the trigger.

She watched his eyes fill with the power of justifiable homicide. She watched his lips twist into a smile that held not one particle of joy.

Lightning struck the tree again the moment Junior Johnson pulled the trigger.

A jagged streak of electricity jumped off the trunk and lit Old Carl like a flash bulb. His hair stood straight out. His arms and legs stiffened then collapsed. A cloud of steam rose from his soggy clothing as he crumpled onto the forest floor.

Glenna watched the preacher holster his weapon and take Old Carl's pulse. She couldn't hear what he said over the thunder, but she read his lips by the light of the two Shiners hovering nearby.

"Dead," the preacher checked the old man for bullet wounds.

There were none.

He started to say something else but lightning struck the tree again. Sparks jumped from the trunk and slapped Glenna's face like a disrespectful child. Foxfire covered her fingers. Another flash of lightning froze the world into a black-and-white image. Green Hickory nuts hit the ground with a sound like a runaway heart.

A finger of electricity thumped her on the forehead, sending her sprawling. All the air in her lungs came out at once, strong enough to blow out every candle on every birthday cake she'd ever had.

She didn't notice when the preacher picked her up, not until she choked on the rain that fell into her open mouth. He carried her toward her open bedroom window, where her Momma, Jonathan, and Uncle Billy posed in the light of a bedside lamp like a family portrait.

Rain fell on Junior Johnson as he carried Glenna to her house, exactly as it had fallen on him while he hid in the forest waiting for an opportunity to see her again. But it felt different, now that he had her in his arms. It felt warmer, softer—a baptismal cleansing.

God was watching. He was dead sure of that. There was no other explanation for the electrocuted pervert lying under the burning tree like a YouTube trailer for the Old Testament. Junior listened for a word of encouragement from above, but all he heard were the sancti-monious tones of his dead wife, complaining as usual.

He couldn't make out exactly what Elizabeth was saying—he'd need a drop or two of Tupa to manage that—but her attitude came through loud and clear. She wanted him to put the girl down in a safe, relatively dry place then walk away before it was too late.

"It's already too late," he told her. It had been too late ever since an ancient heathen Indian drew her picture on some cemetery pots and buried them in a mound where Junior Johnson would hold his Equinox Revival nine thousand years later.

"No way that could be a coincidence." Junior felt heat from the girl's body seep through his soaked clothing and knew this was one of those blessed moments men of God spend their lives trying to find. Everything was perfect except for the fact that looking at her pretty face and holding her so close stirred some feelings he wouldn't want his congregation to find out about.

"Temptation." His eyes filled with water as he turned his face to-ward the rain and winked at the Heavenly Father. Temptations of the flesh filled the Bible from the Book of Genesis to the Book of Revela-tion. God used temptations to sort the apostles from the perverts, so Junior's feelings for Glenna were part of a cosmic plan and nothing to be ashamed of. He stepped through the undergrowth, over Vir-ginia creeper and volunteer elm trees, and around bits and pieces of a ruined cabin that had been built on the property when this part of Oklahoma was Indian Territory. Lightning flashes gave him broken images of the terrain that fit together like a Tupa hallucination. He felt the weight of the bottle in his pocket, nearly full because he'd cut back his consumption since the Equinox Revival when he saw the girl whose picture was on the anthropologist's cemetery pots.

He'd almost forgotten the subtle asymmetries of her face, but they came back to him in electric flashes as lightning filled the air with noise and the smell of ozone.

"Glenna." He said her name aloud just to hear the sound of it because he didn't expect her to wake up anytime soon. Maybe never. Maybe God would take this girl from him, pluck her out of his loving arms. But he felt her chest expand and contract. He felt her heartbeat as he carried her toward her family. She coughed and sputtered and turned her head so the rain wouldn't run into her mouth and nose.

Alive. But what would a simpleminded girl be like after God touched her with lightning a second time?

"The old pervert is dead," he told her. Junior considered taking credit for that but reconsidered. It didn't make sense to strain his already tense relationship with the Lord.

"Pretty girl." He whispered too softly for Glenna to hear in case she was fully conscious. It wouldn't do for her to think there were two old perverts after her.

Her mother stood at the open bedroom window with a man—not Shorty—and a boy Junior didn't know. She didn't look surprised to see a stranger carry her unconscious daughter through a storm.

No one asked him what happened to Glenna. No one asked him what he was doing in the woods in the middle of a torrential rain. He stood in front of the open window, relishing the feel of the girl in his arms and the awe on the faces of her family.

Lightning flashes projected his shadow onto the side of the house. Thunder shook the world like an apocalyptic artillery battle. If Junior could arrange this kind of special effects for his sermons, he'd have his Paraguayan mission paid for twice over.

Two human shadows stood beside his, taller because they walked behind him, thicker because they were the shadows of his Guarani Indian assistants. Too bad such an impressive spectacle was wasted on only three people.

Glenna's family looked ready to run. The boy backed away from the window.

"Jonny," Olivia said.

"Jonny." Junior repeated the name.

The boy ignored them and disappeared into the house.

"There's a dead man in the woods," the preacher said. "The one who bothered Glenna."

The electrical storm intensified as if on cue.

The boy, Jonathan, came back into the room carrying a cell phone. He recorded Junior Johnson handing the lightning-struck girl to her mother. He recorded Olivia refusing to take the child, stepping back and falling to her knees in prayer.

He recorded the man who was not Shorty taking the girl instead, positioning his hands in places a jury of his peers would call inappropriate. "Put her down, Billy." The boy stopped documenting Junior's latest miracle. He looked ready to back up his aggressive tone with action but was too afraid of the Reverend and his ugly twin assistants.

"Her dress is all burned." Billy pulled Glenna against his chest and would have held her there if she hadn't worked an arm free. She clenched her hand into a fist and pounded his nose—once, twice, three times until he dropped her on the floor and ended Junior's miracle with a thump.

The preacher backed into the pouring rain that fell in front of him like a curtain.

"Mine," he whispered to himself and then said the word again a little louder—so God was sure to hear.

"SOME THINGS ARE best forgotten," Momma said. She propped Glenna on a pillow and tucked her under a grandmother quilt with kaleidoscope patterns as beautiful and unpredictable as an electrical storm.

She spooned potato soup into her daughter's mouth and blotted stray dribbles with a napkin.

Forgetting would be simple. The only thing Glenna knew for certain was that it's difficult to eat soup in bed without making a mess. Her head ached. Her ears rang. The skin on her face felt tight and hot the way it did when she'd spent all day in the summer sun.

She ran her fingers across her forehead and found two sticky patches where her eyebrows should have been.

"It's not so bad." Momma stroked Glenna's hair and stirred up a smell like burned chicken feathers. "Could have killed you. Like it killed that man out in the woods."

The image of Old Carl lying dead on the forest floor popped into Glenna's mind, his eyes frozen wide open, his clothes smoldering in the falling rain. She crossed her arms over her chest and felt the stitches in the grandmother quilt push against her skin.

"Naked!" That word bubbled out of her mouth perfectly clear, as full of meaning as the dictionary. She had lots of questions, but they all tried to get out at the same time and only one word that made it out. "Naked." She repeated it over and over again.

Uncle Billy peeked around the doorframe and said, "Sounds like the birthday girl's awake."

Glenna curled her legs and pulled the quilt around her. She tried to hold the cloth so it wouldn't fall across her body in ways that might interest him.

"No need to cover up," Billy said. "Guess I've seen everything now." He wiped a speck of drool from the corner of his mouth. His eyes danced over Glenna's covered body as if he had X-ray vision. He held a driver's license in one hand and a wad of cash in the other and waved them around like a prize.

"Carl Collins." He read the name on the license, slipped it into his pocket, then counted the money, popping each bill between his fingers as he called out the denomination.

"Forty dollars," Billy said. "Figured we ought to get something out of what Carl Collins did to our little girl." He laid a five-dollar bill on Glenna's leg and patted it into place. "Reckon you should come away with something besides shame."

Momma said, "Your birthday dress was burned. Billy had to take it off." She tightened her lips into a thin flat line the way she looked when she tasted sour milk.

"Took off every stitch." He reached for her, but Glenna pushed his hand away. "You were slippery. As hard to hold onto as a girl-shaped bar of soap." He wiped his hand across his mouth again and would have sat down on the bed if Jonathan hadn't come into the room.

"He saw you naked, Glenna," her brother said. "Ain't no way to take that back."

"So did your little fart knocker of a brother," Uncle Billy said. "So did everyone." He held his hands in front of him with his palms up then flexed his fingers into claws to show what a job it had been to hold onto a wet, naked, lightning-struck girl.

"What were you doing out there?" Momma's subtle shift of tone made it more an accusation than curiosity.

Glenna shrugged. That was one of those things best forgotten.

"I'll call the cops soon as it stops raining." Billy crossed his heart as if he were making a solemn promise. "Probably shouldn't mention the forty dollars."

11

Don't Lead Him On

EVERY ROOM IN the house was crowded when Uncle Billy was in it. Glenna kept her eyes in motion, dancing around the kitchen, looking everywhere he wasn't. She kept track of him by his clumsy footsteps and noisy breathing and the hot funk that preceded him a good six inches beyond his reach.

"Pretty, pretty, pretty." He tried to slap her bottom, but she moved too quickly. "You're just as pretty as ever, scorched eyebrows and all."

She made it to the opposite side of the table where Momma stood, holding a stack of dishes. Billy followed her until he ran headlong into an icy maternal stare that stopped him in his tracks.

"Time to set the table." Momma shoved the dishes into Glenna's hands almost hard enough to knock her over and gave her a look that was almost sharp enough to draw blood. She told Billy, "Give my girl some space."

Billy would be more careful if Jonathan were around, but he'd been gone for two days now. As there were only place settings for three, it seemed he wouldn't return for dinner. Glenna wanted to ask where he had gone, when he would be back. She could have done that easily. Words started coming back one at a time right after the police took Old Carl's body away. She could roll sentences off her tongue without so much as a stutter or a misalignment. But she kept that mostly to herself because the last thing in the world she wanted was conversation with Uncle Billy.

Billy feinted to the left and then moved to the right, like a fat, ugly quarterback on the world's clumsiest football team. He brushed his fingers across one of Glenna's breasts without so much as an, "I beg your pardon."

"Stop it, Billy." Those words came out of Glenna's mouth as crisp and clear as the glint in Uncle Billy's eyes. "I'll tell Jonny."

"Well, well, well." He turned to Momma and nodded like he'd just picked a winning lottery number. "E-lect-ro-shock. Didn't I tell you, Olivia? Lightning's done zapped the craziness out of Daddy's little girl."

Momma didn't contradict him about Glenna's mental state or him referring to himself as her daddy. "Jonny's in jail. Billy thinks it will do him some good to spend some time around big boy criminals."

"See if he likes the life," Uncle Billy said. "Kind of an apprenticeship."

The news knocked the breath out of Glenna. Her toes and fingers tingled, her hair filled with electricity almost as much as it had right before lightning struck. She wanted to ask how long Jonny would be away, but her words were lost again. The lightning strike's curative effect vanished and left her speechless—helpless in a room with a man who had plans for her and a mother who wouldn't stop him.

The dishes slid out of her hands. They shattered on the floor.

"Well, well, well." Billy put his arms around her before she understood what was happening. She looked at her mother but her vision was blurred by Billy's greasy face pushing against hers, kissing and nibbling her burned eyebrows.

"Pretty as ever." He wiped a few strands of hair off of her forehead and planted a wet kiss on her lips, full of gum-chewing noises and bad breath.

"You two stop it, now!" Momma clapped her hands to show them what a slap would sound like.

But Glenna couldn't stop something she wasn't doing. All she could do was fight for breath and try to keep her body away from the disgusting man holding her in a bear hug in front of a mother who pretended not to understand what was happening.

"Billy?" Momma's voice turned up at the end.

"Glenna?"

Two one-word questions in a row. That meant no slap was coming. That meant Momma didn't know—*refused* to know—who was at fault while she watched Billy put his hands where they had no business being.

"Sit down," Momma said, calm and reasonable as if Billy hadn't already gone well beyond the reach of reason. "Come on, Daddy. Sit down and have some dinner."

The word "Daddy" stopped him but only for a moment. "Don't want no cookin'," he said. "Not 'til after…." His face scrunched as he tried to think of a way to couch his plans in innocent terms.

Glenna's hair crackled and popped with electricity. Sparks flew into Billy's face and made him step away, far enough for her to kick him in the groin. Men always forgot their weakest spot when they ought to be remembering it most.

She picked up a serving fork and held it like a dagger in case he still had kissing on his mind.

Nobody wanted cookin' after that.

———

WHEN BILLY WAS the only man in the house, there was no such thing as privacy. Momma ran hot water into the tub while Glenna tried to decide if it was safe to be naked with nothing but her mother and a bathroom door to protect her.

Momma sprinkled vitex berries into the tub, "to wash impure thoughts away." As if Glenna was the one with a dirty mind.

Billy's shadow moved back and forth underneath the door.

"He won't come in," Momma promised.

Floor planks creaked as he shifted his weight. His breathing was noisier than water running into the tub. He mumbled words under his breath. Dirty words—Glenna could tell from the juicy noises that came between them. He'd mix in an occasional moan, as if she was the cause of a much deeper pain than a kick in the groin.

Being quiet was no protection when a man like Uncle Billy knew exactly where to find her. Glenna faced the door, prepared to fight if he came inside. And why wouldn't he? The only thing preventing him was a conscience he'd temporarily misplaced.

"Shouldn't have kicked him," Momma told her. "That kind of violence stirs up a man's emotions."

As far as Glenna could see, Billy's emotions didn't take much stirring. She put her ear to the door, listening for bad intentions turning into action, but all she heard was the bathtub filling and the beginning of another thunderstorm.

She took off her clothes slowly, so her mother could see the bruises on her legs, her breasts, her bottom. They started showing the day after she was struck by lightning. The day after Billy undressed her and put her in bed under the Grandmother quilt with everyone watching. The bruises turned green and red around the edges, the perfect copy of Uncle Billy's hands.

Her mother went silent, the perfect copy of Uncle Billy's regrets.

Glenna pointed to an especially vivid mark and looked at the bathroom door. She wanted to ask her mother if she watched while he did those things to her, but all she could manage was a single word. "Naked?"

"He'd act different if you'd call him Daddy," Momma said. "Put fatherly ideas in his head instead of the ones he has."

The vitex berries gave the water a pale blue color and made the air smell sweet. Glenna wondered if the scent would make her more attractive to Billy. Her skin tingled as the hot water covered her body. A cloud of steam rose as she settled into place. Her muscles relaxed in spite of the fat old man having a disgusting conversation with himself a few feet away.

"Got to see if I can find a way to get you back into school." Momma shook her head yes as if she were agreeing with someone else in the room.

Glenna looked for Shiners, but the lights were too bright.

"Ain't healthy for a man like Billy to be cooped up all day with a girl like you."

The muttering on the other side of the door grew louder, clear enough so Glenna could make out the forbidden words the old man mixed with her name. She shivered in spite of the warm water.

"Some things are part of a man's soul," Momma said. "Glued so tight there's no way to break them loose." The bathroom door eased open. She leaned against it until it closed again. "Sometimes girls turn pretty all at once. Sometimes they turn pretty in a special way. Once men like Billy see them, they never can forget." Momma crossed her arms and looked like she was coming to a decision—whether to throw Uncle Billy out of her house or try to forget what she already knew.

Glenna stepped out of the tub and covered herself with a towel so her mother wouldn't have to ignore the bruises any longer.

"Don't lead him on," Momma said. "It don't take much to lead men like Billy where you don't want them to go."

The floor creaked outside the bathroom door. Clumsy footsteps moved down the hall. Glenna couldn't tell which direction, only that they were going away and that was good enough. She listened for the length of time she could hold her breath—only thunder, rain, and wind. When no footsteps returned, she exhaled.

"Men just naturally turn their attention to the prettiest girl in the room." Momma looked a little angry about that. "The more they watch, the more they want to see." She tugged and rearranged Glenna's towel to cover all the parts that might especially interest Billy.

"We never had that talk mothers and daughters are supposed to have. Thought because you were special...." She opened the bathroom door and looked both directions. "All clear." After adjusting the towel again, she stepped into the hallway. Glenna ducked behind her, trying her best not to lead Uncle Billy on as Momma walked her to her room.

"Best if I stay here while you dress for bed." Momma stood in the doorway scanning the hall as if that were the most natural thing in the world.

The grandmother quilt was pulled back. Pillows were plumped. Everything about the bed was inviting but the memories.

"Pajamas would be best." Momma stepped into the room, closed the door gently, then leaned against it. "Gowns might be seen by some men as an invitation." She looked under the bed while Glenna buttoned a pair of flannel pajamas up to the neck—threadbare at the knees and elbows, the least inviting nightwear she owned.

Rain blew against the bedroom window. Lightning flashed across the sky. Thunder rumbled in the deep, predatory way of winter storms that crawl to Oklahoma from the Gulf of Mexico. There'd be tornados somewhere before the night was over—houses destroyed, tree limbs shattered, lives carried away like runaway kites.

Glenna climbed into her bed then pulled the grandmother quilt up around her neck and pretended it would protect her.

Momma kissed her good night. "Everything will be all right," she promised before backing out of the room, keeping watch until the door was shut.

Glenna listened for retreating footsteps. After a minute or so, she heard them. She ran her fingers through her hair and was relieved to feel the tingle of static electricity. Shiners were nearby, the way they always were during storms.

If she was quiet, she could hear them whispering in the wind and rain. The words were incomprehensible and comforting like the lullabies her mother used to sing when Glenna was a toddler—when she showed such promising signs of being normal.

For a few moments, she lost her fear. Everything would be all right, just like Momma said. But then her closet door creaked open, the one place her mother hadn't searched for monsters.

Uncle Billy stepped into the room, smiling like a dog that hasn't decided whether to be frightened or vicious. "Storm's getting worse. Just wanted to see you were okay."

Just wanted to hide in your closet. Watch you through the keyhole. See what you do when you think no one is looking. Wait for exactly the right time.

The tip of his tongue ran along the edges of his front teeth. Testing to see if they were sharp enough to break the skin of a young girl who's pretty in that special way that men like him found so appealing.

Glenna tried to follow Momma's advice and call him "Daddy" so his mind would fill with paternal thoughts and perhaps a bit of shame, but even the simplest words were out of reach. She pulled the grandmother quilt around her neck, the way she protected herself from pretend monsters when she was a little girl. But Billy was too real for quilts and covers. He stood in front of the open closet, holding his hands toward her, leaning forward as if he were being drawn by an irresistible force.

He moved across the room, one nervous step at a time, like a man about to jump across a chasm deep enough to kill him if he didn't do it exactly right.

"Such a pretty girl."

She pulled the quilt over her chin, over her mouth, over her nose. She would have pulled it further, but she needed her eyes to see what Billy would do next. Even though she didn't want to see. Even though watching wouldn't stop him.

"Gonna be a bad one." He pointed to the storm outside the bedroom window but he kept his eyes on Glenna. "A real bad one." His eyes roamed the kaleidoscope quilt that wasn't going to slow him down a bit. Looking for an easy place to touch. A place so easy it looked like an invitation.

As his hand moved toward her face, a spark of static electricity bit him on the finger.

Shiner voices were lost in a sudden downpour. The lights flashed off and on then dimmed to a steady red glow that turned Billy's face the color of the devil's.

His hand moved close enough to draw another spark, longer and stronger than the last. Miniature lightning. A warning to anyone smart enough to listen.

Glenna tried to threaten Billy from underneath the grandmother quilt. Her mind posed perfect arguments no sane man could ignore— forensic evidence, the testimony of a simpleminded girl, the life of a pedophile rapist behind prison walls. But those arguments were reduced to squeaks by the time they reached her lips, except for one word that came out intact.

"Momma!"

It was accompanied by a crash of thunder that sounded like the start of the apocalypse.

Uncle Billy paused. He studied the hand that had been reaching for Glenna as if it might burst into flames. For ten seconds he looked at it. Twenty seconds. Thirty. A very long time for a man like Billy to consider making a new plan.

"Coincidence. That's all it was." As he reached for her again, another thunderclap shook the house. The lights went out.

Billy was lost in darkness.

Glenna could hear him breathing, could feel the air moving around the hand she knew was coming for her and didn't have very far to go. Electricity crackled in her hair, building up a charge she knew wouldn't be enough to discourage him this time.

She took a deep breath and prepared to scream.

The bedroom door burst open. Momma stepped into the room, illuminated by a series of lightning flashes as she moved across the floor. The electrical storm spaced her steps out so she disappeared in one place and reappeared in another.

She held a butcher knife in her hand.

"Olivia." Billy took another look at his offending hand and dropped it to his side. He backed away from the bed and surveyed the room, looking for a place to run.

"Brought you this," Momma handed Glenna the knife, handle first. "A girl feels safer with a butcher knife under her pillow."

She turned to Billy, who was backed against the wall, remembering what it felt like to be kicked in the groin. "Let's go, Daddy. You don't have to keep my girl company any longer."

"Sure thing, Momma."

She walked him out of the room hand in hand, like a U.S. Marshal cuffed to the most wanted man in the world.

12

Isn't That Right... Daddy?

THERE WAS A note stuck to the refrigerator door. *"Gone to bail out Jonny."* Glenna read it twice to be sure.

Her brother was not quite a man, but he was man enough to stand between her and Uncle Billy. She'd be safe when he came back—safer, at least. Words would find their way back to her lips. She'd point to her bruises and accuse Uncle Billy loud enough that Momma would have to listen, and if she didn't, Jonathan would.

A breeze blew across the kitchen table and tipped a box of Wheaties on its side. The breakfast of champions—white gymnasts, African American basketball players, Asian ice skaters, Hispanic runners, gay divers, lesbian tennis players. None of them like Glenna. Not one frightened Choctaw girl with a dangerous "uncle" her mother didn't want to hear about.

The breeze was strong because someone had opened the front door. Three pairs of footsteps—exactly the number Glenna expected—moved toward the kitchen, slow and easy, so she had plenty of time to work out how she'd convince Momma that Billy had to go.

The words lined up in her mind, ready to come out in single file.

Understandable. Undeniable.

The first word balanced on her tongue like a high diver on a Wheaties box, ready to set a new world record.

Someone else spoke first. "It's Jonny's crazy sister."

Glenna said, "Uncle Billy," because those two words had already taken shape. Nothing else followed.

The three boys spread out so they stood between her and every way to escape. She sat on the floor, shrank into a girl so small and pathetic she wasn't worth the trouble.

One of them said, "She's kind of hot." His voice reminded her of Uncle Billy's. His hand felt moist and nervous when it touched her on the shoulder.

"You okay?" He rapped his knuckles on her head, the way Momma tested watermelons to see if they were ripe.

The only answer she had was a groan, almost too soft to hear.

"Jonny says she don't talk much."

Glenna couldn't tell which boy said that.

They traded looks. They moved in closer. Took turns touching her gently and only on the shoulders, like cats teasing a mouse into thinking it has a chance.

"She can talk."

"She said 'Uncle Billy.'"

It didn't matter who was speaking. The voices were all the same, taunting, full of rut and arrogance.

Glenna brought her knees against her chest. Pulled them closer with her arms. Curled herself into a cold, tight, unappealing little ball.

"She didn't make no sense, and she ain't saying nothing else."

One of them ran his fingers through her hair. No sparks.

"We could take her with us."

She closed her eyes and listened for Shiner voices but all she heard was static. She pretended hands weren't lifting her. Carrying her through the house.

"Jonny's gonna be pissed." One of them had lost his courage, but the one who carried Glenna had enough to go around.

"She's soft," he said. "Smells good, too."

The other two boys sniffed the air like a pair of hounds tracking a raccoon.

"Smells like candy."

"Smells like a wet dream."

They didn't notice she was crying until two of them wedged her between them in the back seat of their car. One boy touched a tear with his fingertip and tasted it. "Sweet."

"I'm pretty sure we shouldn't do this," the other said.

The driver didn't say a thing, but Glenna thought he was "pretty sure we shouldn't do this" too.

They took her to 888 Pushmataha Road—assuming the address painted in Chinese red over the door of the house was correct. There were holes in the roof and broken windows, but the lights worked and there was a telephone.

One boy moved lamps away from the windows. "Storm coming. Don't want to blow the fuses." When he was finished moving lamps, he paced in circles around the room.

The other two sat beside Glenna on the floor, a pair of guards keeping watch on their prisoner.

"Maybe this wasn't such a good idea," the pacer said. "Kidnapping, you know. Way serious."

"Only if someone finds out." One of Glenna's watchers put a hand on her shoulder and let it slide toward a breast. He pulled it back when she sobbed.

"So what are we going to do with her?" the pacer asked.

One watcher said, "We could take her back. You know, pretend it was a joke."

The other—the worst one—wasn't finished touching. "We can take her back after."

Storm clouds moved in. Drops of moisture blew through broken panes of glass along with a noise as shrill and annoying as a dog whistle.

The worst boy's mind was all made up. The other two could have been persuaded by a single "please" but Glenna couldn't say it. Shiner voices coaxed her as the storm clouds turned dark and the wind blew harder. They whispered around the room in languages spoken hundreds of years before she was born. The words were mysterious but the meaning was clear.

This is what happens to Choctaw girls who can't say please.

A gust of wind blew shards of broken glass onto the floor, sharp-edged and dirty. Perfect for ending the life of girl who turned pretty in a special, unbearable way. Cold clear fragments shaped like fractured ice. Easy for a simpleminded girl to pick up and hold without cutting any part of herself that isn't fatal.

The worst boy saw her reach for it. "Stop her!"

She held it tight with her thumb and fingers on the flat parts so she could change her mind before it was too late.

The worst boy's hand closed around the sharp edges in a desperate grab as she pulled away, determined to save the broken glass for a time when things got worse. Like the storm was getting worse with every passing minute. Rain blew through the broken window in a rush, so filled with Shiner voices she could barely hear the worst boy scream.

"He's gonna bleed to death!"

"Put pressure on it, man!"

"It'll stop. Give it time."

The storm blustered while they made their decision. The air chattered with Shiner voices and panic. Cold water didn't work. Making a fist didn't either. Or a belt tourniquet. Or a sincere prayer to Jesus.

Three blood-soaked T-shirts later, the boys made up their minds. "Emergency Room."

The sound of three frightened hoodlums coming to the same conclusion in harmony.

"What about the girl?"

Glenna sat in the middle of the floor and watched them swirl around her. Calm in the center of the storm. Comfortable with the electricity and voices in the air. No longer afraid. No longer struggling to say, "Please."

The word "Go" took shape on her lips, like she was an actor in a silent movie who didn't need subtitles to tell her story.

A gust blew more glass onto the floor. A wind-chime solo backed up by thunder. The lights flickered and went out.

"Well, what about her?"

Tree limbs blew against the house. Hailstones bounced off the roof. The sky turned the same green color as the boy who'd lost too much blood.

The green boy fell backward on stiff legs. His friends didn't think to catch him until it was too late. He bounced on the wooden floor.

The storm stopped when they picked him up. They carried him out the door then across a yard littered with hailstones and broken limbs. The weather held its breath long enough to get him into the backseat of the car.

"What can the girl do? She can't even talk." The boys didn't say another word about Jonathan's little sister, who'd turned pretty all at once in that very special way they hadn't been able to resist.

"Sorry!" one of them shouted before they slammed the car doors and drove off, leaving deep ruts in the mud.

The foxfire glow of a Shiner hovered outside a broken window, waiting for an invitation. Glenna's hair puffed with static electricity, not enough current to clear the way for speech, but enough for a single word.

"Come."

The luminous cloud floated between the sharp edges of the broken glass. It glowed brighter as the lights flashed and dimmed, or maybe that was an illusion. The difference was meaningless to a girl whose vocabulary was trapped inside her head. Everything in the world was a story she couldn't tell.

The Shiner hovered over items in the room, one at a time—a worn out couch, broken glass, lamps with old fashioned bulbs that pulled too much current from the wires—evaluating, rejecting, moving on, until it reached the telephone.

Lights flickered off then came back on a little at a time, orange at first, then yellow, then blue-white. Much brighter than they were ever meant to shine. The temperature dropped a few degrees. Hailstones clattered on the roof. The word telephone took shape in Glenna's mind.

She picked up the receiver and listened to the dial tone. The kind of sound power lines make when they bleed electricity into the air. She practiced speaking because when she finally called someone, that's what she'd have to do.

Help me. That's all she'd have to say. The words were there, but she couldn't push them out. Nothing. No sound. Not even a whisper made it through her lips.

Lightning flashed outside the window followed by thunder that rumbled across the sky. She'd been able to speak after the lightning strike. What had Uncle Billy said? "Lightning's done zapped the craziness out of Daddy's little girl."

Plenty of electricity in the air. Enough to make the hair on her arms stand out straight, enough to send a spark to whatever she touched, but not enough to demagnetize words so they wouldn't stick inside her head.

The lights flashed. Four times off. Five times on. A steady blue-white burn. Glenna took it as a sign. Why not? When everything else fails, the supernatural is still there.

She took off her shoes, walked through a puddle of bad boy's blood, careful to avoid the broken glass. The light bulb burned her fingers but she unscrewed it, anyway. She tossed it on the floor. Put her index finger in the empty socket.

The jolt ran up her arm and made her teeth chatter. Yes. Not as good as lightning but good enough.

"Hello." The word slid easily off of Glenna's tongue when Momma answered the phone.

"Glenna? Where are you? Why didn't you leave a note?"

The answer was too complicated. "888 Pushmataha Road."

"What happened sweetheart?" A little anger now that Momma knew her daughter was alive. Now that Glenna was talking to her almost like a normal girl—a girl who disappeared and didn't tell anyone where she was going.

"888 Pushmataha Road." Lightning would have given her a bigger vocabulary, but all she had was enough electricity from the Southeastern Electrical Cooperative to blow a twenty-amp fuse.

"Shouldn't just go off like that," Momma said.

There was talk of long stays in her room. Talk of corporal punishment administered by Uncle Billy.

"Daddy's serious this time," Momma said. *"He knows how to deal with a willful girl."*

A willful girl he watched through the keyhole in her bedroom closet.

"888 Pushmataha Road." Things would change when Momma saw the blood and the broken glass and the broken girl who could barely talk on the telephone.

"You stay put," Momma said. *"Daddy will be there in a little while."*

Glenna hung up the phone and listened to Shiner voices as the second act of the storm began. The only dry place was a dirty couch in the middle of the room. Safe from branches that blew in through the windows, safe from sheets of rain, safe from balls of ice that bounced across the floor like ping pong balls.

Glenna curled her bloodstained bare feet under her body and waited for the storm to run its course. Part of its course was Uncle Billy stepping through the front door, drenched to his oily skin. The air that followed him smelled of ozone and sewers backing up.

"Glenna." His voice was rough and cold. The sound of ice crushed in a blender. He stepped into the puddle of bloody rainwater that filled the center of the room.

"You've caused a lot of trouble, little girl." Didn't ask if she was all right. Didn't ask how she had gotten to this place, miles from home. It didn't matter, her answer to every question would be the same—888 Pushmataha Road.

Billy's hands drifted to his belt buckle, the Western kind made of polished silver set with semi-precious stones. Lightning flashes made his hands look jerky as he unfastened it and pulled the leather strap through the loops on his wet pants.

Foxfire moved across the puddle as Billy snapped the belt against his leg. As he prepared himself for the sound it would make on the skin of a girl who was pretty in a very special way.

"Your Momma ain't here to try and change my mind. Your brother ain't here, either." His voice trembled with the need to punish.

Thunder rolled out of the east like a runaway locomotive. A thunderclap shook the house as Billy reached for her. A spark jumped between them as she took his hand.

"Glenna?" Not so sure of himself once she had him in her grip. Once he could feel the electricity filling up the room.

The flash struck the puddle where Billy stood. So bright it cast their shadows on all four walls of the room. So hot it burned their skin. So cold it froze them into suspended animation.

Glenna woke to the sound of birdsongs and the smell of singed hair. The setting sun was framed in the open door. Uncle Billy lay in the center of a pool of water the color of Oklahoma mud. His chest rose and fell in hitches and starts, the way a lung-shot deer breathes when it's looking for a peaceful place to die.

He moaned. Nothing that resembled language.

"You okay, Uncle Billy?"

"Gah?" His eyes popped open.

One side of his face tried to smile. The other stayed slack and dead as if he'd had a dentist's anesthetic.

Glenna watched him until the telephone rang.

"Hello, Momma?"

"Star sixty-nine. Finally remembered how to call you back." She still didn't ask if Glenna was okay, but she didn't sound angry any longer. *"Storm got pretty bad. Worried Daddy might not make it."*

"He made it." Glenna told her. She carried the phone to the middle of the puddle. She put the receiver against the smiling side of Uncle Billy's face.

He puzzled with his lips for a little while before he gave it up. Glenna took the phone back and told Momma he couldn't talk right now.

He lifted his hand and moved it toward her. Slow and deliberate, but this time it didn't scare her at all.

"He's indisposed." Words fell into place as if a dictionary had been blown into her mind by the storm. She looked at Uncle Billy as she talked into the antique phone. "Isn't that right... Daddy?"

13

Incontinence Could Take the Shine
Right Off a Miracle

TAKING PHOTOS OF Glenna was a complicated matter but
well worth the trouble. Each picture of the girl included at
least one glowing circle of light floating beside her or behind
her like slightly offset halos.

"A light leak or a miracle?" Junior Johnson asked himself the question with as much skepticism as he could muster. He looked toward
heaven and apologized for his doubt.

Men like Dr. Fred Bennett never doubted their view of the world.
The anthropologist would attribute the Glenna illuminations to defects in camera bodies. They'd back up their claims with graphs and
charts and quotes from Albert Einstein that sounded pretty convincing outside of a revival tent.

He pinned the photographs to his bulletin board the way serial
killers do when they construct a shrine for their next victim. It would
be easy for a casual observer to misinterpret his intentions, so Junior
completed his project in secret.

He wanted her. That's all. He was meant to have her. She was part
of a cosmic plan that was coming together a little at a time. His final goal

was hazy but getting clearer with every drop of Tupa he consumed. In the end, she'd be with him in Paraguay, far away from the constraints of American laws and judgments. After that, who could say?

Junior was forced to shoot the pictures with a telephoto lens—the kind favored by bird spotters and spies—while hiding in the woods near her house. The bulletin board would be full soon. He'd have to start a new one if he and the Good Lord didn't come up with a suitable Glenna arrangement.

"God, give me patience." That was the best kind of prayer. Something simple, said aloud so it would be sure to get the Lord's attention. Something that didn't sound like a demand but made his desires clear. He'd have the girl when all was said and done. He was sure of it.

"Amen."

He gave his shrine one last look then checked his watch. It was almost time to start the service.

People came—the way they always did—with the blank expressions of true believers expecting to see cripples walk across the revival-tent stage. A preacher with Junior's reputation couldn't do an ordinary sermon. Thanks to iPhone photos and videos, he was an internet sensation. True believers had seen him stop the rain on YouTube. They'd heard rumors of an old pervert struck down by lightning at Junior Johnson's command. Money had been flowing into his PayPal account, enough to fully fund his Paraguayan mission.

Trouble was, people always wanted more.

Back in the old days, one big miracle would carry a holy man for a decade or more. Loaves and fishes, walking on water, raising Lazarus from the dead—those were all time favorites, but how long would they have lasted if people could click on a link and watch them anytime they wanted?

Conditions were perfect for another miracle. A spring storm moved up from the gulf and microbursts of wind shook the tent. The gathering congregation gave off the bittersweet chocolate scent of a God-fearing crowd drunk on the Holy Spirit. Hundreds of Kool-Aid-stained paper cups lay on the grass between the rows of wooden folding chairs.

Junior turned his microphone on and cued the organist. After eight bars of "I'm So Glad," he had the crowd's full attention. They swayed to the music for a couple of beats then went into a wave like football fans who knew ESPN cameras were watching. Faces twisted into expressions that couldn't decide between ecstasy and terror. The way people look when they ride a rollercoaster, when it feels like they're going to die but know that won't really happen. Some of them looked toward the cooler wondering if there was time for another cup of Jesus Juice.

The Reverend Junior Johnson could have taught Jim Jones a thing or two. The secret to a successful Kool-Aid operation is lots of sugar. Sweetness opens the door and invites the medicine to come in. A spoonful is good. Two spoonsful are better. Big spoons are preferred.

For now, his ugly assistants stood in front of the podium at ten and two o'clock like an electrified fence until Reverend Junior signaled it was time to start the show.

"Pedros! It's time." The Reverend barely needed the Holy Spirit's help after his congregation was properly Tupafied. He saw love in their dilated eyes and heard faith in their voices as they climbed to the hallucinogenic peak.

"How much did you boys put in that Kool-Aid?"

The Pedros ignored Junior's question the way they ignored everything he said.

No matter. He wouldn't have understood their answers anyway. They moved into the crowd like Paraguayan Jaguars in tall grass, completely invisible in a matter of seconds.

People were already speaking in tongues. Dancing the St. Vitus Foxtrot. Shouting praise.

Junior pulled his bottle out of his pocket. He looked toward heaven and hardly blinked as he applied a drop to his right eye. After a momentary sting, Tupa shook hands with the preacher's soul.

The first few seconds were the best. He was tempted to do another drop but held back.

"Save it for later," he told himself. And it was a good thing he showed restraint because spirits were already coming through the canvas.

The organist quit playing and the congregation got quiet the way they always did when the time was right for a telegram from God.

Junior did a Tupa moonwalk behind the podium like he was channeling Michael Jackson. His wife's ghost floated up on the stage and shimmered beside him. Peripheral vision was all she'd allow most days. He supposed that was his punishment for killing her.

"It was an accident, pure and simple." At least as much her fault as his, but Junior could never figure out how Elizabeth was going to act. Whether she'd smile and blame him, or smile and tell him all was forgiven, or smile and let him wonder.

"It's okay, Junior. This looks like a good night." There was almost as much sugar in Elizabeth's voice as Junior put in the Christian Kool-Aid, but it didn't completely hide the bitterness.

Trouble was, Elizabeth could read his mind. Could do it when she was alive and could do it better now that she wasn't.

He held up his arms the way politicians do when they've cheated their way to the top of an election. The congregation went dead quiet. They listened to Junior like he was reading to them from a new, improved version of the Ten Commandments.

"Thou shalt not kill," he said, because Elizabeth was still on his mind. The congregation echoed the commandment in unison. The faithful in this part of Oklahoma were Old Testament kind of people. They waited for him to say more, as if he was on the verge of reporting the latest breaking gospel news. As if he was about to tell them when the world was going to end and how to get a first-class seat on Rapture Airline.

"Wouldn't happen again, Elizabeth. Not in a million, zillion years."
Not since Junior had learned to manage Tupa.

A man couldn't put a jungle drug on a time clock. Tupa worked on
its own schedule. Junior knew that now. Depending on the weather,
depending on the hour of the day, depending on the ideas it met when
it arrived at its destination.

Junior and Tupa were old friends now. Business partners. The
drug and the internet were making him rich and famous. Richer than
Billy Graham and Oral Roberts put together. His wife was the price he
had to pay. Godly prices were always steep.

"At least you're in a better place, Elizabeth."

"It ain't that good," she said.

He turned his head toward her so quickly there was no way she
could fade into the shadows. But she popped like a soap bubble. Even
a Tupafied preacher couldn't sneak up on a ghost.

He hopped off the stage and walked among the congregation,
laying hands on everyone he passed. Some of them danced. Some of
them fainted. He spotted the Pedros in the back, breaking up a fight.
The spirit took everybody in different directions.

But when the screaming started, they all came together.

A woman's scream. Wasn't it always a woman? The man beside her
pitched onto the paper cup-littered grass. His arms and legs thrashed
like insects caught in a spider web.

He was still by the time Junior reached him.

"Dead!" The woman screamed loud enough to convince everyone
under the canvas.

Junior put a hand on the man's neck the way he'd seen the mission-
ary doctors do when Elizabeth passed. He shook his head solemnly,
even though he felt a pulse. It wasn't a lie if he didn't put it into words.

"Je-sus!" Junior gripped the man's shoulders with both hands. He
shook him slowly at first but gradually picked up speed until the two
men vibrated like a paint shaker in the Home Depot.

The stricken man kept moving after Junior quit shaking him. He moved right through his grand mal seizure into being wide awake.

"Praise the Lord." It was a preacher's duty to share credit with God—even if nothing supernatural really happened.

The *resurrected* man had peed himself while his spirit was in heaven. Junior held him close so people wouldn't notice until their enthusiasm was in high gear. Incontinence could take the shine right off a miracle.

The resurrected man stumbled to his feet so full of halleluiahs he couldn't keep them bottled up. That started an avalanche of "Praise the Lords" and the only thing to do was let it run its course.

Lots of noise. Lots of motion. Junior sat on the floor, the way Buddha posed for the brass statues the Vietnamese sell in their grocery stores. He closed his eyes and waited until everything got quiet.

Meditation combined with Tupa nudged Junior Johnson all the way to the frontier of Nirvana. When he opened his eyes again, he was the exact center of a circle of U.S. currency. Ones, fives, tens, twenties. A couple of hundreds if Junior wasn't mistaken. And lots of coins.

The Pedros stood in their usual ten and two o'clock positions like a pair of cigar store Indians sulking about the Cuban embargo.

"We had a pretty good night," Junior said to no one in particular "Healing services are good, but Dead Raising services are way better."

"You need to lighten up on the Tupa, boys," he told the Pedros.

Not a spark of comprehension in their eyes. They hardly ever spoke and when they did, they mostly spoke Guarani. The jungle language was full of throat catches and animal grunts, punctuated by wheezes and squawks, like a pair of five-year-olds with duck calls.

"*Entiende?* You understand me, Pedros?"

Probably not. They stared straight through him like he was one of the ghosts that could only be seen through a healthy dose of Tupa.

"How'd you boys follow me from Paraguay, anyway?"

Not a grunt. Not a shrug.

"Wasn't like I invited you." One night he had walked out onto his stage and there they were, standing in front of him the way they'd been ever since.

"Creo," one told him.

"Conozco," said the other one.

Junior figured those were names, but he couldn't really be sure. The Indians brought Tupa with them when they came. He knew what that was all right. Junior and Elizabeth had started on the jungle drug back in Paraguay. Innocently at first. A local witch doctor passed them a cup at one of the heathen ceremonies.

The Pedros were there. At least Junior thought so. God made white men all different, but Paraguayan Indians looked like they'd been put together in a factory with only one set of human blueprints. Long black hair and saggy breasts for the women. Long black hair and loincloths for the men. Until the natives started dressing in Goodwill imports. Then it was Pittsburgh Steelers jerseys, pajama bottoms and flip flops for everyone.

Indians at the Paraguayan mission listened to Junior's sermons the way old-time English Catholics listened to Latin masses. Words didn't matter as long as they felt the spirits moving in the trees. After they shared some Tupa with Junior, he could feel the spirits too.

He hadn't meant to incorporate the drug into his Oklahoma services. Hadn't meant to use the drug at all after it killed Elizabeth. But somehow, he had.

14

In Your Watchful Care

A FAMOUS FIRE and brimstone evangelist had just folded up his tent when Junior's team arrived in Idabel.

"This is one tough town." Reverend Daryl Thomas specialized in prophecies. He spread his arms wide, turned his eyes to heaven, and prophesized that Junior wouldn't draw much of a crowd, despite his internet fame. "Evangelists from Arkansas and Texas come through Idabel regular. Local Christians have drunk their fill."

Junior wasn't worried. He'd been in town for several days, fluffing the community with rumors of signs and wonders, and his fans kept him all over Twitter and Facebook. There were gifs and shorts of him carrying Glenna in from the woods, all lit up with holy light that followed the girl through every digital image she was in. And a YouTube video of Junior raising a "dead" man with a touch and a prayer had reached a million views.

"Hugo's a better bet," Reverend Daryl said. "Traveling preachers hardly go there. Hugo Christians are hungry for the Word."

Junior pointed to a flat piece of ground and signaled his crew to get started.

"Lazarus miracle," he told Reverend Daryl. Maybe that was bragging, but bragging was a little sin and raising up the dead was a big miracle. Even if the man he raised was only nearly dead. "Resurrection is the point of this whole business. Ain't it?"

He gave Reverend Daryl a triumphant smile, making sure to get his lip line high enough so the fire and brimstone preacher would get a good look at the gold inlayed cross on his front tooth.

By six p.m., cars and pickup trucks were already pulling in.

The impending storm wouldn't keep the crowds away. Hadn't Junior already proved he could stop the rain?

He could see the western horizon through the entryway of his tent. Clouds turned the light of the setting sun pea-soup green. Thunder rolled across the sky like a slow-motion avalanche.

"Something big will happen tonight." He looked up as he spoke so anybody who noticed wouldn't think he was talking to himself as he stood behind the podium.

His gospel girls mingled with the congregation. The sweet young things had shown up in droves after his dead-raising miracle. In more sinful parts of the United States, they'd be following rock-and-roll bands. But in the southeastern corner of Oklahoma, it was evangelists. And Junior was the man of the moment.

The Idabel crowd was mostly Choctaw, with a scattering of African Americans and a handful of white stragglers. None of them was talkative, but almost nobody would turn down conversation from a pretty Christian teenager. The girls collected information from the crowd. They told Junior who'd passed away. Who was sick. Gave him an idea of what kind of miracles would impress the locals. They spread rumors about aching teeth filled with heavenly painless root canals, brain tumors that vanished with a touch of Junior's hand, and withered limbs that straightened up so fast nobody thought to take a picture. A half dozen pretty girls could manage a crowd better than a pack of German Shepherds, and nobody needed first aid afterward.

Junior put a drop of Tupa in his left eye, because the right one was still blurry from his last application.

"All things in moderation," he told Elizabeth.

She materialized in his peripheral vision and drifted forward as the drug took hold. The spirits had a solid look tonight. Some of them floated around the halogen lights like helium balloons. Some of them buzzed the stage. Some mingled with the gospel girls.

Elizabeth put her fists on her hips and tapped her foot the way she always did when Junior turned his thoughts to pretty girls.

"I only go as far as the Bible allows," Junior told Elizabeth's ghost, and if things got a tiny bit inappropriate now and then, he had no doubt his good works made up for his indiscretions. The Bible provided for considerable latitude.

The Pedros moved away from the stage, traveling through the crowd like icebreakers sailing through an Arctic freeze. Each one took a different aisle so the congregation was forced toward their seats.

There weren't many cups on the grass. No people gathered around the cooler. Wrong flavor? Lemon lime worked last Wednesday night in Poteau, but the Idabel crowd wasn't drinking.

A thunderclap shook the world. Horizontal sheets of rain blew across the entryway.

"Maybe the storm is one of those signs you're always going on about," Elizabeth whispered.

The Idabel Christians prayed with Junior. They sang hymns and said their halleluiahs as he walked among them.

He drank two cups of Kool-Aid to set an example. He fed the congregation information collected by the gospel girls and a few facts he was pretty certain had a bona fide supernatural origin. He knew middle names of dead cousins. He knew slights that needed forgiveness. He knew which husbands had wandering ways and which wives had a taste for gin.

Spirits fluttered around him like bats sweeping insects from the air.

If the congregation saw them, they gave no sign, and when everything was finished, they sent the offering basket back with some coins and a couple of crumpled dollar bills.

"Reverend Daryl Thomas had it right," Elizabeth said. "There ain't enough money in that basket to fill a pole dancer's G-string."

No matter what he tried, Junior couldn't excite the congregation. Couldn't make them rededicate their lives, go into trances, or pledge support for the Paraguayan mission. The gospel girls would have to settle for forehead kisses and promises of better times ahead.

After the service, Junior leaned against the central tent pole and tried to steady his Tupa-rattled world while he whispered a silent prayer thanking the Lord for his PayPal income, which kept going strong even when revival nights failed.

"Sorry, ladies."

The G-girls understood—his respect meant they wouldn't be getting any money.

"Hochatown is next Sunday's stop." Junior was careful not to phrase it like an invitation. "Sure to be better offerings there." He reached behind him and gripped the tent pole with both hands. "I should say there'll *probably* be better offerings." Not even a prophet like Reverend Daryl could predict the future in the evangelist business.

"I know you girls don't do it for the money." Junior wasn't doing it for the money, either. Not any longer. His bank account was full and running over. There was plenty of cash to move his operation down to Paraguay, where he could really make his mark. A prophet couldn't reach his full potential unless he was far away or long ago. That's how legends were started, how names were written in the holy books, how men like Junior Johnson were put on an equal footing with the apostles—dare he say even equal with Jesus.

A feminine rain had replaced the deluge. The girls reached into their handbags for rain hats and miniature umbrellas. They filed out of the tent in pairs.

"God's work is never easy." Tupa made Junior's words circle his head and echo off the canvas. He closed his eyes and counted to ten. When he opened them again, the girls were gone and the world spun a little slower.

"Nasty little girls," Elizabeth said, as if she knew what went on in the adult section of Junior's mind. Jesus might pardon a man for having natural thoughts, but Junior's dead wife never would.

"Preacher." A real voice. A female voice. Probably a gospel girl, but he couldn't be sure.

She stepped in front of him, too close for him to look away. This girl had furrows across her brow and a hard set to her mouth. At least eighteen. Old enough to vote. Old enough to think grown-woman thoughts. She looked a little bit like Glenna, but then all pretty girls looked a little bit like Glenna. Junior would figure out her name later on.

"That old Tupa's gonna make my head throb." Elizabeth laughed behind Junior's back when he said that. Gospel girls didn't know about Tupa. Not for sure, anyway.

The Guarani moved behind the girl. They'd grab her if Junior wanted them to. Drag her into the rain and scare her so bad she wouldn't think of spreading rumors. They understood Junior's body language. They recognized his moods, even if they didn't understand his English.

The gospel girl got the message, too. "Think I'll go back home for a little while. Honor thy father and thy mother, you know." She backed away from Junior. The Pedros stepped apart so her path was clear.

"Daddy's passed, But I still have to honor momma. Right?"

"Tupa," Junior answered. "Tupa, Tupa, Tupa." He leaned harder against the tent pole and pretended he was speaking tongues.

The world wobbled like a top running out of spin. The spirits flickered like cheap special effects in a fairgrounds ghost house. Junior could walk away from the tent pole if he wanted to, but Tupa was prone to tricks.

"Visitors." Elizabeth's voice blended with the rolling thunder.

Junior followed the direction the Pedros' eyes had turned and found a woman walking toward him, too blurred to recognize. Still, she looked familiar through the haze. He heard two sets of footsteps, but Tupa did things like that.

He scooted around the tent pole so she was directly in front of him. He let go with one hand, then the other, but remained ready to grab for the pole again if the world tipped over. He held his arms straight out at his sides, the way a man keeps his balance on a tightrope.

"Set your feet apart," Elizabeth told him. "Point your toes out."

"Thanks." The world felt steadier, but the woman stopped at least six feet away, unwilling to come closer to a man who talked with people who weren't there. She stood quietly and stared at a puddle of water at Junior's feet long enough for her face to find its place in his memory.

"I'm Olivia Anoli." She stepped aside so Junior could see Glenna had been hidden behind her mother, like a secret treasure.

Junior stepped forward and extended his hand, anxious to touch the girl who had never left his mind since the Equinox Revival. When his hand was three inches from her face, a spark jumped the gap with a pop that sounded like a cap pistol being fired.

"Careful, preacher." Olivia Anoli's tone was flat and dull as if she'd said nothing unusual.

Junior stared at her long enough to make her blush.

"Glenna started in a lightning flash, and it never strays too far." Her gaze shifted toward the Guarani Indians. They shuffled behind Junior, taking their usual spread-out positions so the woman had to dart her head back and forth to keep track of them. "One man killed. You were there when that happened."

Junior shifted his gaze to Glenna. She stared back at him like polite Choctaw girls never did.

"A teenage boy's been hurt real bad," Olivia said. "My Billy's so addled, I have to care for him night and day."

Junior reached for Glenna again. Got another shock.

"A simpleminded girl with her looks makes men act foolish," Olivia said. "They should know better, but they don't."

Junior understood completely. He took a step closer to Glenna, close enough so he could feel her body heat rising beside him but not close enough for another shock.

"I've known she was special since the start," Olivia said. "Too special for a woman like me." She backed away as smooth as a ballet dancer moves across the stage with no sign of motion above the waist.

Junior watched her getting smaller, listened to her voice growing faint.

"I'm leaving her with you, Preacher." She stood quietly at the entryway of the tent for an uncomfortably long moment. "In your watchful care. It's only right. You were with her before the she was even born."

Then Olivia Anoli stepped out into the rain.

There was a dangerous, exciting feel about the girl. Glenna had her own face—unlike most pretty girls—full of subtle asymmetries. She stood out from her background, perfectly focused like an image in an old-time stereopticon.

Junior felt the hair on his arms and legs stand up. Pulling him toward her. The girl had a power his senses couldn't register. Like ultraviolet light that remained invisible while it cooked your skin, or X-rays that brushed against cells too gently to be noticed but hard enough to turn them into cancer.

It was clear to Junior Johnson that Glenna was meant for him. He knew it with the certainty of a mother picking out her baby in a nursery. The girl's body was designed by God to fit into the preacher's arms.

Energy filled the air around her. An irresistible, electrical, reproductive force that made gravity look like a suggestion. Junior Johnson was doomed to fall under Glenna's influence the way a meteorite falls into earth's atmosphere. He could feel his skin beginning to catch fire.

The hair on the girl's head swelled like a pufferfish that's been threatened. Junior heard the snapping and popping of static discharges.

"Careful," Elizabeth warned. "Don't get too close."

But he'd had already gotten too close. He breathed too fast. Too much oxygen turned his blood alkaline, but he couldn't slow it down. A humming noise came from the tent pole that had steadied him, a high lonesome whine like a circuit that's been overloaded by a surge. The smell of ozone filled the air. Junior turned toward the pole and raised both hands like a burglar surrendering to the police.

He didn't mean to catch the lightning flash that jumped from the pole, but that's exactly what he did. A two-handed catch. Bright sparks. An explosion.

When Junior Johnson opened his eyes again, Glenna was still there, standing between the Pedros.

"What happened?"

Nobody answered. Junior's Tupa had completely worn off, so he couldn't hear Elizabeth.

The palms of his hands burned as if they held a matching pair of coals. Where the lifelines joined the love lines, charred flesh cracked open and bled, a miracle as easy to understand as one drawn on the pages of a Classics Comic Book.

He closed his eyes and aimed a thank you at the top of his tent. He hoped God wouldn't hear the doubt in his voice.

...two years later

15

It's a Goddamned Miracle

"**G**O ON, TOUCH her hand." The Reverend Junior Johnson nudged Glenna toward the group of sweaty pilgrims climbing off the Paraguayan chicken bus. "The girl won't mind."

The crowd was mostly senior citizens with the latest iPhones in their hands. They looked at the screens, consulted mates for technical advice, then started taking videos and photos.

Junior pushed Glenna again, a little too forcefully to suit the wide-eyed Christians. They gathered in a frightened knot, afraid of the jungle, afraid of the local Indians watching them from the trees, even a little bit afraid of the pretty girl with the black wavy hair and the lopsided smile moving toward them.

"Injuns are safe." The preacher gave her another push. Made her stumble. She knew why—so the pilgrims would give her their full attention. So they wouldn't notice he was also checking out the forest.

She tried to make eye contact, but several of the new arrivals found more exotic things to photograph—capuchin monkeys, scarlet macaws. A couple of digital cameras focused on the gold cross inlay in the smiling preacher's front tooth.

Everything was more interesting than the silent teenage girl in the Bob Marley T-shirt being steered in their direction by an evangelist who the pilgrims hardly noticed was wearing rubber gloves.

"She's just a simpleminded girl, even safer than the Injuns. Go on, touch her hand."

Glenna was on a collision course with an older man wearing gold-rimmed glasses. He had kind eyes and a little tremor that wobbled his head back and forth as if he were trying to refuse. He backed against his fellow pilgrims but they were packed too close for him to work his way inside.

"You'll see," the preacher told him "Go on. Put your hand out."

The old man's eyes darted back and forth behind his gold-rimmed spectacles. His tremor picked up speed. It looked like he might bolt into the jungle, but the Indians were scarier than Glenna. He put on a brave face and held out his left hand, carefully, the way he might try to make friends with a stray dog.

"Perfectly safe," Junior reassured the man. "Long as you don't have a pacemaker. You don't, do you?" When the man didn't answer, Junior gave Glenna another, more gentle push, anxious to get first impressions over with.

"Daylight's burnin', girl. You know what to do."

She raised her hand slowly, deliberately. She ended the motion with a dramatic flick of the wrist that captivated the pilgrims' attention. When her fingertips were an inch from the older man's, a bright spark of electricity jumped the gap. It snapped like a firecracker. He pulled his hand back and rubbed his wrist. It took him a few stunned seconds to notice that his watch had stopped.

"It's a goddamned miracle," he said, confusing religion with static electricity the way pilgrims—and the preacher, for that matter—always did.

The old man held his hand up for everyone to see. The sweeping second hand on his Rolex was stuck on the number twelve. He took the watch off and passed it among his fellow travelers.

Glenna smiled for the crowd so she'd look good when they got around to posting her on Instagram and Facebook. She'd seen their reactions before. Some of them kissed the watch crystal. Some of them pressed it against their foreheads. One woman held the ruined watch next to her heart, paid a half-second of attention to each of the cell phones pointed in her direction then, like she was reading from the preacher's script, said, "Twelve is a holy number."

Glenna wanted to tell her holy arithmetic had no place in the Paraguayan jungle, but it was dry season and the words came out in a nervous stutter.

"My girl doesn't talk much, but she's a regular little sparkplug, all right." The preacher pulled off his rubber gloves and held up his hands so everyone could get a good look at the scars on his palms. That meant Glenna's part of the show was done.

"Stigmata." He pushed his hands forward for some close-up photographs. The braver pilgrims touched them.

"Sometimes they bleed, but they never throw off sparks. Ain't that right, Glenna?" He took a moment to shoo her away with one of his holy hands. "Go on back home, sweetheart. We'll see you at the service later on." When she was too slow to respond, he slid a glove back onto his left hand and shoved her toward the compound. "Thanks darlin'." He turned back to the new arrivals, "While you all get your luggage off the bus, I'll tell about some other miracles."

Glenna watched a flock of black vultures circle the clearing where the pilgrims unloaded their bags. Junior's southern accent got thicker as he dug into his sermon. He talked about curing cancer, restoring vision to the blind, and bringing back the dead.

Glenna knew the dead never come back—not like the preacher meant, anyway. The vultures knew it too. The pilgrims would probably figure it out eventually.

An old woman with bright-red hair and a Nike sweatsuit asked Junior, "Where's the nearest cell tower? I don't have any bars."

All the pilgrims checked their phones. Some held them up like offerings to a jungle god. They stared into the screens with stunned expressions at the miracle of a place on the planet without cell reception.

"Plenty of bars when you get back to civilization," Junior told the nervous Christians. "You can live without Facebook 'til then."

He asked for a minute of silence to thank the Lord in advance for all the miracles they would see later on. A minute was a long time for Americans to be quiet, but most of them managed. By the time the preacher said, "Amen," Glenna was halfway to the compound. Junior's words to the new arrivals carried through the jungle. "Let's get on back to the compound before…."

She knew exactly what he wanted to say. "Before the spirits come out." But he didn't. Junior Johnson didn't talk about the spirits to anyone but Glenna.

"Weird things happen after dark," he said.

She could testify to that. Everything that happened in the Paraguayan compound was deeply weird.

DARKNESS CAME SUDDENLY in the jungle. Glenna watched the red rim of the sun dip below the canopy and leave the moon alone in the sky. When the last sunlight disappeared, that moon and Reverend Junior Johnson were in charge of the world.

Junior shook a gourd rattle and danced between the rows of ancient burial pots that stood in the middle of his compound. He walked in circles around one in the center—the same one every time. Glenna could tell because that one was tipped and the others stood as straight as German soldiers.

Junior circled the pot four times, counting his laps in Spanish.

"Uno, dos, tres, cuatro." The local Indians were accustomed to things like that, but everything the preacher did was brand new to the pilgrims. He knuckle-rapped the crooked pot, cupped his hand over his ear, then paused to listen. He nodded his head as if he'd picked up the latest news from the spirit world and mouthed a soundless complicated word that none of the pilgrims would be able to figure out.

Elizabeth.

Even Glenna was impressed by the Junior Johnson show, and she'd watched him do his act a hundred times. The pilgrims had seen it on podcasts downloaded from the preacher's website and on YouTube, but watching magic happen on a tablet screen didn't come close to the real thing.

The full moon peeked around wisps of clouds that drifted in from Argentina. Animal sounds moved through the trees. The pilgrims were so nervous they hardly noticed the preacher's two ugly native assistants mixing a cooler full of cherry Kool-Aid.

"Faith is thirsty work," Junior Johnson told his flock. "You all help yourselves." He did a Michael Jackson spin and held his hands up so the moonlight reflected from his stigmata. He wore an Aloha shirt with the dolphins swimming around the buttons. The hem fluttered in the breeze that never quite stopped blowing during Paraguay's dry season. The shirt rode up enough to show the grip of the nickel-plated revolver none of the pilgrims had noticed until that moment.

The preacher shook his rattle so it blended with the jungle noises. He sputtered vowels and consonants that sounded like words struggling to be born. Every now and then a little English slipped out—quickly, so people hardly noticed. Complicated words that came from the vocabulary calendar on his desk.

He looked at heaven and said "Glenna," so the pilgrims weren't sure if he was praying to a saint they hadn't heard of or talking to the mute captive girl who lived with him in the vicarage.

She didn't think Junior was sure either.

There weren't enough torches, so the congregation filled the darkness with imagined things—especially after they had a little Kool-Aid.

"Tupa," Junior named the jungle drug at least one time during every night service. He started doing that shortly after *disclosure* came up on his vocabulary calendar. Disclosure meant telling all the facts. Glenna didn't think it counted if people thought you were speaking in tongues.

"Tupa, tupa, tupa," He ran the words together. They echoed off the rows of burial pots lined up like ceramic angels guarding the gates of heaven. Everything he did came back to the ancient jars in the end—the central props in Junior's special brand of charismatic religion.

He reminded the pilgrims that every pot had a skeleton inside. "Bones put away like peach preserves. So charged up with spirit power, they glow."

The symbols scratched into the pots might explain everything if anyone knew how to read them. Might be the dead people's names or when they were born and died. Might be their stories. Might be nothing but an old-time alphabet. No one knew for sure.

With the dry season moon, burial pots, and mute captive girl full of electricity, the preacher had no trouble holding the pilgrims' attention. The Americans gasped when he moonwalked around the skeleton pots. Glenna didn't think they'd be so impressed if they watched him practice in front of an old Michael Jackson DVD on the vicarage television.

The preacher's dance didn't impress the local Indians. They'd been waiting generations for something they weren't sure would happen in their lifetimes. They were still waiting to see if Junior Johnson was an ordinary white man with bulldozers and smallpox or the holy white visitor their gods had promised them when the pot skeletons were still alive.

Reverend Johnson timed his service so it ended when the moon settled behind the edge of the jungle. The moon's face was mushroom-white, with a jagged line across her chin drawn by the sharp points of palm fronds and Kapok leaves.

Corpse Moon. The Indians had names for every lunar face. English or Spanish names for things they thought were important enough to share with white men. This moon looked like the face of mother death peering through a tunnel at the end of the world, making sure her skeleton children were safe inside their pots.

When everyone's attention was focused on the moon, Junior Johnson squeezed an English sentence out behind his rattle noise. "Fear the priest." Borrowed from a movie about a little girl with the devil inside her. Priest is a powerful word, much more powerful than preacher. It's how he wanted his congregation to think of him.

Glenna wondered if he'd forgotten how that movie ended.

"Fear the priest." He said it so softly the congregation heard it without noticing.

Subliminal was one of the words Glenna learned from the preacher's vocabulary calendar. A way to sneak feelings past the eyes and ears.

The service was almost over when Junior Johnson drew his nickel-plated cowboy pistol. He pointed it at the moon and fired a shot. An orange flash exploded from the barrel as bright and noisy as a lightning strike. It was the preacher's way of reminding the Indians that men like him have power that doesn't rely on prayers. He pointed the weapon at the trees and sprayed the world with fire and smoke. When he stopped shooting, all the animal noises in the jungle went silent.

The Americans covered their ears, but the Indians didn't bother. There was no way to stop the ringing once it started.

A limb cracked deep in the forest. A heavy weight dropped to the ground. The preacher had killed a canopy dweller. Maybe a sloth. Maybe a howler monkey. He'd killed something without trying. He popped open the cylinder of the cowboy pistol and emptied brass cartridges on the ground. Like magic, a troop of white-faced monkeys raced out of the trees, collected the hot brass, then disappeared in all directions.

Like magic, but Glenna knew it wasn't magic. Monkeys valued shiny things the way pilgrims valued holy men. Burnt paws and the smell of gunpowder didn't discourage them.

Another heavy weight fell to the jungle floor. A howler monkey

alarm cry followed. The congregation turned its attention to the forest—even Glenna—wondering if this would be the last life the preacher
would claim that night. When they looked for Junior Johnson again,
he had disappeared.

The pilgrims went silent. A few raised iPhones to document potential miracles. When they watched their videos later, they would see
Shiners floating among the trees and wonder why they hadn't noticed
them earlier.

The Indians whispered among themselves—short sharp words that
sounded like an asthma attack. Everybody was afraid, exactly as the
preacher planned.

Men want people to be afraid of them. Glenna had figured that out
a long time ago. They called it respect, but it only comes after violence
and threats of violence. Men want money too. Sex, fear, and money—
nothing matters to a man but those three things. Junior got them by
pretending he was God's best friend. Sometimes he pretended so well
he convinced himself.

A bright light flashed in the rainforest, moonlight reflecting off of
the preacher's pistol. He kept the weapon in his hand when he night-
walked in the jungle. Glenna could make out his shape when she con-
centrated. She knew he was watching her, so she smiled—a lopsided
twist of her lips that had nothing to do with joy. She held the expression long enough to give him time to work it over in his mind. To
ask himself, one more time, whether she was simpleminded or clever.

Simpleminded. She imagined the thoughts taking shape on his lips.
Slow-witted. Crazy. Almost mute.

She knew the preacher smiled back at her, pretending to be in control. She held her right hand up so he could see sparks jump between
her fingers. She pointed at the tipped cemetery pot—the only one that
hadn't stood up straight through the centuries—and knew the smile
was sliding off of Junior Johnson's face.

The congregation had no idea what to do after the preacher did his disappearing act, so they waited quietly for something more to happen. Reality and imagination traded places in the failing moonlight. Animal noises sounded like warnings. Breezes took on the shape of words. Shiners floated at eye level among the trees. Some were as bright as new silver coins. Some were the dull, tarnished color of ancient gold. Glenna saw them clearly, even without Tupa. She heard them, too, reciting words no one had understood for centuries.

"*Pombero.*" She said one of the words out loud. It had the impact of a shout because she hardly ever spoke. The preacher's twin assistants, Creo and Conozco, moved beside her like a pair of ugly bookends. The pilgrims' eyes turned to Glenna so they didn't see the luminous boy standing under a mango tree.

Not one of the local Indians. He wasn't dressed in American Goodwill cast offs. His skin glowed like the dial on a pilgrim's wristwatch. Most Shiners were shapeless blobs of flickering light, but this one took a perfect a human shape.

A very handsome Indian boy. Glenna watched the sharp lines on his body where his muscles rippled just below the surface. Anatomy. She remembered that word from the preacher's vocabulary calendar but had never thought of it this way. The boy's body was made of curves and lines, but his face was smooth and symmetrical, like a movie star in the teen magazines delivered with the mail on chicken busses from Asuncion.

Too pretty to be real.

His hair hung over his wide shoulders. Not naked—more's the pity— he wore a loincloth. Glenna wondered how he'd look without it. The boy was quiet and confident like a cat who knew he wouldn't be seen by anyone he didn't want to see him.

A breeze blew around him and carried the scent of fermented mangos across the compound. Fruit so ripe the sugars had already begun turning to alcohol. Glenna had seen this boy before, many times, circling the compound during night service the way the preacher circled the tipped cemetery pot.

But he'd never been so close.

"*Pombero*." When she said the word again, the pilgrims moved further away and the local Indians gathered closer. Creo and Conozco tried to hold them back. One of the assistants reached out to touch her. A spark jumped from her hair to his hand. It lit up the Indian circle like a miniature flashbulb.

"*Pombero*." The word slipped between Glenna's teeth like the dying breath of an ancient whose ghost is trapped inside a jar. She was already walking toward the jungle. The circle of Indians popped like a soap bubble. They wouldn't risk one of her magic sparks.

Thunder rumbled in the distant west the way it often did in dry season. The preacher's ugly assistants followed her to the edge of the jungle, but they stopped where the trees began. Flashes from iPhones followed her for a few feet, documenting the magic for Instagram and Pinterest.

The *pombero* boy called Glenna in a voice so subliminal only she and the pot spirits could hear it. Moonlight outlined him in silver. She saw his eyes clearly and knew exactly what he wanted.

What all men want—and she just might let him have it. His smile filled her mind and stayed with her even when he turned his back and led her down a path that was invisible until illuminated by Shiner light. Then the path was clear.

A lot of things were clear to Glenna as she followed the *pombero* boy down a corridor of ferns and trees.

He stopped in one of the thousand tiny clearings in the Paraguayan jungle, small circular spaces where trees and ferns chose not to grow. This one was no more than a mile from Reverend Junior Johnson's compound, but it might as well have been on the dark side of the Corpse Moon. A solitary pot stood in the center of the clearing, shaped like the ones in the preacher's compound. No symbols were scratched into surface of this one. Pictures covered it, drawings from another era—jagged lightning bolts, a pair of hands with marks on the palms, a bearded skull. There were spirals too, clockwise and counterclock-wise like hurricanes in opposite hemispheres. A female figure was in the center of it all—primitive, not much more than a stick figure with breasts and a pregnant belly.

The boy touched the female figure. He tried to touch Glenna, but a spark of electricity stung him when his hand was still an inch away, so he pulled back... even though she didn't want him to.

Nothing would happen in this clearing unless she made it happen.

They sat and watched the shadows cast by the light of the Corpse Moon as it set behind the trees. He reached for her again. No spark this time, but he pulled back as soon as his fingers touched her shoulder.

Glenna edged closer. Smiled so he'd know it was all right. He didn't touch her again—not yet—but she thought he would when the time was right. The air was full of insect noise. Thunder rumbled in the west. The moon disappeared below the western horizon, and everything was soaked in darkness.

She felt another touch. A pair of lips against her cheek. Not a kiss exactly, but the boy was so close she could feel his breath on her face, moist and hot, like the wind in rainy season. It carried the scent of overripe fruit that must be eaten soon or it would spoil. His lips brushed against her cheek again, harder, more insistent, like a cat demanding to be petted.

No beard.

He touched her shoulders with both hands—still no static sparks, so it must be all right. Glenna pushed her breasts forward, hoping his hands would slide down and touch them, but his fingers moved into her hair instead, slowly, carefully, looking for permission. She let her head fall onto his shoulder but didn't move her arms because they might chase him away and she didn't want him to go.

The Shiner voices spoke to her. Glenna didn't understand the words but understood the warning.

The boy understood the warning too.

She wanted to tell him not to go. Now was not the right time, but that time was coming soon. *Very soon*, she wanted to tell him, but it came out, "*Pombero.*"

They stood together beside the cemetery pot as the moon sank below the edge of the world. Darkness was complete except for stars and insects with luminescent tails hovering above the undergrowth like miniature Shiners.

The boy put something in her hand, a stone as smooth as polished glass. He backed away. Two steps and Glenna could only see him because she knew he was there. Four steps and he was completely gone except for the scent of fermenting mangos.

She wondered if he'd been there at all.

16

There's No Such Thing
as Magic

THINGS WEREN'T GOING the way Junior planned. Night service was supposed to end with pistol shots. Glenna was supposed to stand up after his disappearing act. She was supposed to walk to the vicarage, brushing against the pilgrims on her way, throwing sparks and stopping watches. It was Glenna's job to end the show like a curtain falling after the third act of a play but, instead, she stayed in her circle of Indians and stared at him. Glenna looked right at Junior so anyone who followed her gaze could find him standing in the trees. Hidden but not invisible. Stealthy but not magic. Impressive, but not the kind of night service that made Americans pull out their checkbooks.

He circled the compound, weaving through the trees like a frustrated boa constrictor, trying to make his failed final act look like it was part of God's plan. The pilgrims followed his progress, still hoping for something that would be worth the price of an airline ticket to Paraguay. The Indians focused on the cemetery pots.

Junior looked at the heavens and whispered, "Everybody is a critic." A flash of lightning would be nice. A comet streaking across the sky.

Any little thing would do. His stigmata itched like a bad case of poison ivy, a reminder of the last time he had asked God for a favor. By this time, he should be sitting in his cave, safe from wandering spirits, waiting until the Indians had gone wherever they went after the night service, waiting for the Americans to slip into Tupa-troubled dreams that would make them believe what Junior Johnson did had been a miracle. If only his little sparkplug girl hadn't gone off script.

I'm the one. But it didn't matter how he tried to convince himself. Glenna, the simpleminded mute girl, had stolen Junior's show.

Lit up by foxfire. That was how she looked as she walked into the trees, her hair puffed out, sparkling with electricity. Much scarier than a man in a Hawaiian shirt brandishing a pistol.

He considered firing a few random shots. Considered shooting an Indian or two, just to demonstrate that spirits weren't the only dangerous things in the jungle. But the damage had already been done, and loud noises might attract the attention of things Junior didn't want to think about. Nothing to do but take center stage again and go on with the show. He walked out of the trees like a businessman late for an appointment then moved through the skeleton pots as smoothly and efficiently as a down-hill skier on a slalom run.

Not too late.

The Reverend Junior Johnson could still make this thing work. He stood dead still, held his hands up—palms out—so his stigmata reflected the failing torchlight. His silence pulled the attention of the crowd away from the simpleminded girl, brought them back to the holy man standing among ancient, bottled-up skeletons. A little inspiration was what Junior Johnson needed, something to get the night service back on track. The problem was, he didn't have an alternative plan.

He rotated in a slow circle and looked into the dark spaces between the stars. "Jesus, send me a sign."

Preferably one that doesn't leave scars this time.

He ran over a list of promises, ways he would scratch God's back if the Good Lord would nudge him over this rough patch in his religious act. That kind of thing usually didn't work, but it was worth a try, and lip-synching prayers added a little much-needed drama to the scene.

He gave Jesus exactly twenty seconds and, when no message flashed onto the celestial teleprompter, he pulled his Tupa bottle from his pocket. This batch was particularly strong but ought to be safe enough if he restricted the dosage. A single drop in his right eye, another in his left—the quickest route of administration short of IV injection.

Tupa users didn't build a tolerance. Not like smoking opium or snorting cocaine. The jungle drug didn't lose its power with practice. If anything, it got stronger. Junior felt the hallucinogenic key fit into the lock and heard the tumblers click. In a few seconds his pupils were so dilated the planet Venus looked like a spotlight over the western horizon. No dizziness, no sensation of falling. So far so good.

Pilgrims were documenting the preacher's act again. Phones came up, even an old-fashioned video camera or two.

"The show must go on." It didn't matter what he said after a double dose of Tupa. The Indians couldn't understand him, and the doped-up Americans would believe anything.

There were no seats in the compound's amphitheater. The pilgrims were tired from standing through the night service and weak from the metabolic byproducts of Tupa. Eventually they'd seat themselves on the dirt, putting their knee replacements and arthritis medications to the test. Sitting would be a form of surrender, an admission they didn't have the strength to stand in the presence of the Word.

The Indians squatted in a circle around the empty spot where the Glenna used to be. They wrapped their arms around their knees, ready to bolt for the forest at a moment's notice—afraid of the cemetery pots, afraid of the preacher, afraid of the Americans, and afraid of Glenna, even though she was no longer there.

The double dose of Tupa had tears dripping from the preacher's chin as if he were a televangelist who'd been caught with a prostitute.

His teardrops glittered like bioluminescent bones inside the cemetery jars. They splashed in the dust around his shoes.

Jungle drugs brought out the spirits—ghosts, demigods, disembodied voices—depending on what was on the preacher's mind. And what he had on his mind at that moment was his dead wife. He should have been talking about withered limbs made straight and eternal life, but what he did was defend himself against accusations no one heard but him.

"My only sins are committed in my dreams." His tongue felt thick. His eyes stung. His ears burned with the expectation of Elizabeth scolding him. He didn't have to wait long.

"Liar," she whispered. "Murderer. Adulterer."

How much of her was real and how much was Tupafied nerve cells firing sparks of electricity through the parts of his brain that still felt guilty about the accident?

Junior cleared his mind with a soliloquy delivered in dead languages. He followed with a string of complicated words that probably didn't fit the situation, but he liked the way they sounded. "Abrogate, bibulous, catholicity." College words, and not from a Bible college either. Words that didn't need meanings because they had so many syllables.

Tupa spun the world vertically. Junior reacted with a moonwalk through the cemetery pots to keep from falling down. The world spun for the pilgrims too, even though their doses were minimal. Most of them had lowered themselves to the ground, staining their clothing with red Paraguayan dust.

The skinny ones crossed their legs and posed in a rickety parody of far eastern mystics. The fat ones slumped on the ground like broken dolls, legs spread, bodies propped on arms so they didn't topple over. Ugly caricatures of people who hoped to discover the meaning of life in the Paraguayan wilderness.

The Indians were beautiful by comparison, balanced on the balls of their bare feet, each identical to the next, like synchronous dancers frozen into place. All men. The women stayed home when Junior started ending his night services with gunfire.

Did they hear the spirits whispering in the cemetery pots? Dead people speaking an ancient language that leaked out through microscopic cracks? Perhaps they did, but Junior's ears were the only ones that registered Elizabeth's accusations.

"It was an accident," he told her once again, even though he knew it would do no good. He held his hands together like the Shoalin monks in the Kung Fu movies he watched when the satellite TV was working.

"Accident!" He shouted the word, but nothing was loud enough or good enough for Elizabeth.

"And I never touched the girl." He looked at the empty place where Glenna used to be so Elizabeth would know who he was talking about. The pilgrims would figure out that part, of course. Glenna was the only "girl" within a hundred miles.

"Liar." Shrill, the way Elizabeth always sounded after a double eyeful of Tupa.

The trees were full of glowing spirits, come to watch his wife accuse him. He saw them clearly through properly dilated eyes. Most were nothing more than flashes. Electricity moving between the trees like sparks jumping in Glenna's hair.

"Bones!" the preacher shouted for no particular reason. He pointed at the cemetery jars and babbled like an auctioneer. His body temperature climbed, the way it often did after too much Tupa. He counted off degrees in centigrade, "Thirty-seven, thirty-eight, thirty-nine...." It rose too fast for perspiration to correct it. His brain heated to the religious boiling point and spirits came out of places they'd been hiding since men first came down from the trees.

Febrile seizure. Junior knew exactly what was happening. Not dangerous. It would pass.

"Not always," Elizabeth told him. Her voice bounced inside his head as his body began shaking. "Sometimes there's an accident."

Junior fell twitching on the ground. His bladder let go. His voice was full of phlegm as he recited a list of words and dates. "Grandiloquence, March 7. Ignominious, December 8. Legerdemain, October 6. Mendacious, January 25."

It sounded like witchcraft to the Indians and prophesy to the pilgrims, but Junior was remembering pages from the vocabulary calendar on his desk. Substitutes for an education the Lord thought he didn't need.

Junior's faith was double-strong, the way it always was with Tupa. He squinted his eyes shut and promised himself he'd never use the drug again. He promised Elizabeth, he promised God. He promised to stop dreaming about Glenna, as he'd promised so many times before.

This time I mean it.

He wanted to say the words but couldn't. His mouth was being pried open with a metal hook. Junior opened his eyes and saw the hook was on the end of a prosthetic arm, and the arm was worn by a giant of a man with khaki pants and a safari shirt and an expression on his face that said the preacher was a fool.

Junior recognized him immediately—Fred Bennett, scientist, atheist, troublemaker who had no business in Paraguay.

The hook-handed man slipped a stick between Junior's teeth, even though the seizure was almost over. He shined a flashlight into the preacher's eyes and said, "You really put on a good show, preacher. Even better than I remember."

The pilgrims stood in a circle around the two men. Junior could see by their faces they were sure what happened was supernatural.

The scientist played the flashlight over Junior's palms. "You didn't have the stigmata last time we met. Did you make them yourself?" He helped Junior to his feet. Stood beside him so everyone could see the preacher was the smaller man.

"What are you doing here?" Junior's voice sounded weak and he felt like he might throw up. The wet spot on his pants was turning cold, and the scent of urine was too strong to ignore.

"Investigator for UNESCO," Fred Bennett said. He told the pilgrims he was an anthropologist sent there to evaluate the site. He turned toward the few local Indians who hadn't disappeared into the forest and muttered a few indigenous words. They showed no sign of understanding him, but they were clearly interested in his hook.

He opened it and closed it for them—a regular puppet show. Not as mystical as an epileptic seizure, but Junior had to admit it was impressive.

"Who brought you here?" The preacher shoved his pointing finger into Bennett's face like an accusation.

"This place brought me here." The anthropologist opened the double hook on his prosthesis and made a halfhearted pass at Junior's finger. "It's the mirror image of the pre-Columbian site I excavated in Oklahoma. Had to come once I saw photos of the skeleton pots on social media."

"Nobody drives the jungle roads at night." Junior kept his finger to himself this time but his hand drifted to the butt of his pistol.

"Pretty flashy the way you use the burial jars," Bennett said. "Fusion of Christianity with indigenous theology. Impressive."

"I didn't hear any cars drive up. You didn't come here by magic."

"You were busy having a seizure, and there's no such thing as magic."

With scientists, it all came down to that in the end. The Indians turned toward a noise in the forest. Nothing unusual as far as Junior could tell—a monkey call, a gust of wind from Argentina. They drifted away without exchanging a single word. Choosing to be far away when trouble started between white men.

The pilgrims were frightened by the stranger with the hook hand who walked into the compound when no one was looking, but they might have been more frightened by the cemetery jars, the sparkplug girl who could stop watches with her touch, and a preacher with a pistol who suffered epileptic seizures.

An American woman stepped out of the circle. She took Junior by his arm. "Time to go home now. Preacher. You and the scientist can sort things out tomorrow."

"Right," the anthropologist said. "Go home and take a bath. You've pissed yourself."

17

Just Electricity

THE SUN HAD already peeked over the canopy when Glenna walked out of the jungle. Creo and Conozco waited exactly where she had left them. They looked angry, but their expressions softened when she showed them the slick stone the *pombero* boy gave her before he disappeared.

It looked like a capuchin monkey perched on the palm of her hand. Green, like the stone local Indians used to make their Tupa pipes. Smooth, as if it had been shaped by water spirits instead of an artist's hand, carved over centuries, one delicate line at a time.

When she pushed the stone monkey toward Creo and Conozco, they stepped back. Fear invaded the edges of their angry indigenous faces in a series of erratic blinks and twitches. They backed away from Glenna like a pair of fiddler crabs who had met their match. She backed them through the preacher's cemetery jars, Walking them backward through the compound, savoring the feel of power from within the stone. The sensation traveled up her arm and filled her with electricity.

The matching pair of Indians separated and escaped into the trees on opposite sides of the compound. Glenna had never seen them do anything like that. She'd never seen them more than twenty feet apart.

She turned the monkey so its stone eyes looked at her. Its power made her ears ring. Flashes of light danced across her peripheral vision like shooting stars she wasn't quick enough see straight on. Would she be stuck in that spot forever, standing among the cemetery pots, absorbing power from the stone, her hair so full of electricity it puffed around her head like a crown?

Words ran through Glenna's mind and came out through her lips, loud and clear—the opposite of subliminal. Words so old nobody understood them. They fit together like a language filled with clicks and throat catches. Complicated syllables tumbled over her tongue like a witch's spell. Electricity built inside her as if she were a radio with a short circuit pulling in signals from another world.

The dark side of power.

When Glenna held power in her hand it also had a hold on her. Until the spell was broken by three words.

"What is that?"

Three American English words in a voice from Glenna's past. "Where did you find it?" The hook-handed man from Equinox Revival night moved in front of her, too big to ignore. He towered over the preacher, who stood beside him. They both towered over the local Indian men who lined up behind them in a single row.

Handsome, was the first word that came to Glenna's mind. The hook-handed man was made of hard lines and angles, nothing like the *pombero* boy and nothing like the preacher. The tall man had a straight back, broad shoulders, and a face that radiated strength and patience.

The Indians turned their attention to the new white man who might be the one their legends promised. He was big enough, strong enough, and white enough, and he had one special attribute that filled them with fear and wonder. He opened and closed his hook-hand. Held it so the Indians, the preacher, and Glenna could see it clearly—a strength that would have been a weakness in a lesser man—and smiled to show he was aware of the effect.

"Now that I have your attention," he said to Glenna, "What's that you've got?"

The big man looked her in the eyes as if he expected an answer. When he didn't get it, he answered for her. "It's a fetish."

A new word she'd never seen on the preacher's vocabulary calendar. She tried to say it. The lip movements felt right but they came without sound.

"Sometimes the monkey is a rainmaker. Sometimes it brings fertility. Sometimes it transports spirits of the dead." Hook Man looked Glenna over, the way men always looked her over, but he didn't try to hide it. "The monkey is a multipurpose fetish."

"She won't understand you." The preacher stepped between them. He started to touch Glenna but pulled his hand back at the last moment. "The girl ain't right." He used his pointing finger to draw circles at the side of his head.

The big man eased preacher aside with his hook-hand, as simple and smooth as power steering.

The Indians behind them inhaled simultaneously.

Glenna understood what they saw. Hook Man was stronger than the preacher with his Aloha shirt and nickel-plated pistol. She offered the stone monkey to the big man, but he didn't take it right away.

"I'm Doctor Fred Bennett," he told her. "Doctor of Anthropology. Do you know what that is?" His eyes traveled up and down her body, investigating every curve—gently, almost asking permission. His smile said he appreciated what he saw.

Glenna wanted to tell him she knew all about anthropology. She wanted to tell Fred Bennett a lot of things. But the only word she could manage was, "*Pombero.*"

"See there." The Preacher tried to move between her and Fred Bennett again, but the big man shoved his hook in the preacher's way.

He eased him aside as if the minister were weightless then opened the double hook and let it snap shut.

Everyone jumped at the sound except for Glenna.

"*Pombero* is a Guarani tribal word." The anthropologist looked at Junior Johnson as if the preacher were the simpleminded one. "Means 'spirit people.'" He reached for the fetish with his right hand, paused, then moved his hook a few inches from the stone monkey. Moved it slowly as if he knew something would happen. When the hook was an inch from the capuchin fetish, a spark jumped the gap. The sharp snap caught everyone's attention—even the preacher's.

"A handy handicap." Hook Man grinned at Glenna. "Think you can show me where this came from?" He took the fetish into his right hand now that the charge was gone. His eyes explored it the way they had explored Glenna a few minutes earlier.

She smiled and shook her head yes.

"You're a very pretty girl."

EXCEPT FOR THE beads of perspiration on Junior's upper lip, his face was emotion-free as he watched Glenna shower. He followed her into their shared bedroom and watched her dress in threadbare safari pants and a Goodwill T-shirt with Bob Marley's smiling face on the back and *LIVELY UP YOURSELF* printed across her chest—castoffs from a culture five thousand miles away that had never heard of monkey fetishes and Guarani Indian spirits.

She put on her secondhand running shoes, took her time tying perfect double bows. She jumped a spark between her pointing finger and a table lamp to remind him to keep his distance.

"E-lectricity." Junior pronounced the word with a capitol *E*. He respected Glenna's little sparks. They reminded him of lightning. And defibrillation.

Electricity was a matter of life and death, and a man of God never knew which way things like that were going to go.

He held the door for her. Backed against the wall so she wouldn't brush against him, careful to touch her with nothing but his eyes.

MIDMORNING WAS THE best time to ask his North American visitors for money. Creo and Conozco were burying the pilgrims' doubts under mounds of scrambled eggs and drowning their fears in Tupa-flavored mango juice.

"Just enough to keep our congregation in a supernatural frame of mind," the preacher reminded them. "Don't want them to get so generous their checks bounce."

He wrangled Glenna across the compound with rubber glove-insulated pokes and nudges. She was the star of his daytime services. She'd charm the Christians with her smile and stop their watches with sparks of static electricity.

"People like to look at pretty girls," Junior told her. "Give them permission and they'll do it every time."

Glenna couldn't say no. It was dry season, and her vocabulary was dormant.

"My little sparkplug." He walked her through the cemetery jars to remind the Americans that sooner or later every battery runs out of juice. "Touch her folks. She doesn't mind." Their watches stopped, the way their hearts would stop eventually.

Thunder in the west sounded like a case of indigestion that might turn into a trip to the emergency room. The preacher faced the bank of clouds that hovered over the Argentina border. He held his arms up, spread them wide so he looked like a capital letter Y. Turned his palms toward the clouds, as if he and his rubber gloves were the only things holding back the violence.

Storms seldom crossed the border in dry season. Glenna knew that. The local Indians knew it, too. But the pilgrims didn't, and they were the ones with checkbooks and ballpoint pens. Lightning cooperated and filled the western sky with fireworks. The North American Christians held their smartphones in the ready position and documented everything.

Glenna's hair inflated with electricity. She pointed her finger at one pilgrim after another. Sparks jumped the gaps. One inch, two inches. No matter how many watches Glenna stopped, she could always summon another spark. It was a very good day for the preacher but a very bad day for keeping track of time.

Dry-season lightning and Glenna were the only props Junior had that could withstand daylight inspection. When the sun came out, everyone could see he was a stoop-shouldered man with a pot belly, the cemetery jars were just jars, and the bones inside the pots were just bones—even if they did glow in the dark. But Glenna was Junior's pretty little sparkplug girl, and the electrical storm over Argentina was.... Well, the pilgrims were glad he had the power to hold it back.

The anthropologist was the only one aiming his smartphone at the cemetery pots. He ignored Junior, Glenna, and the dry-season clouds boiling up in the western sky, ruining the day service with critical observation.

Fred Bennett would not eat Junior's food or drink the Tupa-laced mango juice. He wasn't looking for a backstage pass into heaven. He photographed the cemetery jars from every angle, close up and far away. He inspected them for cracks and fingerprints. He paid special attention to the tipped jar with all the footprints around it.

"This one's damaged." The anthropologist ran his hook around the lid. "Looks like the seal's been broken." He said Junior shouldn't tap on jars or touch them or lean against them. Called the pots "historical world treasures" and said, "I'm the first UNESCO anthropologist, but there'll be more if things check out."

He talked like the mission compound never really belonged to Junior.

"This is Guarani tribal land no matter how many Paraguayan bureaucrats you have on your payroll," he told Junior, "and the cemetery jars don't belong to you either."

He framed Glenna in his cell phone screen. Told her to smile. She was one more thing he was there to document, to photograph from every angle. She was one more thing the preacher didn't own. Fred Bennett said that with his eyes.

"Can't fight the United Nations." The anthropologist turned off his phone and slipped it into his pocket.

"Syria, Somalia, Rwanda, Iran, Sudan, Sierra Leone." Junior named a long list of countries that fought the United Nations just fine. He turned to his ugly twin assistants. "Bring our friend a cup of coffee." By the time Fred Bennett finished his coffee, he'd forget all about the United Nations and cultural treasures.

But the anthropologist sniffed the drink and poured it on the ground. "You're not some rogue nation with guns and missiles. You're a half-baked holy man in the company of a girl who might not have the capacity to give consent."

Glenna moved closer to Fred Bennett. Too close, as far as Junior was concerned. Her hair crackled with electricity, but the anthropologist was too busy arguing to notice.

"Holy men have been doing the same tricks for thousands of years." The anthropologist didn't shout, but he spoke loud enough for the pilgrims to hear. "Claim to know things they can't possibly know. Make promises they can't possibly keep." He ran the fingers of his human hand over the top of a cemetery jar. Stroked it as if the jar was a feral cat he meant to tame.

He reached for Glenna with his hook.

The local Indians retreated toward the trees. The pilgrims drew a breath in unison. A blue spark jumped three inches from Glenna's hair to Fred Bennett's double hook. He moved the prosthesis closer so the spark kept going until all of her electricity had bled away.

When her hair was flat again, he announced to his audience, "Just electricity."

The preacher moonwalked away from the anthropologist. The move looked clumsy in the daylight, but it was good enough to recapture the pilgrims' attention.

A thunderclap followed a distant flash of lightning by several seconds. He took it as a sign it was time to forget about Fred Bennett and put the daytime service into gear.

"What if you knew exactly when you were going to die?" Junior asked the Americans. He ignored the local Indians, who moved to the edge of the compound. Ignored the anthropologist, who wasn't going anywhere. Tried to ignore Glenna, but his gaze kept drifting back to her.

There were a dozen pilgrims gathered among the cemetery jars, their pupils dilated and their minds open to persuasion. The American Christians wanted to believe what the preacher told them, but he had to speak with more authority than usual because the anthropologist was watching. Fred Bennett was a scientist. Men like him built the airplanes that had flown the travelers from Houston to Asuncion. Scientists invented the cell phones that seldom had reception in the jungle. They designed the watches Glenna stopped with electric sparks.

Things could go either way, so Junior walked up to each of the pilgrims and looked them in the eyes. It would have worked better in the moonlight. It would have worked better if the anthropologist wasn't taking pictures, but it worked well enough.

Fred Bennett followed him on his journey from pilgrim to pilgrim. He took continuous video with a cell phone as he used the cemetery jars as props in his religious show.

"From dust thou art and to dust returneth." Junior reminded the Americans why they came to Paraguay. He pulled off his rubber gloves so they could see the bloody stigmata on his palms.

He'd picked at them, scratched at the tops of the scars so he'd leave bloody palm prints on the pilgrims' skin where he touched them. There was always a lot of touching when it was time to ask for money.

"What if you had three days to live?" He slapped the top of a cemetery jar to remind the Americans there was a skeleton inside, to remind them how long death lasts once it happens.

"For-ev-er." He stretched the word to the breaking point then lapsed into silence for an uncomfortable sixty seconds. "How many minutes in eternity?" He gave them another sixty seconds to ponder the long division of non-existence.

The anthropologist took pictures of the bloody splotches Junior's stigmata left on the pilgrims' shirts, and on the jars. He shook his head and said something into his phone.

The wind lifted the hem of the Junior's Aloha shirt so everyone could see his pistol. The grip was bone—like the bones in the cemetery jars. The finish was as shiny as a brand-new silver coin. The holster's tooled leather was the color and texture of a local Indian's skin.

"How 'bout you, Mr. Scientist?" The preacher's hand brushed across his pistol grip. "What would you do if you had just three days to live?"

The pilgrims didn't know what to say when the preacher asked them questions. They'd stumble over a sentence or two and then start writing checks. But Fred Bennett kept on taking pictures. He snapped one of Glenna—close up. He took headshots of Junior, Creo, and Conozco. He took several zoomed-in images of the bloody smudges on the last jar Junior touched.

"Guess I'd make funeral arrangements." The anthropologist reviewed the pictures on his phone. "How about you?" He held his right hand against his hook as if he were about to say a half-robotic prayer and turned his attention to Glenna. Full, unwavering eye contact. Most men, if they looked at her at all, looked at her feet or her breasts if they looked at her at all. Not Fred Bennett. And she held his gaze until he blinked—ten seconds at the most before he looked away.

Glenna understood the mathematics of eternity as well as Junior.

"Sure would like to see where that monkey fetish came from." The anthropologist spoke to her directly. Didn't ask the preacher for permission the way the pilgrims would. "Think you could show me?" He gave her time to answer. Didn't rush her. Didn't presume she'd do what he wanted. After a while he said, "Please?" then waited a little longer. No one said please to Glenna. No one asked her permission. Certainly not Junior. He had never imagined she had any appreciation of such niceties, but he was wrong.

She turned and walked toward the path.

18

Sympathetic Magic

GLENNA WALKED IN front of the preacher and the anthropologist. They moved in single file down the narrow path with Creo and Conozco bringing up the rear.

The anthropologist talked about UNESCO Heritage Sites and indigenous treasures that need international protection. The preacher talked about private property, freedom of religion, and grants from the Paraguayan government.

"We shouldn't follow her like this." The preacher was out of breath as he always was after venturing a few steps beyond the compound.

"Then don't," Fred Bennett said.

The two men swapped words back and forth, each louder than the last. They drowned out insect and bird sounds with their arguments. Lots of talking. Not much listening.

Glenna stopped. She turned and watched the two men argue, far enough away so she could duck through a wall of ferns and vanish if she chose. But this was still Paraguay. There was still no place to go. And Fred Bennett wanted to see where the fetish came from. Although she didn't have the slightest idea why—she wanted to please him.

The two men stopped when she stopped. The preacher and the anthropologist scuffled with each other like naughty little boys who both wanted to be first in line. They reached a truce when they saw Glenna watching them, arms crossed, lips pulled into a thin pink, disapproving line. The men stood side by side in a path so narrow it almost wasn't there. Creo and Conozco stood behind them, still in single file, motionless as trees. The white men fidgeted. Tight expressions on their faces teetered between reconciliation and attack. With monkeys and with men, it was always difficult to tell where a smile would lead.

The preacher shooed Glenna forward as if he were chasing a raccoon away from a trash barrel. "Go on then."

"Leave her alone." The anthropologist showed the preacher his hook, opening it like a crayfish claw.

"Don't...." The preacher shuffled away. He took his place in line behind the anthropologist before the hook could do anything more.

Fred Bennett's smile spread so wide all his teeth showed, a monkey-fighting smile for sure, but the preacher wouldn't want to fight. Fred Bennett was too big, his hook was too full of power, and Junior Johnson wasn't angry enough to imagine he could win.

The anthropologist softened his smile for Glenna. "Go on sweetheart. Take your time."

She brushed her hand across the bark of a kapok tree. Her finger came away wet with sugary sap that leaked out of a perfectly round hole. A bullet hole. The trees in this part of the forest were riddled with them from the grand finales of night services. This was a fresh one.

When she was sure of the anthropologist's full attention, she moved forward, stepping around and over fallen limbs like a dancer. One motion flowed into the next as if she'd practiced every step.

Beautiful. She could almost hear Fred Bennett's thoughts as he appreciated the way her fully extended arms brushed jungle leaves aside, the way her body blended into pleasing curves like the lines in a painting of a young woman flirting with an older man.

Not that much older. She felt the touch of the anthropologist's gaze, gentle, curious, nothing like the preacher's attention crawling over her like a pair of spiders. She wondered how Fred Bennett's lips would feel against her cheek. How his hand would feel on her shoulder? His hook?

Glenna smelled fermented mangos as she stepped into the clearing with the painted burial pot in the center. Maybe the scent was all that remained of the *pombero* boy after the sun had risen. She'd almost forgotten the monkey fetish—her only proof the boy was real. She placed it on the burial pot and gestured the way pretty girls on gameshows do so the audience's attention will move to the prizes.

"Holy shit." The preacher pointed to the pair of hands drawn on the pot. He touched the marks on the palms. "Do you see this?"

The anthropologist took out his cell phone and snapped pictures of the hands, the lightning bolts, and the stick figure from every angle. "I've seen art like this before. Rock art. Petroglyphs near my Oklahoma excavation." He spoke into his smart phone as he walked around the jar. "Solitary burial pot...." His lips kept moving but no words came out.

Glenna understood. In dry season, words were as hard to find as rain, but after a few sputters, the anthropologist found all he needed.

"Will you look at this?" He pointed his human hand at the drawing of the bearded skull. "Black pigment, as rich and dark as if painted last week." He scratched at the picture, touched his fingernail to his tongue, then shook his head. "It looks new, but I think it must be very old. Even older than the pots in the compound."

"You're looking at the wrong picture." The preacher held the palms of his hands so the anthropologist could see. "Isn't it obvious?" He spread his fingers and moved his hands over the drawings on the pot. "I tell you, it's a goddamned miracle. Like the Ten Commandments with pictures."

The preacher's hands were a perfect fit, but the anthropologist brushed them away with his hook.

"Don't touch," Fred Bennett opened and closed his hook-hand. He held it so close to the preacher's face he had to cross his eyes to focus.

Glenna had seen fights before. This is how most of them started. One man moved too close. Heads bobbed within inches of each other. Voices shifted into lower tones like a pair of aggressive dogs warning each other off. Before threats turned into violence, the scent of fermented mango grew stronger in the clearing. A boy-shaped shadow moved between the trees. A flash of luminous skin, the sound of bare feet stepping over deadfalls. The *pombero* boy was much more interesting than two white men fighting over an old pot. He retreated into the forest, and Glenna followed.

Behind her, angry American words filled the clearing. An argument between religion and science laid claim to something that was partly both. The preacher used Old Testament words, but Fred Bennett's scientific vocabulary had a much sharper edge.

A hundred yards into the jungle and she couldn't hear them anymore. The only sounds were birds, insects, and broad green jungle leaves slapping against the boy who led Glenna to another place she'd never been. Her Nikes slipped and slid. She didn't move like a dancer anymore. She could hardly keep up with the sound of bare feet weaving between cashew and mango trees.

He followed a game-trail marked by marsh deer hoofprints and scat. Glenna navigated by shadows and noises. It was easier when she stopped trying. Easier after she admitted the jungle boy might not be real. No more real than the voices she heard when no one spoke or the glowing balls of light no one else could see.

Shiners. A word for something that might exist only in her mind. Had she actually seen the boy? His scent was clear in her mind, but his face shifted and rippled in her memory like a reflection in a restless pool of water.

Real enough.

Real enough to make noise on the trail ahead. Real enough to caress her shoulders and her hair, to brush her cheek with his lips, to heat her skin with breath that's warm because it was inside him. Not as real as Fred Bennett perhaps, but real enough to make her want to feel his touch again.

By the time she stepped into another hidden clearing, she could scarcely pull enough oxygen out of the thick jungle air. So much heat, so much pollen, so many scents—the earthy aroma of compost, the decomposing proteins of small animals, the overwhelming odor of ripe mango. Intense sunlight felt like a poke in the eyes after so much time in the shadows of the rain forest canopy.

Another solitary burial pot sat in the center of this one, exactly like the last. The images were similar. A bearded skeleton, hands with marks in the palms, jagged lightning bolts, and a pregnant girl.

The girl on this pot had more detail. The same pregnant belly, but in this picture she had a face—two eyes, a nose, two ears. She had long black hair that fell over her shoulders in waves and curls. Her mouth curved into a smile that rose on one side more than the other.

Like mine. Glenna placed a fingertip on the picture's lips and felt pressure on her own mouth in exactly the same place.

Sympathetic magic. The local Indians believed in it. Part of the old religion Spanish Catholics couldn't chase away. The Indians carried charms with locks of hair and baby teeth and bits of umbilical cord to keep their lovers and their children close. The girl on the pot was like those charms.

Not me, but like me.

The colors on the pot were bright, as if they'd been refreshed many times since the pictures were drawn a thousand years ago. Sharp and clean, not washed thin by rain or faded by the sun. She walked around the pot, appreciating the hues and shapes. Some of them were impossible to understand. Some of them were easy—pretty things like the pregnant girl, powerful things like the lightning bolts, evil things like the bearded skeleton man whose eyes followed her as she changed position... the way the preacher's eyes had followed her from the first day he took her into "his watchful care."

Glenna forgot about the boy until she felt his hand on her back. She didn't look at him, afraid he would be gone.

She closed her eyes as the boy turned her, gently, the way a male ballet dancer would spin his partner, then he laid her down beside the burial pot. She felt the shadow of his arm pass over her face. Felt his fingers touch the picture girl. Hesitant, magic, almost imaginary touches.

When his hand moved from the picture to caress her skin, the change was so gradual she couldn't be sure it really happened. So smooth the boy almost had permission, even though he didn't ask.

Time slipped by as she lay beside the *pombero* boy—seconds and minutes indistinguishable from hours. It was impossible to tell how long the touches moved across her body—she knew only that she didn't want them to stop. Glenna didn't complain when the boy undressed her. As natural as breathing, as sleeping. Slowly and efficiently, he worked buttons and zippers as if he'd done this kind of thing many times before.

His hands were warm and smooth. His body wasn't heavy as he lowered himself onto her then guided her along another kind of path. A path she wasn't sure existed until that moment, but the instant she was on it, she knew exactly where it ended. Glenna's emotions curled into a ball and rolled downhill so fast the law of gravity was suspended and her soul—for the first time in her life she knew with certainty there was such a thing—blended with the sounds of jungle birds and the scent of mangos.

It's done. No reason for Glenna to open her eyes even when the *pombero* boy's footsteps disappeared into the jungle. No point in opening her eyes when everything was perfect. No reason to work vision into a world of senses that were already complicated. She lay on her bed of composting leaves beside a burial pot decorated with pictures painted before Columbus accidently found America. Didn't move because when everything is perfect, there's no place to go that isn't worse. And in that perfect moment, she fell asleep and dreamed of luminous spirits whispering a secret.

This is why we brought you here.

19

Naked

JUNIOR JOHNSON WALKED among his cemetery pots and rubbed the place on his arm where the anthropologist scratched him with his hook. His stigmata seeped blood, his head throbbed in time to a Christian hymn he remembered from the good old days before the spirits of long dead Indians buzzed inside their burial pots like hives of African killer bees.

Things were going wrong. Junior saw that clearly, the way he'd seen things were going wrong just before Elizabeth's Tupa overdose. He looked into the future like a gypsy fortuneteller and saw nothing but trouble.

"Sorry, Elizabeth, for how things worked out," he said much louder than he'd planned. The Indians hardly noticed, but the North Americans exchanged troubled glances, trying to decide whether Junior was a modern-day Joan of Arc or a schizophrenic who'd gone off his medication.

Elizabeth remained silent for the moment, letting the accusations build up enough speed to break the sound barrier. Before long the false charges would come rushing out. She'd accuse him of murder. She'd accuse him of sleeping with Glenna. She'd accuse him of a thousand shameful ideas that had never ventured beyond the realm of fantasy.

Ghosts didn't differentiate between what a man wanted and what he did.

"A man can't turn away unwelcome thoughts." He looked at the pilgrims who had gathered around him. Some bowed their heads as a sign of respect. Others averted their eyes because they were embarrassed.

"When a girl is in a preacher's watchful care, he has to watch her all the time." Junior maintained a conversational volume, which was better than shouting, but not as good as whispering.

He shrugged, spreading his arms like a fledgling bird that didn't want to fly. "If she's a pretty girl, ideas take root and grow."

The American women moved closer to their husbands. The American men crossed their arms and frowned. Local Indians smoked native tobacco and marijuana in green stone pipes that had been passed from father to son since the cemetery pots were new.

"It's difficult for a woman to understand." Junior could see from the expression on the American women's faces this was a massive understatement. Living white women were as quick to judge Junior Johnson as Elizabeth. There was no point in trying to explain the movies that play in a man's mind when the pretty girl he's watching is asleep. When she's not watching him back, just lying on her bed, sparkling with electricity. Who could blame him for putting on a pair of rubber gloves and moving close enough to look after her properly? Who could blame him for dreaming he could feel the girl's electricity running through his body like the 220 voltage of the Lord?

"She would have cried out if anything had happened." That's how Junior knew it was all a dream. "Even a mute girl would cry out."

He desperately needed someone who wasn't a local Indian or a pilgrim, someone who might understand how Glenna walked away while her spiritual custodian wrestled with an anthropologist. One more thing Elizabeth would blame on him in the end.

"Got to go find her." Junior saw nothing but fear and confusion on the pilgrims' faces. He hadn't told them she was missing. He hadn't told them anything, and the more he babbled, the less they wanted to know. He reached for his bottle of Tupa. Squeezed a generous drop onto the bloody center of his left hand and made a fist. His palms still stung from the last few drops.

There was no way to judge the concentration of the Tupa. No way to control the size of the drops. No way to adjust the wildly different absorption rates, and he'd lost count of the drops long ago.

"Accidents happen," Junior told the pilgrims. His words came out much louder than they should have, and the North Americans backed a few steps further away.

Tupa seeped into his system the way spirits seeped through cracks in thousand-year-old cemetery jars.

He told Elizabeth, "Christians are supposed to go to heaven when they die, not hang around and torment their loved ones." He'd given her a proper burial—in the forest, right in front of his secret cave.

"Said my goodbyes private and personal." The way it should be between man and wife. He'd recited a verse from the Book of John while he shoveled dirt onto Elizabeth's face. "In my Father's house are many rooms...." He did that so she'd remember he did things properly.

He laid her in the grave so she'd face east when Gabriel woke her with his horn. Covered the freshly turned earth with stones to keep wild dogs away. Put a cross at the head of the grave and promised to bring flowers on Memorial Day.

But death didn't work the same in Paraguay as it did in Oklahoma. Once a body was put into the ground, ants and beetles began their work. When the bones were clean, the spirits were free to walk the world. Unfortunately for Junior, Elizabeth was never one to wander far from his side.

"Something had to be done." He heard dry bones scrape against the kiln-fired clay burial pots, shifting position so the empty eyes of the skulls lined up with microscopic cracks that weren't wide enough to let a ghost slip through but were plenty wide enough to let their voices out. Spirits had a lot to say after being sealed inside their jars for a thousand years.

Should he close his eyes the way people back in the U.S.A. talked to the dead? As if the whole thing were made up....

In the night services, a little Tupa made him look like a holy man. In daylight, he looked more like a drug addict on the verge of an overdose. His tears, the jittery way he shuffled his feet, the jerky movements his head made when he searched the forest. Everything reminded the Americans of meth users they'd seen on episodes of Cops. Everybody kept close watch on Junior—the local Indians, the pilgrims, the anthropologist. Some of them were afraid to turn their backs on him. The rest sensed a train wreck coming soon and didn't want to miss it.

Fred Bennett came up behind Junior, clearing his throat so he didn't take him by surprise. The anthropologist used his calmest suicide hotline voice. Lots of soft vowels, not so many hard-edged consonants, modulated tone, the meter of his sentences divided into hypnotic segments guaranteed to suffocate anxiety. His movements were as slow and measured as an animal control officer who's been sent to take a pit bull into custody.

"Sorry." He placed his human hand on Junior's shoulder, but moved his hook hand close to Junior's face in case things went wrong. "About the fight, I mean."

Elizabeth was reading the moving pictures in Junior's mind, a wide screen Technicolor feature film of Fred Bennett and Junior Johnson wrestling around a solitary burial pot. Of Junior Johnson losing the fight because the anthropologist's double hook caught his arm between its jaws. Of the two men rolling against the pot, tipping it. Of Creo and Conozco pulling them apart. Of the ugly twins pointing at the underbrush simultaneously and speaking one stereophonic word. "*Pombero.*"

The girl had wandered into the jungle. How long would it be until her bones were picked clean and a young energetic ghost was following Junior?

"Got to find Glenna." The preacher's voice was on the shrill edge of a scream.

"She'll come back." Fred Bennett gestured with his hook, talked about the local Indians who knew every tree and every rock of the rain forest. "They'll find her if she doesn't come back on her own."

The anthropologist believed he had the Indians figured out because he knew their history. He knew a few words of their language and some details of their ceremonies, but he didn't understand the locals at all. Junior understood them perfectly, especially after Tupa opened his mind.

"Spirits," he told the scientist. One word that said it all. One word that said more about the jungle and the Indians than every anthropology text the scientist ever read.

Doctor Fred Bennett had more important things to worry about than a simpleminded girl who wandered off. He tapped a pot with the tips of his double hook then opened and closed his prosthetic hand as if he were taking hold of something no one else could see.

He told Junior, and anyone else who cared to listen, why he'd come to the religious compound. "Ghosts of kings and queens, princes and princesses had been bottled up by holy men and stored for the day when their savior would come and let them out. Put away like canned goods with no expiration date on the promise. Death and resurrection. Not much different than Christian theology."

The anthropologist had the details all worked out, but he clearly didn't believe any part of it.

Junior showed him his bottle of Tupa. "A drop of this in one eye and you'll see things in a different light."

Fred Bennett was far too sure of himself to give the jungle drug a chance. He pushed the preacher's hand aside with his hook then opened and closed the jaws as if the prosthesis were a robot snake that could swallow every spirit in the jungle. He moved the hook closer to Junior's eyes—too close to pretend it wasn't there, especially after the Tupa concentration in his brain had reached the point of enlightenment.

Junior heard spirits moving in the trees like predatory cats. He reached beyond the hook and grasped the plastic cup that fit over the scientist's stump. The prosthesis looked magic, but it felt like a flimsy bandage covering a disability. He wanted to ask the anthropologist what happened to the bones of his amputated hand. Did he keep them close the way a Guarani Indian would because they held a piece of his soul?

He wanted to tell Fred Bennett how he had removed the luminescent bones from a pot and scattered them in the jungle. How a ghost boy glowed in the trees at night, angry with Junior for releasing him too soon, like a spiritual abortionist.

Junior put one hand on the butt of his revolver, loaded with special silver bullets.

"Don't do anything crazy, Johnson," Bennett said.

But crazy was the only sensible thing. The Indians and the spirits understood that even if the American scientist didn't.

Junior smelled mangos on the verge of going bad, the way he had when Glenna disappeared. He pointed his revolver first at the scientist, then at the burial pots.

"The quick and the dead." He felt the Indians and the pilgrims and the anthropologist move away from him. He heard capuchin monkeys chattering in the canopy all around the compound, waiting for him to fire his pistol and spill hot, shiny brass onto the ground.

Junior's stigmata tingled, as if he were touching Glenna. His heart bounced against his chest. Elizabeth's voice recited a list of grievances in his ear. The scent of over ripe mangos stung his eyes.

His vision blurred, but he saw movement in the undergrowth. A trace of white moved in the shadows. A human form. An arm. A leg.

The butt of Junior's revolver was slippery with stigmata blood and unabsorbed Tupa. He cocked the hammer back and heard the satisfying mechanical click as the weapon locked into killing position.

Could a spirit be killed? No guarantees from the Bisbee, Arizona, new age ammunition store. For fifty cents a bullet more, Junior could have had a verse from the book of Revelation engraved into every slug, but this was not the time to regret his thrift.

When the spirit showed itself, Junior would squeeze the trigger. He took a step forward, because he was not a practiced marksman. He never aimed at the end of night services, but this time he would.

"See there, Mister Scientist?" He kept a firm grip on the pistol butt with his right hand, pointed with his left at the figure moving behind the elephant ear leaves. Could the spirits hear how fast his heart was beating? Would the ghost look like a collection of dry bones in daylight?

"Hold your fire, Johnson," Fred Bennett said.

Junior released the grip of his spirit-killing pistol. There would be no gunfire in the compound, at least not yet.

Glenna stepped out from behind the elephant ears—naked, walking his way, voluntarily—just as Junior had been imagining she would since she came into his watchful care.

20

That Nasty Man

"NAKED WHEN WE found her."

Glenna knew that's what the preacher's American congregation would say, even though they did no *finding* at all. Notice her is what they did when she walked out of the jungle.

"The speechless girl" is what they'd call her, as if she didn't have a name. The pilgrims had made a point of not noticing her before. The preacher's little sparkplug girl, no more interesting than an old-time roadside attraction—a two headed chicken, a petrified dinosaur turd. Glenna was something to look at then look away before it was too late to ignore what was happening right under their self-righteous noses.

They couldn't very well ignore her when she stood at the edge of their religious compound *in all her glory* as the pilgrim women liked to say. Glenna carried her clothing—her pants, her shirt, her underwear— folded in a neat bundle. She walked past the preacher who mumbled nonsense and held a pistol in his hand. She hardly noticed him because her head was spinning with memories of the boy. She didn't hear what anyone said. Couldn't if she wanted to because her ears were full of ghost noises leaking from the cemetery pots.

She walked directly to the anthropologist and said, "I'm back," as clear as the weather report on satellite TV. Much clearer than Fred Bennett's brain when he saw her naked body. Much clearer than the Tupa-fogged mind of the preacher who stopped in the middle of talking to himself. Both men were more speechless than Glenna until a polished stone fell out of her bundle of clothing. Then Fred Bennett found some words.

"Another fetish."

The crowd of white Americans whispered all at once. Words like "rape" and "molestation" and "prison" were the easiest to make out. They talked about suspecting "something like that was going on" then got really quiet because no one had done anything to stop it.

Glenna swept her gaze across the crowd and watched Americans avert their eyes. The women looked ready to apologize for being blind. The men looked ready to deny being cowards.

A man in the crowd asked, "Who'd have guessed?" then looked at his watch as if the time of day made any difference. Even if it did, the watch wouldn't help him because Glenna had stopped it long ago with a magic touch that had moved everybody's mind away from rape and onto miracles.

The Indians backed to the edge of the compound. The careful ones stepped into the trees and vanished. The curious ones stepped into the shadows and were difficult to see.

Fred Bennett picked up the fetish with his human hand. He held it up for the Americans and the curious Indians to see. Green pipestone like the first. Another monkey.

"Exquisite." He held the stone monkey so it caught the morning sun. Green light reflected from its polished surface and colored the faces of the white Americans who were trying their best to ignore the naked girl standing in the compound. The anthropologist ignored her too—until the preacher snapped on his rubber gloves and reached for her.

Glenna let his fingers almost touch her before she pulled away. "No."

Another word, loud and clear. She moved to Fred Bennett's side. Made him drop the monkey fetish and put his arm around her naked shoulders. He pulled her closer with his large right hand. His palm was rough and calloused, almost big enough to cover her.

She pushed her body against the hand and Fred Bennett held her tighter, pulled her closer—even though that seemed impossible— comforting her, protecting her, promising her with his sandpaper touch that she'd be free of Junior Johnson in a little while. Fred Bennett stood beside Glenna, not like the *pombero* boy who made love to her then ran away.

Fred Bennett was real. Solid as a kapok tree with his hard muscles and hook-hand. She could see him in sunlight with her eyes open. Fred Bennett didn't smell like overripe mangoes. He smelled of male musk and laundry starch and Old Spice aftershave.

She smiled at the anthropologist—the same lopsided smile as the girl on the painted burial pot. She reminded him how pretty she was, how smooth her skin felt against the palm of his giant human hand.

"Go." Glenna pointed an accusing finger at the preacher. "Go." She said it softly. Hardly more than a whisper. But it seemed like a shout because everyone else was too ashamed to talk.

Creo and Conozco pushed through the circle of Americans and stood behind the Reverend Junior Johnson, far enough away from the preacher so they'd have time to change sides if things didn't go his way.

The anthropologist showed the twins his hook-hand. How they could be frightened by something they'd seen so often, she couldn't fathom, but the trick worked again. He stepped toward them. Backed them and the preacher across the compound until they scampered in three directions like a clutch of rabbits that had seen the shadow of a hawk.

When he lowered his hook hand, Glenna kissed it. A spark of

static electricity jumped between the metal and her lips. Wind blew from the west and spun leaves in a circle around the two of them. Clouds followed the wind over the top of the canopy, west to east, on a collision course with the morning sun.

"Come on honey," one of the American women stepped out of the crowd and took Glenna by the hand. "That nasty man won't bother you anymore."

Glenna held on to the anthropologist's hook-hand. Warmer than she expected. Comforting. Powerful. "Nasty man." No combination of words from the preacher's vocabulary calendar described Junior Johnson so perfectly.

The American woman pulled her away from the anthropologist, gently but persistently, the way gravity pulls ripe fruit from a tree. Glenna followed her for the same reason she had followed the preacher to Paraguay. For the same reason she followed the *pombero* boy. Because she had no choice.

"Looks like it's going to rain," the American woman said as the first drops of water fell. The large tear-shaped raindrops plopped onto the compressed red dirt of the compound's plaza. Enough rain fell to wash the grime off the cemetery pots and make the pilgrims' clothing cling to their bodies.

"Magic," Glenna told her because it never rained in the dry season. Not since the preacher brought her to Paraguay. It stopped as suddenly as it started, and the grey clouds receded over the Argentina border.

GLENNA SLEPT ALONE for the first time since her mother put her into Junior Johnson's watchful care. She showered alone. Lived in the vicarage by herself, though she supposed it wasn't a vicarage now that the preacher wasn't there.

She had no idea where Junior Johnson spent his nights. There were plenty of empty dormitory rooms now that the Americans were leaving, but the preacher was unkempt—especially in the morning—unshaven, disheveled, dirty like a homeless alcoholic standing by a U.S. highway with a cardboard sign that said *Anything Helps.*

He probably slept somewhere in the jungle, where there was no running water and no protection from the bloodthirsty Paraguayan mosquitoes. Would he work his plight into one of the sermons? He still preached to the local Indians, the anthropologist, and—of course—to her. Cast out like Adam from the Garden of Eden, patiently waiting for Eve to join him.

Glenna would have cast him out long ago if she'd known how easy it would be to turn him from a holy man into a nasty man. Just a matter of walking out of the jungle naked, pointing at him, and saying, "Go!" A one-word spell.

The preacher still watched her from a distance. He hung back like a stray dog, close enough to notice but too far away to be hit with stones—as if Glenna had an order of protection. She learned about those on the American Judge shows she watched on rare days when satellite TV could find a signal.

According to the judges, legal papers don't always keep nasty men away—but Glenna's order was the supernatural kind. Junior Johnson *had* to pay attention.

The white congregation evaporated like a pool of water at the end of a hot dry season day. No reason to stay after the preacher became one more disgraced charismatic evangelist on a long and growing list.

The departing Christians took their iPhones with them full of video miracles that looked ridiculous now that they understood how they'd been duped. How many would turn up on Facebook and YouTube? How many would be woven into the fabric of social media, undoing the legends of Junior Johnson? How many would be deleted, flushed into the endless sewers of the internet?

"*E pluribus unum.*" She pointed an accusing finger at the preacher and quoted the Latin phrase printed on the U.S. money that was leaving with the Americans as they climbed into their private cars and rode off to Asunción. It would be easy for them to forget how they were fooled when the windows in their automobiles were rolled up and the air conditioning was turned on. Easy to forget about Glenna too—the pretty, simpleminded girl still living in the compound.

Some of them said goodbye to her. Some wished her luck. One slipped a twenty-dollar bill into her hand and said, "You really ought to leave this place," but didn't offer his hired car because even though there were empty seats, "It wouldn't look right." And things already looked bad enough.

The Americans, all but Fred Bennett, packed their bags and said their prayers and flew back to the U.S. with their checkbooks and bank balances and injured pride. The only thing they left behind was one simpleminded girl and a lot of threats—*extradition, incarceration, litigation.* Glenna knew all of those words from Junior Johnson's vocabulary calendar.

Menstruation is another word that Glenna knew. Her period used to be as regular as the lunar calendar, but it went away with the American pilgrims. Even a simpleminded girl understood exactly what that meant.

Glenna was as pregnant as the girl on the solitary burial jars.

She held one hand over her belly as she walked across the compound beside Fred Bennett, protecting her baby the way no one ever protected her. She held the anthropologist's hook so everyone could see which white man she had chosen.

The Indians all knew a baby was on the way. The preacher and the anthropologist didn't have a clue.

21

Kills Don't Count
Unless You're Aiming

"**B**AT SHIT!" JUNIOR never noticed how bad the stuff smelled until he started sleeping in the cave. The little critters didn't bother him much. They flew through the jungle all night long and in the daytime hung upside down in the deeper regions. But the bat shit.... Drops of it spattered on the floor in a disturbingly regular pattern that reminded him of a leaky faucet. The ammonia stench drifted toward the entrance in the evening when the temperature dropped outside.

"Still, it's not so bad." An unconvincing lie, but even the most transparent lies would start sounding like the truth if he repeated them often enough.

"The cave has everything I need." That lie had quite a way to go before it reached the self-delusional threshold. It was closer to the truth to say the cave had everything he needed except for comfort. No electric lights to read the Bible—or to properly appreciate the three classic issues of Playboy Magazine in the box underneath the lawn chair recliner he used for a bed. No mosquito netting, no front door to discourage nosy animals, and—the worst thing of all—no bathroom.

"Plenty of toilet paper. That's a blessing." Junior said a prayer of thanks even though he ordered the toilet paper on the short wave, paid for it himself, and carried it from the compound in the middle of the night. He took every opportunity to thank God because he desperately needed to be on good terms with someone.

"*Papel de Hygenico.*" He read the large print on a family pack of double-ply rolls. He frowned at the taste of Spanish on his tongue. *Way* too lyrical for a nitty-gritty item like toilet paper. As if he were wiping his ass with a poem.

Junior used to keep words like ass out of his mind because sooner or later one of them would slip out and the pilgrims might hear it. That didn't matter now. The pilgrims had been carried away by the private hired cars that descended on the compound like a biblical plague. So, he could think words like ass as much as he liked. He could say ass out loud—shout it if the notion took him. But Junior had sunk too low to shout. Lower than when Elizabeth passed. Even lower than when her ghost started nagging him from the other side.

Was he depressed or simply facing facts? Probably depression. There was a lot of that going around these days. He'd read all about it in the magazines that came with groceries on the chicken busses from Asunción.

Depression made people lose their taste for life, and that described him perfectly. After a few days sleeping in the cave, he'd lost his taste for everything—even canned Tex-Mex chili and Meals Ready to Eat in their foil pouches that could be brought to a digestible temperature by dropping them in boiling water.

"Ambient." Junior reminded himself of a word from his vocabulary calendar that belonged to Glenna and the scientist since the troubles. It was a useful word. He ate everything at ambient jungle temperature because building a fire was not easy without a gas stove.

He had plenty of wood, but it was too damp, even in dry season. He collected it and stored it in his cave the first day, but the wood was full of bugs. Consequently, in a few hours, the cave was full of bugs. Junior almost asked God to help him out with that, but with so much in the balance, he hated to waste a prayer on something that could be handled with insect spray and citronella candles.

He tried to make a list of things to bring back on his next visit to the compound, but one of the things Junior didn't have was a pen and paper. Those were back on his desk with his vocabulary calendar and the list of Paraguayan officials he'd been bribing so nobody like Fred Bennett would show up at the mission.

He squeezed a drop of Tupa into the palm of his left hand and ground it in with a knuckle. He didn't mind the pain.

Tolerating pain was something he had in common with Jesus. A beard was another thing, although Jesus probably kept his better trimmed. Junior ran his fingers through his scruffy facial hair and imagined how he looked. Pretty cool, he bet. Wild and mystical and a little dangerous, like an old-school holy man.

The Bible wasn't clear whether Jesus heard voices, but He probably did. He had seen the devil for sure, the way Junior saw ghosts after a drop or two of jungle drug. They moved through the forest like foxfire, impossible to bring into focus but equally impossible to ignore.

Elizabeth hovered a few feet outside the cave entrance, brimming over with Glenna-accusations he wasn't in the mood to hear.

"Didn't do it," he shouted loud enough to make the birds and insects around the cave shut the hell up for a minute.

"Did, too," she said.

Sometimes he thought Elizabeth was just a bad side effect of the jungle drug, but—side effect or not—she had his dead wife's character down cold.

Capuchin monkeys gathered in her spirit glow, ready to steal anything Junior left unattended. They resembled humans. Charles Darwin was right about that, but anyone who'd been around capuchins knew the nasty little creatures had no souls.

He pointed his pistol at an especially brave one that edged into the cave, smiling the way they always do, ready for a fight. Except for the pinched face and pointed teeth, the little bastard looked like one of those black silhouette targets cops practiced on back in the U.S.A. Junior could almost see the circles and numbers on its chest. If he had another drop of Tupa, the bull's eye would come in clear and crisp.

"Easy shot." It would be a lot easier if his heart weren't flopping around in his chest like a dying carp.

"Seizure coming," Elizabeth told him. "Grand mal this time. Bet your boots."

Or maybe it was the monkey pretending to be Elizabeth. Pretending he'd evolved far enough to carry the spirit of a disagreeable dead woman. Not a reasonable idea, but not many things were reasonable lately.

The monkey hopped in fits and starts the way squirrels crossed roads back home.

"Big mistake, you little cretin." The monkey moved further into the cave, closer to Junior and his nickel-plated revolver with the six new-age, ghost-load bullets in its cylinder.

"Don't waste your ammunition, Junior." Elizabeth's voice, all right. The monkey had his eye on a half-finished can of Dinty Moore Beef Stew.

"You can't hit that monkey," Elizabeth told him. "You never could hit anything."

"What about all the animals I shot out of the trees at the end of night services? Must be a dozen. Maybe more."

"Kills don't count unless you're aiming."

"Means I didn't kill you, then. Doesn't it?" Proof positive Elizabeth wasn't some kind of jungle drug psychosis. A man couldn't out-argue one of his own hallucinations.

He held his pistol in a double-handed grip. That slowed down his trembles a little. The monkey cooperated by picking up the can of stew with his greedy little nearly-human hands that had fascinated Darwin so much. It posed like a wax statue of evolution in Madam Tussaud's Wax Museum.

Junior pulled the hammer back. He held his breath. He timed the final ounce of pressure on the trigger to coincide with the lulls between his heartbeats.

The noise of the gunshot reverberating off the cave walls caught him by surprise. A column of fire swallowed everything in front of him as the weapon jumped.

Yellow spots spread over his visual field. He listened for dying monkey sounds and thought maybe he heard something mixed in with the neurological alarm blaring in his head.

He held the pistol in front of him, pointing as if he could see a target. Capuchins have sharp teeth. If this one was wounded, he'd certainly attack.

Nitrocellulose smoke burned his nose. Tiny fragments of gunpowder residue were trapped in his beard. His stigmata throbbed, and the pistol seemed to weigh fifty pounds.

The ringing in his ears subsided into a harmonic rhythm, like a pair of tuning forks held close together. His heart adjusted its rate to match. A searing pain traveled from the fingertips of his left hand to the center of his chest.

"Call 911," he said as if he were dying in a crowd of Americans.

The cloud of gun smoke settled on him as he collapsed onto his cave floor. Insects scampered around him, getting ready to move in when the time was right.

As soon as the shaking started, he knew it wasn't a heart attack. He clenched his jaws so tight he chipped the cusps on his back teeth—a regular feature of his Tupa seizures. Then came the incontinence. Another useful vocabulary calendar word. He thought he had a change of clothing in the cave but couldn't be sure until the seizure passed.

When Junior opened his eyes, he saw two of everything. Two

caves. Two pistols lying beside him. Four stigmata covered with grime that was sure to be loaded with bacteria. No dead monkey on the cave floor. A wasted bullet, a wasted seizure, a wasted nasty bump on his head. How the hell could he go through all that and miss the capuchin?

"Told you." Elizabeth was waiting for him, naturally. Seizures only lasted a few minutes, and they loosened the mind so the Tupa could dig its way in deeper. He could almost see her shining in the corner of his left eye, but it might be a symptom of a concussion or the beginning of a detached retina.

Junior worked his way to his feet then replaced the spent bullet. He tried to check the time on his wristwatch, but it wouldn't hold still. Images separated and merged in ways a preacher would think of as metaphysical and a physician would think of as neuropathological.

He wiped at a wet spot on his mouth and smeared a streak of blood across his lips. His tongue was lacerated and raw. His eyes burned as if he had doused them with Tupa. The sun had already dropped below the canopy, but the red aura oozed through the trees so his body cast a blue shadow as he left the cave and lurched toward the compound like a zombie.

The Indians turned his way as he stepped out of the trees. They mumbled words he couldn't understand and spread out among the cemetery pots so he could only focus on one individual at a time. As if he were a wild animal with a sudden taste for Indian blood.

"The Lord works in mysterious ways." His tongue was thick and swollen, so the words were slurred. The Indians didn't mind. They were more interested in the miniature blood clots trapped in his beard and the urine-soaked circle between his legs, trying to decide whether he was sick or magic. Afraid of him either way.

Creo and Conozco looked fearful, too, and disappointed—understandable, but also unforgivable.

Junior spit a bloody wad of mucous between the cemetery pots. He faced the east, held his hands up so his body was a gigantic letter

Y, just as the moon peeked over the canopy—or two moons from his double-vision point of view, with two ancient stone faces like crude portraits of Creo and Conozco.

"Perfect timing."

The matching pair of lunar discs joined into a single moon. It looked like magic to Junior, and it sure as hell looked magic to the Indians. If it looked magic to Glenna and the anthropologist, so much the better.

22

The Truth is Different
in the Jungle

GLENNA WATCHED JUNIOR Johnson's night services while Fred Bennett stayed in the vicarage trying to figure out the shortwave radio. She sat on the ground with the local Indians while the preacher stumbled among the cemetery jars and entertained an indigenous congregation that had never heard of tax-deductible contributions.

He ranted like a homeless drunk trying to come up with an excuse for his deplorable condition. Sprays of saliva accompanied his esses and effs. He slurred his vowels. A film of blood coated his teeth and stained his shirt.

Creo and Conozco passed around cups of Tupa-laced Kool-Aid, not fooling anyone since the Americans had gone back home. The locals had no reservations about combining drug consumption with religion. They'd been doing it for thousands of years. They'd be doing it for thousands of years to come.

The preacher screamed, *"Elizabeth!"* He walked in a sloppy elliptical orbit around his favorite cemetery pot and talked nonsense about ghosts and skeletons and bullet-proof monkeys.

Glenna watched moon-shadows in the trees. She waited for the *pombero* boy the way pregnant girls waited for their boyfriends in tele-novelas. She hadn't seen any of them all the way through, but she'd seen enough to know that love stories and tragedies had the same endings.

The preacher held his hands around his mouth, shaped them like a megaphone, then sang Glenna's name in two exaggerated syllables. He pulled her attention away from the trees and gave her a big al-pha-male smile. Blood on his teeth only spoiled the effect a little. His eyes danced over the Indian congregation but kept coming back to her. His lips twitched as if he might speak in tongues, but finally he settled on English. "Always took good care of you."

Euphoria and *cadence* were two words Glenna had learned from the preacher's vocabulary calendar. They hadn't seemed all that useful at the time, but when he started praying, the meanings came right back to her.

"Never touched you." He looked at the sky and put his voice through paces holy men have always used to pull crowds into a religious frame of mind. "Never touched you even though I could have."

Another lie. Glenna thought God must be tired of hearing them. She certainly was. Every Indian head turned her way when she stood to leave. They didn't say her name, but they discussed her in the coughs and wheezes that made up their language.

Important is what the coughs and wheezes meant. All of them had seen her image on the painted burial pots, so they kept track of her in jerky glances too brief to offend the spirits. The Indians divided their attention between Glenna and the preacher. They didn't notice the *pombero* boy step out of the trees, but she did.

Finally.

Thunder rumbled in the west, threatening a storm no one be-lieved would happen so far into dry season. Lightning put on a show in the western sky. It pulled the locals' attention toward the heavens.

Glenna measured the time between the flashes and the claps of thunder by naming an American river that is exactly one second long. "One Mississippi, two Mississippi."

Lightning bolts jumped between the clouds, yellow and jagged like the ones painted on the solitary burial pots. The preacher held up his hands so the Indians could see his stigmata, pretending he was part of the electrical storm. The wind lifted his stained Aloha shirt, uncovered the pistol everyone already knew about. The air filled with humidity and the smell of ozone.

Thunderclaps followed flashes by less than one Mississippi. Scattered drops of rain sounded like half-hearted applause against the canopy—not falling on the compound yet, but soon.

Junior Johnson wrapped his hand around the grip of his nickel-plated pistol as if he could end the storm with one of his silver bullets. He backed away from the sound of rain. not moonwalking this time. The preacher staggered among the pots, ricocheting from one to another like a steel sphere in an old-time pinball game.

"Frenetic." Glenna repeated the vocabulary calendar word out loud. She pictured phonetic symbols that taught her how the letters sounded. So many perfect words on squares of paper that counted days with European names and Arabic numbers. The word sounded magic to the Indians who were already a little bit afraid of the pregnant girl their ancestors had painted on burial jars before Columbus came along and ruined everything.

They were more afraid when the preacher stumbled into the tipped pot—the Elizabeth pot—and knocked it over, spilling the bones on the ground. The Indians gasped all at the same time. They edged away from the cemetery pots, bumping against each other as they chose evacuation routes.

So much magic coming at one time—a storm in the dry season, a goddess saying magic words, a cemetery pot knocked over so its spirit could escape.

The Indians bolted for the forest when Junior Johnson drew his pistol. A minute filled with so much confusion, it was the perfect time for Glenna to go with the *pombero* boy again.

She could hardly see him in the darkness that came between lightning flashes. They ran toward the thunderstorm, away from gunshots that filled the quiet gaps between thunderclaps. Bullets slammed into tree trunks and branches.

Chain lightning turned the rainforest into an old-time movie. Local Indians stumbled between Glenna and the *pombero* boy. One of them stopped in front of her, his face frozen into a horror show advertisement. He drew his hand to his chest over words printed on his cast-off New York Yankees T-shirt. A rose-shaped splotch of blood spread around his fingers. Bubbles formed at the corners of his mouth as he tried to recite a prayer.

Another pistol shot. The Indian fell to the forest floor. Glenna stepped over him and followed the *pombero* boy.

Too many lightning strikes, too much thunder, too much panic to count the gunshots, to know if the preacher had run out of bullets, to know when it was safe to stop running.

But finally, they did stop running. The storm passed and Glenna stood with the boy in a circle of light under the jungle moon. Another clearing. Another solitary burial pot, but this one was broken. A double-handful of delicate bones lay in the center of destruction, glowing like mother of pearl under a black light.

What will Fred Bennett think?

Then the *pombero* boy kissed her, and she forgot all about glowing bones, broken burial pots, and anthropologists.

TINGLING SENSATIONS RAN through Glenna's body, exactly the way she felt the moment before lightning struck. Insects swarmed around her, attracted by the faint glow from her electrical field, but they didn't touch her flesh. The winged creatures that dared to fly too close died in miniature flashes of blue light.

Glenna covered her belly with both hands and felt the current drain into her center where it found a place to hide until needed again. She suspected she might need it very soon.

The sun pushed over the eastern canopy when she stepped into the cleared area of Junior Johnson's compound. Her insect escort vanished the way night fliers do when morning comes. Her glow faded into the first light of the day. Only an echo of the tingling sensation remained.

Fred Bennett sat cross-legged beside the pot-bones the preacher had spilled the previous night. Local Indians stood in a broken circle around him as he photographed the remains with his smartphone.

Glenna looked for Junior Johnson. She was ready for him, charged with electricity and a new kind of power she had never felt before. A pointed finger and a single word were all she needed. *Murder*—she arranged the vowels and consonants perfectly in her mind, prepared to accuse him of a crime he probably didn't know he had committed.

Fred Bennett's phone made artificial mechanical shutter sounds as he documented each bone from the desecrated burial pot. He didn't acknowledge Glenna until she placed a hand on his shoulder and said, "Preacher?" A two-syllable question that might have been a statement except for the way she ended on a high tone and raised her eyebrows.

"Preacher?" She repeated herself, eyebrows and all.

"Gone," Fred Bennett said.

She kept her hand on his shoulder and looked into his eyes so he didn't dare stop without a more detailed explanation.

"Ran into the jungle, the way he always does. Hasn't come back. If we're lucky, he's gotten himself lost."

Or maybe he knew he'd killed someone. Not a howler monkey this time. Not a sloth. The preacher had killed a man.

Fred Bennett went back to photographing the bones. Didn't ask her where she'd been. Didn't seem interested in where the preacher was. Not very curious for a scientist.

"This skeleton is female," he told Glenna. He proved it with words like "supraorbital ridges" and "external occipital protuberance." He lifted the pelvis with his hook, held it up for the locals to see. Glenna understood he was showing off, the way men always do. Proving he was more powerful than a pile of bones that used to be someone important.

"Nullipara." The anthropologist said the word slowly with exaggerated movements of his lips so Glenna could watch every letter as it was formed. "Means she never had children."

All her life, Glenna had watched boys and men pretend to be smarter than they really were. The anthropologist used Latin words to mystify simple things for the very same reason the preacher had spoken in tongues.

"Greater trochanter." He pointed to a section of a long, thick bone that looked like the end of a ball peen hammer. "Signs of osteoarthritis, perhaps a trace of osteopenia. Means this one was probably in her forties. Old for the era if...." He poked his hook at a yellow band at the end of one of the long bones. He turned the skull over and inspected the upper molars. "Well, this...."

The wrinkled brow, the slack lips waiting for a thought to bubble to the surface—Glenna had never seen a look that suited him more. Scientists didn't go silent unless they found something that proved they weren't so smart after all.

The anthropologist was like the preacher in so many ways, desperate to be admired by people less educated than himself.

But not less intelligent. Glenna remembered what the scientist forgot. Education is a collection of facts. Intelligence is figuring out which facts are true. Fred Bennett had forgotten that truth is different in the jungle.

"Both fibulae are missing." He picked up a new thought without finishing the old one. "Also the sternum and the mandible. Probably carried off by scavengers." The anthropologist looked at the circle of vultures overhead. "Not much nourishment in old bones like these."

The Indians watched Fred Bennett drop the woman's skeleton back into the jar, one piece at a time, then seal the lid with wax they'd made from the sap of local palm trees. They stood motionless and silent, as always, while he recited the bones' Latin names before he pushed the lid into place.

The anthropologist hadn't listened to them chanting while they harvested dry brown flakes of sap from slits in the central spines of palm fronds. He didn't watch them mix the sap with drops of their own blood. Didn't see them inhale the smoke when they cooked the mix into sealing wax. Didn't share the visions that made their efforts strong enough to keep a restless spirit inside a jar until the time was right.

Fred Bennett was almost as good at ignoring Indians as the preacher. He was very good at measuring them and weighing them and counting them and thinking they had nothing to tell him worth knowing. He didn't notice the gap in the circle of Indians where one of them should have been standing.

Had anyone missed the dead man in the Yankee's T-shirt? Surely his people knew he was gone.

Fred Bennett tipped the jar into place. Walked around it. Photographed it. Documented his ceremony with comments into his cell phone—something about carbon dating, biometric measurements, and racial characteristics. Could he have been so calm if he knew there was a dead man not a hundred yards away? Someone who died last night, not centuries past.

There were so many things the anthropologist didn't know. But soon he would. Glenna meant to show him. The local Indians didn't mind being ignored, but she did.

"Fred." The word slid off her tongue as delicate as the lines on a pipe-stone fetish. A spark jumped the gap between her fingers and the anthropologist when she touched his hand. Electricity still worked.

He looked at Glenna and his features softened. Maybe he remembered how pretty she was, so much prettier than a jar of bones. Another spark flashed when she kissed him on the cheek. No spark at all when she took his human hand and placed it on her belly. No words needed to tell him what the local Indians—despite their lack of college degrees and urban sophistication—had known all along.

"Pregnant?" The anthropologist couldn't find a Latin word to help him out of this situation. He stood and put an arm around Glenna. Held her with his human hand. "The preacher?"

Instead of answering, she moved his hand over her belly again. Let him draw his own conclusions. Let him make the pieces fit into a puzzle he understood.

He ran his hook through her hair, teased out the tangles left by the dry season storm. Glenna let him cherish her because a girl needs a man like Fred Bennett when she is pregnant. When she is living in the Paraguayan jungle, surrounded by spirits, stalked by an obsessed preacher with a pistol.

He kissed her on the forehead the way men do when it's too late for them to make decisions but not too late to take responsibility. "I should have...."

There was nothing the anthropologist should have done, but she didn't tell him that. He wanted responsibility—the way men always do—so Glenna gave it to him.

"Come with me," she told him. Clearly a command, even though she sang it like a lullaby. Pregnancy gave back bits and pieces of Glenna's voice with the same hormones that took away her period. It changed the way she thought, the way she walked, the way men looked at her. Pregnancy was more powerful than electricity.

"Come with me, Fred."

There were more ways through the woods than one. Thousands of game trails intersected like interstate highways, from hunting grounds to feeding grounds to springs that never quit running.

Birds and monkeys chattered in the canopy. Insects buzzed in the air. Trees creaked in the dry-season wind as Glenna led the anthropologist to the scene of the crime. The path had seemed sinister and dangerous the previous night but was peaceful now that the storm and the gunshots were absent.

Rain had washed the trail clean of blood—and there must have been a lot of blood. Too much for the dead man's T-shirt to absorb. Glenna thought she must have gone the wrong way until she saw drag marks.

"Look." She pointed them out, but the anthropologist was too busy hating the preacher to notice.

The local Indians had followed her, too. They looked at the drag marks and then looked at each other. If they took the body away, they weren't telling anyone. Not the white man who had a hook instead of a left hand. Not the pregnant girl whose face was painted on solitary burial jars.

No reason to stand there wondering where a dead man had gone. There were other things in the jungle that would interest Fred Bennett.

23

Lots of Accident for
a Careful Man

THE BONES LOOKED fragile in the sunlight, but they no longer glowed. Fred Bennett pointed at the broken burial pot with his human hand. His double hook opened and closed like the mouth of a hungry robot snake. "This time the preacher has gone too far."

Creo and Conozco stood behind him. The local Indians formed a circle around the edge of the clearing, their faces full of the same horror Glenna had seen on the face of the man the preacher killed the previous night. Fear turned them into brothers.

"Irreplaceable cultural treasure," Fred Bennett said.

He couldn't know about the dead man, so Glenna didn't blame him for thinking the worst thing in the world is a broken burial pot. He spoke into his phone, Latin words and legal terminology. He took pictures of everything from every angle, already wondering how this broken, irreplaceable cultural treasure could work to his advantage.

Glenna didn't blame him for that either. The anthropologist was a nice man, but he was still a man, still trying to be the biggest, smartest, most powerful man in the world. She put both hands over her belly. Too early to feel life, but she thought maybe life could feel her. Men worry over sex, money, and power. Women worry over the next generation.

Fred Bennett teased shards of ceramic away from the bones. Turned the biggest piece over. Picked it up with his human hand.

"Glenna." He held the shard so she could see her face was painted on it. Not a photographic likeness, but her energy and character were captured perfectly. Lips parted in a half smile that looked more like cynicism than joy. Eyes that saw the world too clearly and didn't expect things to change. Hair full of tangles and waves that fell over her shoulders as if it had been blown there by a dry-season storm.

As Fred Bennett traced the outlines of the ceramic likeness with the tip of his hook, Glenna felt polished stainless steel move over her cheeks. He pointed to a conical fracture at the edge of the fragment.

"Bullet hole," he said.

What would it have felt like if the preacher's bullet had struck the image?

The anthropologist took another photograph.

He spoke into his cell phone. "Recent damage. Fracture lines are sharp. No weathering or oxidation. Not older than a month. Maybe as recent as last night."

Fred Bennett turned his attention to the delicate pile of bones exposed to the sunlight for the first time in a thousand years. "This one's an infant."

While separating the ceramic fragments from the human remains, he spoke into his phone. "The pot is broken in too many pieces to reassemble. I'll document and collect the shards later."

He rearranged the ancient ceramic fragments into a near perfect square, fencing in the bones. Sorted the pieces by size and shape so the angles were perfect and the height was uniform. Nudged the shards into place with his hook as carefully as if he were disarming an improvised explosive device.

The local Indians missed none of this.

The infant skull looked up at Glenna from its place at the edge of the ceramic spirit fence. Its eye sockets were too large, its cheek bones as thin and delicate as a cat's. Cusps of milk teeth poked through the ridges of the jaws. Gaps separated the bones of the skull and spread into triangular holes on the front and sides.

Fred Bennett followed Glenna's gaze. *"Fontanels.* Soft spots, you know? This little one died too young to differentiate its sex on gross inspection."

Its sex.

Glenna's hand drifted over the anthropologist's ceramic spirit fence. He moved his hook hand as if he planned to stop her, but an agitated whisper moved around the circle of Indians and distracted him. Her fingers dangled between the eyes of the skull. She offered the dead infant her open hand, peaceful, vulnerable, a primate gesture that's been recognizable even longer than this baby had been inside the burial jar.

A spark jumped the gap between her fingers and the baby, a three-inch discharge that sounded like a slap. She pulled her hand back. Placed it on her belly. Too early for the life inside of her to kick, but she felt it tingle.

"Boy," she told the anthropologist. "The baby is a boy." Did she mean the long dead infant bones, or the living fetus growing inside her? Glenna couldn't be sure exactly which child she meant She knew only "the baby is a boy." About that she had no doubt.

————————————

"BODIES ROT FAST in the jungle. Even worse in rainy season." Junior couldn't resist explaining himself to the corpse he'd dragged to the soft patch of ground in front of his cave. "Nothing personal."

The dead man's mouth hung open as if he'd been interrupted in the middle of a sentence.

"Have to bury the dead quickly." That went double when dying wasn't entirely natural. It was also best to bury a murdered man some place the Indians couldn't find him. Junior wasn't sure the jungle kept secrets from them. There was no doubt the vultures knew all about his crime. They perched in the trees and watched him dig with his U.S. Army surplus entrenchment tool.

Hungry was mostly how he felt after digging for three hours. Hungry and weak and a little bit confused. His Tupa peak had passed, and he was coasting into a valley of depression.

"Crashing is the downside of feel-good drugs," he told the corpse. "A yin-and-yang sort of thing, I guess." Maybe there was something to those silly eastern religions after all.

Junior shook his arms the way he'd seen athletes do on ESPN when they were too tired to go on but had to. He shook a little harder, hoping to rid himself of the heathen philosophies that were working their way into his born-again Christian brain. Shaking didn't help. Tainted ideas swam through his mind like schools of tropical fish, compelled to move one direction or another by tiny shifts in current and instinct for survival.

"I'll work all that out later," he told any jungle spirits who might be listening. He'd had a very busy night. Killed an Indian, spilled the Elizabeth pot, followed Glenna through the jungle. Junior looked at a little piece of the sky that showed through the canopy and wondered if God was looking back.

"Thought I heard someone crying," he told the little patch of sky. "It turned out to be me." Salty tears ran down his cheeks, dripped off his chin. The Good Lord knew he had good reason.

He considered asking for divine intervention, but God's answers to his prayers always seemed to come without a warranty. He sorted through his extensive biblical knowledge—King James only, thank you—but couldn't come up with a single strategy for asking the Lord to help him dig a grave.

"Don't suppose it would do any good to ask for a backhoe." He leaned his full weight on the shovel and watched it sink into the ground. Easier than the last time he dug a grave.

Maybe things were looking up.

Then Elizabeth started in. "Now you've killed an Indian." Her voice seemed much louder since he spilled her bones. "Dumped me in the dirt like so much garbage." His wife's ghost was full of complaints. Full of grudges. "Broken promises. Broken lives." Elizabeth complained that her grave was as empty as her life with Junior. As empty as the unfinished walnut cradle she'd bought on impulse many years ago when Junior had a flat tire outside of Lebanon, Missouri.

"No family," she told him. "That's the worst thing for a woman. Worse than bones strewn in the dirt."

The cramps in Junior's stomach made it hard to stand up straight. The noises coming from his abdomen sounded like an argument between demons and proctologists.

"You'll have company now." He turned over one shovel full of dirt after the next, reopened Elizabeth's empty grave the way he'd reopened it once before.

The dead man's eyes were open. When Junior started digging, they were as shiny as the polished silver bullets in his revolver. They had a matte finish by the time he was done, like a paint job from a cheap fender and body shop.

"Doin' my best, Elizabeth." How much company would this Indian ghost be? Buried in the secondhand grave where his wife started out. That ought to count for something. He'd removed Elizabeth's bones a long time ago, but there would be some bits and pieces of her left. Rotten molecules left behind where her remains had been "disinterred." One of Junior's very first vocabulary calendar words.

Would the dead man give up his Indian ways once the worms and beetles picked his bones clean? Would he jabber like Elizabeth, following his killer around complaining about his life cut short?

"No family is the worst thing for a woman," Elizabeth told Junior again, in case he'd forgotten in the twenty seconds since she told him the last time.

"Too late for that." Junior thought about spilled milk, then he thought about ice cold milk—whole milk—the kind with fat floating on the surface. He thought about Oreo cookies, and whole wheat bread, and tins of Spam in the storage units back at the compound. His stomach demanded food so loud, Junior could almost make out English words.

The scent of death brought a temporary wave of nausea as he rolled the body into the grave. It landed face-up, with a wet, hollow sound.

That wasn't the worst of it.

The preacher had gotten a good look at the corpse's back. The shirt was in tatters. Bits and pieces of it lined the trail from the killing point to the gravesite. The threads and drag marks must have stood out like flashing highway signals to the local Indians. A trail of bread-crumbs through the forest. Junior remembered the story of Hansel and Gretel and started thinking about ovens and gingerbread. That led him back to Oreos and milk.

He could have left the body where he found it. He could have buried it on the spot or let the scavengers disassemble it in some place far away, but here it was, looking like the most recent in a long string of very bad ideas.

"Easier to dig here," he explained to the corpse.

Trying to get on good terms with the dead man, because his ghost was sure to follow Junior around as soon as the ants and beetles finished their cleaning detail.

Rain had faded the blood on the front of the NY Yankees T-shirt to the color of a chocolate stain.

"Chocolate." The word filled Junior's mouth with saliva. There were chocolate bars in the storage unit back at the compound—dark chocolate, chocolate with almonds, chocolate mixed with peanut butter, varieties of chocolate that tasted much better in anticipation than they ever could inside the preacher's mouth.

Junior read Derek Jeter's name through the chocolate-colored stain—one line of calligraphy underneath the tiny bullet hole no bigger than the tip of the preacher's index finger. He hadn't seen an exit wound, so there was a nugget of silver buried in the dead man, pushed against a bone, flattened like a coin that had been crushed under the wheel of a locomotive.

The fat, black vultures in the trees moved to lower branches, getting restless. A couple of brave ones hopped down to pull away bits of flesh before Junior covered it. He swung his shovel at them. Considered firing a shot or two, but gunfire was like a dinner bell for birds of prey.

The loose dirt broke into clumps of peat and loam as he threw it on the corpse, full of tannic acid that was rumored to preserve bodies. Insects scattered as the clots of earth broke open. Beetles, ants, worms, centipedes—all anticipated something soft and rotten.

"You have lots of accidents for a careful man." Elizabeth complained over Junior's left shoulder, much louder than usual. He was pretty sure that meant her bones hadn't made it back into the jar—not all of them, anyway.

Junior felt sure he'd see her if he turned around. He did so slowly, with his eyes closed, because he wasn't sure he'd like what he saw. Ready to apologize again if that's what she wanted. Ready to do whatever she asked.

"So sorry." He considered going for his pistol but couldn't be sure it would work on Elizabeth's ghost, and she was already out of sorts. He kept both hands on his entrenchment tool, holding it over his shoulder like a baseball bat. Not because he believed he could fight off a ghost with a shovel, but because he didn't know what else to do. He kept his eyes closed until he faced the direction of her voice accusing him of "putting a baby in that girl's belly."

When he opened his eyes, instead of Elizabeth, he saw a capuchin monkey holding something in its nasty little paws.

A lower jaw. Elizabeth's lower jaw! Junior recognized it right away. Yellow stains on the back teeth, as bright as the middle light on a traffic signal. Yellow stains from antibiotics that locked onto the calcium of Elizabeth's teeth and never let go. Diagnosed by a dentist in Idabel, Oklahoma.

Tetracycline hypoplasia. College words that would never show up on a vocabulary calendar. "Wonder what the anthropologist would make of that?"

The monkey shrugged, a gesture so human it made Junior furious. He swung the shovel but the capuchin hopped over the blade. Another swing. Another hop. Junior followed the monkey into the jungle, but the creature stayed one hop ahead of him.

Impossible to kill a monkey with a shovel. Junior knew that from the beginning, but once he started, he couldn't stop. That's the way it seemed to go with so many things in his life. Knowledge isn't power unless your aim is good and your reflexes are fast. He kept swinging until the capuchin decided the game was over and climbed into the trees. Junior leaned on the handle of his U.S. Army surplus entrenchment tool, suitable for digging foxholes and latrines and graves but totally inadequate for killing monkeys.

He dared the creature to show itself again, even though nothing good would come of it. The monkey was young and strong. Junior Johnson was weak—and starving.

He lowered himself to the ground using the shovel as a crutch. Remembered he hadn't eaten anything since he lost his half-finished can of Dinty Moore Beef Stew to another capuchin—how long had it been?

He put his hands on the spot where his prosperous preacher's belly used to be and found in its place a concave area crying out for food.

He lay flat on the ground, listened to Elizabeth complain about her incomplete life, and looked into the open sky.

"Clearing." He understood. The monkey had led him to a clearing the way a new star in the east had led three wise men to Bethlehem. God had a use for every creature, no matter how smelly and disgusting. Junior Johnson saw the white pile of delicate infant bones stacked inside a rectangle of broken pottery and knew what he was supposed to do.

"Another accident," Elizabeth said.

"The answer to a prayer. When God closes a door he opens a window. Or sometimes he just breaks something." Junior removed his shirt, laid it on the ground beside the spirit fence and the baby skeleton. He rearranged the pot fragments, created an opening so he could collect the bones with respect, even though it seemed like a superstitious heathen sort of thing to do.

"Respect is everything," he told the monkeys chattering in the trees around him. So much chatter he could no longer hear Elizabeth as he threw the homemade bag of bones over his shoulder before heading back to his jungle home. "Plenty of time for eating later."

Capuchins didn't mind the darkness inside Junior's cave. They plucked open boxes of cereal, popped a couple of pull-tab cans, and scattered papers all over the floor. One monkey seemed particularly interested in the centerfold of Junior's favorite Playboy Magazine. The preacher swung the makeshift bag of bones at the disrespectful little simians and sent them screaming into the forest.

"Sorry," he apologized to the infant skeleton. Meaningless, he supposed, like most social conventions extended to the dead, but a holy man couldn't be too careful where spirits were concerned. Especially when he was asking for a favor. He hadn't been able to give Elizabeth a baby in life, but this one had been waiting for her for a thousand years.

"Hatched out of a burial pot like a chick from an egg," he told her.

That reminded him, there were no eggs in the cave, but there were other things. Soda crackers, canned goods, Meals Ready to Eat, and Tang.

Suddenly, the thought of Tang mixed with algae colored stagnant water sounded better than champagne. Better than a margarita with a salted rim and a slice of lime. Better than Coca-Cola in the small reusable bottles he had stored in the refrigerator back at the vicarage. A man could work up quite an appetite doing spirit work.

Vultures fighting over the partially-buried dead man sprawled in Elizabeth's open grave took Junior's mind off of Tang. The birds had stripped the corpse naked and pulled sizable chunks of flesh from his bones. The females flew into the trees carrying bits of New York Yankees T-shirt and "lightly worn" Goodwill jeans donated by Americans who never imagined their cast-off clothing would be used as nesting materials for carrion birds.

Junior drew his pistol and aimed it at a large ugly bird tearing at the corpse's face. He didn't count the shots and didn't stop pulling the trigger until the hammer fell with sharp, unsatisfying clicks.

All misses—unless Junior counted a couple of extra bullet holes in what was left of the body.

The birds flew away.

Gun smoke hung in the air, gradually seeking a lower level as it cooled. Junior watched it settle in the grave like a special effect in an old-time horror movie. The dead man was mostly there, except for a couple of strips of human jerky and a couple of missing toes and fingers. Naked, but that's how people came into the world, so there was nothing wrong with going out that way.

The preacher shook the baby bones out of his shirt. They fell over the dead man like flakes of Parmesan cheese on a giant Italian sausage.

Ignoring the cramps in his stomach, Junior filled the grave with dirt, gathered rocks and laid them out in the shape of a cross over the loose unsettled mound. His stigmata cracked open and bled so they left handprints on the stones that looked almost identical to the ones on the solitary pots.

"A goddamned prophecy." Junior was sure of it. Too much coincidence to be anything but. He pulled his gun belt a little tighter because his waistline had shrunk to its teenage size.

Who'd have thought a stylish thirty inches would be waiting under all that paunch? For the first time in many years, Junior's legs were longer than the circumference of his middle. He looked for his wristwatch, but it must have fallen into the grave. He fancied he could hear it ticking, but Elizabeth told him, "That's the sound of time running out."

He tossed his entrenchment tool aside and turned to his cave, wanting steak but ready to be satisfied with anything.

It looked like he'd have to be satisfied with nothing. The cave teamed with black-striped capuchins again, carrying off what they could and urinating on what they couldn't. They'd opened his storage chest with their clever little Charles Darwin fingers then scattered to the trees carrying cans of peaches in sugary syrup and MREs in boilable foil packets.

Junior drew his pistol, but he'd used all the bullets. His hands shook too much to reload, and the monkeys mocked him, showing off the cans they couldn't open and the pouches they couldn't unseal.

The food would remain good inside its containers for a very long time. If Darwin turned out to be right, maybe long enough for the creatures to evolve sufficiently to invent the can opener.

"Another brilliant plan," Elizabeth whispered in his ear.

"There's fruit." He walked to a mango tree and selected the ripest one. After a few bites Junior stopped to pick some fiber from his teeth and listened to the sound of a baby crying. Or was it his imagination? Elizabeth sang a lullaby—something by Paul Simon about a bridge and troubled water. Nothing from the dead Indian so far, but that one never talked much even when he was alive.

Dead babies don't grow up.

Junior never thought of that when he fetched the infant skeleton to Elizabeth's grave. Dead babies could cry until the end of time, dead wives never stop complaining, and mangos....

Another thing Junior hadn't thought of. Mangos taste like crap.

24

More Questions
Than Answers

GLENNA WATCHED AS Fred Bennett leaned too close to the microphone of the shortwave radio. He pitched his voice a half octave higher than usual and affected a vaguely southern accent. His sentences were short and choppy. He swallowed too much and cleared his throat too often.

Would his lies be so obvious after they'd been filtered through transistors and copper wire and bounced across the Atlantic Ocean to UNESCO headquarters?

The woman on the other side of the conversation spoke with a French accent that managed to convey charm and still sound official even through the static. She had lots of questions.

"Too early for decisions," the anthropologist told her.

Glenna could tell he was stalling. She imagined the French lady in Geneva understood that as well.

Fred Bennett talked about the preacher but didn't say he'd gone missing. He talked about the burial pot with a skeleton from the modern era inside. "It's the only one that's been evaluated to date."

He didn't mention the modern era skeleton might have been put inside the pot within the last fifteen years and might be the preacher's wife who disappeared under mysterious circumstances. He didn't mention the thousand-year-old burial pot that was shattered by a bullet or the fetal skeleton inside. He didn't mention the pregnant girl living in the vicarage with him.

"*Obfuscation.*" Glenna said the vocabulary calendar word loud enough for the UNESCO lady to hear. Four syllables that summed up the tricks the scientist used to keep secrets from the people who sent him here. She could tell from the look on his face, he didn't like that word at all.

"*Répétez s'il vous plaît.*" The UNESCO woman stumbled over a few English words and finally said, "*Say again, please.*"

When he didn't, she got right to the point. "*Is it time for an investigator? Someone with legal authority?*" Perfectly clear this time. Questions she was accustomed to asking.

"No need." He answered far too quickly. "Still preliminary. More questions than answers. Might not be an important site at all." Rapid fire statements separated by audible swallows and smacking lips, each word enunciated carefully, like an intoxicated man pretending to be sober.

Fred Bennett said most of the cemetery pots "might be much more recent than we thought."

Glenna knew he wanted them for himself, just as he wanted her for himself. Fred Bennett was smarter than the preacher, and nicer, but the two men wanted exactly the same things.

Creo and Conozco had become Fred Bennett's assistants after the preacher left the compound. They stood guard outside the vicarage door, where the anthropologist lived with Glenna. He moved in without an invitation, but—to be fair—she hadn't objected.

He never touched her—except to draw an occasional spark with his hook hand. Glenna understood that would change in time. She might not mind as long as he didn't put a rubber glove on his human hand—the way Junior Johnson had—and poke at her like a third-grade boy working up the nerve to dissect a frog.

Fred Bennett checked Glenna out with quick sidelong glances, the way a man appreciates a sunrise without damaging his vision. He thought she didn't notice. That she didn't feel his eyes shift to follow her as she walked in front of the radio.

He was ashamed of wanting her but wanted her just the same.

Glenna didn't blame him. Fred Bennett was a man, and a man's senses were fine-tuned to pick up every nuance of a pretty girl. Education made men more deliberate but didn't change their nature.

She showed the anthropologist her lopsided smile so he'd understand he could hide nothing from her. That she knew what thoughts ran through his mind every minute, every hour. That she could read him like the words on the vocabulary calendar, which was still on the preacher's desk. His desk now, since the preacher disappeared into the jungle.

Prevaricator was the word of the day. She tore it off the calendar and held it in front of Fred Bennett while he told the UNESCO woman his choppy transistorized lies.

"It'll take another month at least." He raised his voice and spoke much more slowly than necessary. He put his lips so close to the microphone his breath fogged the polished metal surface. That's how men tell lies to women—much too close and much too loud.

The UNESCO woman's voice sounded like a poem even over the low-end radio speaker, full of vowels and music.

Incomprehensible. Glenna couldn't remember when she'd learned that vocabulary calendar word, but it described the UNESCO woman's voice perfectly. Incomprehensible and pretty. The French were the only people in the world who could turn a collection of lyrical sounds into a language.

Fred Bennett raised his voice to the breaking point. "At least one month. Maybe two." Any louder and he'd be shouting. He didn't tell her dry season was coming to an end. Roads would turn into shallow rivers between the compound and Asuncion, becoming impassable. So, he'd have the burial pots and Glenna to himself for three more months at least. By then, perhaps the UNESCO woman would have other international treasures on her mind.

Glenna said, "At least one month. Maybe two," with exactly same inflections as the anthropologist. She watched his face change as he heard his lie played back. So obvious. So transparent.

Deception. Glenna thought that might be a word from the vocabulary calendar, but it sounded too simple. She repeated it but added southern diphthongs. Deception sounded more believable from that part of the world.

Glenna put both hands over the baby bump that was still so small it might be her imagination.

She opened the vicarage door and counted the local Indians standing among the cemetery pots. Twenty. Probably twenty more hidden behind buildings and in the trees. Every dark, almond-shaped eye turned her way.

She walked between the ugly Guarani twins standing on either side of the door, so much like statues the jungle insects didn't want their blood.

Glenna brushed her hand through a swarm of gnats that gathered around her face to drink the hormones in her breath. Tiny sparks flashed through the cloud of insects and sent them tumbling to the ground. The Guarani moved apart, out of Glenna's reach. Dry season could end without warning. Glenna's sparks could turn to lightning strikes. Dead Indians could be scattered around her as easily as dead gnats.

The locals moved toward the trees as they almost always did when she stepped into the compound yard, clustering in small groups like sheep that have caught the scent of a wild dog. They gathered into fearful little knots. Their bronze, weathered faces turned her way, but they kept their eyes on her baby bump so they didn't have to meet her gaze.

Bits of gold sparkled on the tops the cemetery pots.

"Offerings," Glenna said loud enough to make the Indians pull back a little further. Cast and hammered golden images of ancient gods. Not the first offerings left for her.

"As old as the pots." She told the Indians what the anthropologist told her. They didn't understand her, but they listened, anyway. Words came easier for Glenna, now that dry season was almost over. Now that pregnancy had a firm grip on her body. Borrowed words came easiest of all.

"Golden images of gods so old no one remembers their names." She repeated what the anthropologist said, even though he got it wrong. The Indians remembered everything. They remembered promises the gods made to the ghosts of their ancestors who were waiting inside the cemetery pots.

The ugly assistants followed her though the rows of pots. Watching her. Watching the locals. Watching for the preacher who was still loose in the jungle with his pistol and plenty of bullets.

Glenna walked to the Elizabeth pot, the one spilled by the preacher and resealed by the anthropologist. The offering posed on that one was a feathered serpent. In Mexico it would be Quetzalcoatl, but Glenna had no idea what this god called himself in Paraguay. She dangled her fingers over the effigy the way noodlers tease hungry catfish out of holes along riverbanks.

Bright blue sparks jumped the gap between the effigy and Glenna's fingertips. The Indians scurried deeper into the forest. The ugly assistants moved among the cemetery pots, collecting the golden offerings for their new boss. They stopped when they came to the object Glenna charged with magic, afraid to pick it up but afraid to leave it too.

A pistol shot made their decision easy. The preacher stepped out of the trees and pointed his revolver in their general direction. He told Glenna, "Stand clear of Elizabeth." His hollow eyes darted back and forth over cheekbones that looked sharp enough to penetrate his skin.

His face was covered with an uneven mix of black and gray whiskers, like a late blooming suicide bomber who's anxious to please his seventy-two virgins. He pushed his tongue between his lips and tightened the muscles in his jaw, but that didn't help him hold his pistol steady.

The Guarani abandoned the golden Quetzalcoatl effigy. They reached for Glenna instead because she was the most valuable treasure in the compound.

Sparks jumped between her and the Guarani's hands. They stepped in front of her, a bulletproof Indian barrier to protect her from the preacher.

Junior Johnson laughed and stepped back into the trees, abandoning whatever task had brought him. Glenna heard him talking to himself long after she lost sight of him. His voice got louder as he moved further into the jungle, until he ended his conversation with another pistol shot.

"Rainy season will put an end to him." She told the ugly assistants what the anthropologist told her.

A half-dozen capuchin monkeys moved out of the trees where the preacher had disappeared, led by an alpha male.

"A congress," Glenna told the Guarani twins. Her easy way with words was a reminder that the dry season was coming to an end. "A herd of deer, a gaggle of geese, a school of fish, a *congress* of monkeys." The anthropologist thought that was very funny. Glenna never understood exactly why.

The alpha male monkey walked around Glenna and the twins. He hopped onto the Elizabeth pot, touched the Quetzalcoatl effigy. Didn't pull away when he drew a spark.

The monkey took the offering in his hand, inspected it carefully. Held it over his head so it reflected the sunlight. He jumped off the cemetery pot and scampered into the jungle with his congress chattering behind him.

25

Clear

CLEAR. THE WORD rang in Junior's mind like a dinner bell as he moved through the rain forest in the middle of the night. He couldn't say what time it was—midnight, early morning. Time had slipped a gear or two since everything started falling apart. That much was clear.

Surprising how many things a word like clear could mean—a cloud-free sky, an unambiguous message, a pure note of music, an unobstructed trail.

Clear was how millions of lightning bugs looked floating through the jungle, calling to their mates with bioluminescent flashes that reminded Junior of the sparks of electricity in Glenna's hair.

No flashlight for the Right-Reverend Johnson as he bumped through the trees using one hand to hold up his pants and the other to reassure himself his pistol was safely tucked in his holster. He felt the empty place on his wrist where his watch used to be—now buried with the newly-dead Indian and the long-dead baby in Elizabeth's slightly-used grave. He pictured the watch's luminous hands—green like the flashing lightning bugs—counting the next hundred thousand seconds of eternity until the last volt of electricity was gone.

Hunger fine-tuned his reception of supernatural broadcasts. Enlightenment rode the fine edge of starvation.

Perhaps the lightning bugs were messages from God. Junior tried to make sense of them, because lightning bugs weren't supposed to come until the end of rainy season. Not in such numbers, anyway. He caught one, crushed it, rubbed the bio-luminous goo across the palm of his hand. It mixed with stigmata-blood and itched like poison oak. For the first time in a very long while, he wondered if the marks were signs from God or simply an eczema that wouldn't clear up.

As Junior speculated about the nature of signs and miracles, his pants slid below his hips. He visualized the religious nuclei in his brain switching off like streetlights in a rolling blackout. Everything would eventually go dark, and Junior would be another animal foraging in the jungle.

Clear. The word became a mental twitch, a repetitive idea, like a song that that runs through the mind so long it leaves an indelible mark on the brain. It reached the audible level, a remote sound, like something carried over an impossible distance by a trick of the atmosphere.

Clear was the word the Emergency Medical Technicians shouted to each other when they tried to shock Elizabeth back to life. The EMTs were husband and wife. They had traveled all the way from Antlers, Oklahoma, to meet with Junior Johnson.

That was before Glenna came into the preacher's watchful care. Before stigmata blossomed on his palms. Before he learned the unpredictable side effects of Tupa.

When it was clear Junior couldn't raise Elizabeth from the dead, the pair unpacked the defibrillator they'd "borrowed" from the Antlers Fire Station Number 2. They bared Elizabeth's breasts, burned circles on her chest, made her dance like a marionette controlled by a spastic puppeteer.

She opened her eyes for a second, sniffed the smoke from her cooked skin. She looked at Junior and said something that might have been "Ecclesiastes." Or maybe "electricity."

He wanted to ask her what she meant, but before he could think how to put the question, Elizabeth's pupils shrank to the size of periods. The perfect punctuation for the end of life.

"Clear!" The pilgrims rubbed their paddles together and waited while the charge built enough to reanimate her one last time, but the Antlers Firehouse Number 2 battery had run its course.

"We've done everything we could do," one of them told him. Junior couldn't remember whether it was the husband or the wife.

People abandoned him then, too. Dribbled out of the camp over the next two weeks. Junior went back to Oklahoma, temporarily, until his faith and his bank account built up enough charge to bring him back—this time with Glenna, his little sparkplug girl.

Now she had slipped out of his grasp. Stolen from him by the anthropologist the way the monkeys stole his food. Junior drew his pistol. Watched the lightning bug reflections in the nickel finish. His pants slid down when he reholstered it, again. Junior cinched the belt a little tighter, but there was no fat for it to sink into. His body was stripped to the frame. When all his tissue finally wasted away, scavengers would scatter his bones, and his soul would walk the world beside the jungle spirits.

He heard Elizabeth complaining. Knew he didn't want to hear her more clearly. Most of her soul was still trapped inside the Elizabeth pot, and he wanted to keep it that way as long as possible.

At least the ghost who used to occupy Elizabeth's pot wasn't talkative. That luminous spirit slid through the trees, glowing like ectoplasm in the moonlight. As mute as Glenna was in dry season. Waiting for something Junior didn't understand.

The preacher removed the bottle of Tupa from his pocket, squeezed a drop into each nostril, and sniffed. It opened his sinuses. Opened his mind. Made his hunger feel more like determination. But it also made him feel like he was being watched—and not only by Elizabeth.

Junior suspected the Indians were stalking him and was pretty sure it wasn't just a paranoid side effect of Tupa. Nothing in the jungle happened without them finding out. He felt their bodies displacing air as they changed position. The lightning bugs adjusted their flight patterns and left dark, man-shaped spaces that moved in slow motion. The Indians watched Junior the way Jaguars watched agouti. Not ready to spring, but the time would come. They'd think a long while before they acted. When they did, it would come as a surprise. Like the death of a loved one when an EMT from Antlers said, "We've done everything we could do."

But wasn't there always a little more that could be done? One more thing, like sneaking into the compound in the middle of the night? Junior was four sticks of beef jerky away from thinking clearly. A box of powdered eggs away from sanity. A perpetually fresh pack of Twinkies away from a logical mind.

Ah, the mathematics of low blood sugar.

He stepped into the compound on the balls of his feet, moving in fits and starts like a salsa dancer who had lost his rhythm, silent except for the pistol bouncing against his leg.

"Should have left the gun behind." The voice came from the Elizabeth pot. A swarm of sphinx moths flew above the jar, recharging their spiritual batteries with energy from the grudge she held since he came back to Paraguay with Glenna.

"Predators are never as stealthy as prey," she told him.

He knew she spoke the truth. An armed hunter's confidence shines like a hundred-watt, sealed-beam flashlight.

Creo and Conozco spotted him ducking through the cemetery pots. They separated and approached from opposite directions—impossible for him to focus on both at the same time.

He moved quickly. Tried to keep the maximum distance between himself and the ugly pair until he realized they were wrangling him across the compound the way wolves isolate a straggler from the herd.

The generator sputtered and coughed behind the vicarage, complaining like an old man who'd given up cigarettes too late. Junior saw a light behind a window. He might have seen a silhouette behind the lace curtains, but that could be a trick of shadows and jungle drugs. If so, the trick was a good one. The silhouette looked like Glenna. He'd not been this close to her in... he didn't know how long.

Junior tasted tears at the corners of his mouth. "A side effect," he told himself. A side effect of Tupa, or starvation, or fear of the two ugly Indians who used to be his allies but now....

He backed against a storage shed. "My destination all along."

One of his ugly assistants, Creo or Conozco, stood in front of him. Impossible to tell which and it made no difference because there was no place left to run.

He put his hand on the butt of his pistol and tried to order the Guarani to stand clear. But suddenly that word, which had dominated his mind all evening, was stuck at the back of his throat.

Junior stepped away from the storage shed, ready to draw and fire like an old-time Western gunfighter. He pulled the hammer back while the pistol remained in his holster. A satisfying mechanical *click,* like a door opening to new afterlife possibilities for the ugly twin who stood in front of him.

An even louder *click* came from behind him. Real tumblers in a real door being unlocked.

Creo, or Conozco—the one he wasn't going to kill a moment ago—pulled the door wide open. A stream of drool formed in response to the scent of grains and chocolate. Saliva dribbled into Junior's beard. He released his pistol butt and wiped the goopy mess on his wrist.

One of the ugly twins handed him a Bible. A page from his vocabulary calendar marked a passage. Junior tried to thank him but his words turned into gibberish.

The other twin shined a flashlight into the storage unit so he could see the wonders inside.

All was not lost. Creo and Conozco had not abandoned him, at least not totally. He reached into an open box and grabbed a Hershey bar with almonds. Suddenly it was the best thing in the entire world. For a moment he considered dropping his Bible and grabbing a double handful.

"How would that look to the Indians?" Elizabeth said.

He peeked out of the storage shed. Her jar was still intact, sphinx moths still flew in circles around the top.

Creo and Conozco were the only Indians Junior could see, but they'd been joined by a capuchin monkey with something in its hand.

Clear. The word was back in Junior's mind. It was crystal clear what the monkey had. A bone. A long bone—the anthropologist would know which one—but it wasn't very long because its owner died so young.

The bone was thin and light. It glowed a dim green bioluminescent color from mold fibers that had replaced microscopic bits of tissue over the thousand years it was sealed inside the cemetery jar.

"Another accident," Elizabeth complained. Junior must have dropped the bone on the way back to his cave.

He pushed his chocolate bar and the Bible toward the monkey so the animal could make a choice.

"Trade." He kept it simple, the way Glenna talked. One word and a gesture that couldn't be misinterpreted.

"Trade." He gave the monkey the choice between the chocolate and the Bible. Not a real choice. Something sweet or a collection of dry promises. Sugar, or a different sort of sweetness only an evolved mind could taste.

He edged closer to the animal, stepped away from the food scents behind him. He heard the door to the shed close. Heard Creo and Conozco move away. Their footsteps retreated toward the vicarage.

The monkey reached for the chocolate bar, but Junior pulled it back.

A monkey tantrum followed, loud enough to bring an unambiguous pair of silhouettes to the windows of the vicarage.

The monkey tossed its bone into the air—much higher than Junior thought was possible. It tumbled like a bioluminescent pinwheel before bouncing on the ground. He reached for it with the hand that still held the Hershey bar.

A blue spark made him jump backward.

When he looked up again, the compound yard was full of Indians. They didn't stop him as he ran into the jungle. He dodged tree limbs and vines, jumped logs and ducked around tree trunks like a rabbit escaping from a pack of dogs.

The Indians weren't following him. At least, he didn't think so.

Junior ran until he reached his cave. He sat in front of it and licked the last of the Hershey bar off the foil wrapper. It brushed across an old silver filling and gave him a jolt. He wadded the foil into a ball and tossed it on the grave.

Only then did he realize he had dropped his Bible. Its pages flipped back and forth like a slinky warming up for a trip down a flight of stairs. The bookmarked passage was lost in the chaos.

Another accident. The page from his vocabulary calendar lay on the ground beside the Bible. The wind lifted a corner and dropped it again.

Junior's hand trembled from the rush of Hershey energy, but he grabbed the paper before the wind had another chance to snatch it away. Big print. Big enough to read in moonlight.

"Barcarole." He said it like a contestant in a spelling bee.

"A boat song of Venetian gondoliers." Junior tried to make sense of it, but the Hershey bar didn't have enough sugar to bring order to the world. "What's it mean, Elizabeth?"

"It means nothing," she told him. "What did you expect?"

Junior looked at the sky and tried to think of a clever way to ask Jesus for another Hershey bar.

26

Death Song

THE LOCAL INDIANS trickled into the compound from the surrounding forest. Their eyes swept the outbuildings and burial pots then finally settled on the picture window of the vicarage. Glenna stood behind it, keeping watch.

"Trouble," she told Fred Bennett.

The anthropologist sat at his desk, making notes in a five-subject spiral notebook he'd found among the preacher's belongings. He scratched out one word, scratched in another, and mumbled something about "solitary pots."

He wrote a word on the page, underlined it, and told her some useless bit of information about the Pai Tavytera Indians in the Amambay hills.

"Trouble." Glenna opened the front door of the vicarage so the anthropologist could hear the locals mumbling in their breathless language.

Creo and Conozco stood outside, bracketing the door. They held their heads at uncomfortable angles so they could watch Glenna and the locals at the same time. Their eyes darted back and forth, trying to keep track of everything at once.

"Trouble," she said again.

"What do they want?" Fred Bennett asked, the question white people have pondered since Columbus found the New World and realized it was already spoken for. "The Indians, I mean. What do they want?"

"Trouble," Glenna said, as if the Indians hadn't been dodging trouble of one sort or another since 1492.

Creo and Conozco twitched their heads in identical synchronous movements, searching out the most likely starting place for violence. They clenched and unclenched their fists, mirror images of panic.

"The jungle," she told Fred Bennett. The body language of the locals was as easy to read as words on a vocabulary calendar. Every head turned toward the path that led to the broken burial pot.

"The baby." Glenna covered her belly with both hands. She knew Fred Bennett would imagine she was talking about the baby inside of her, not the infant spirit he'd fenced in with shards of the broken pot.

He gave her a nervous smile and touched her hair with his hook hand, a surprisingly tender act. After her static charge was spent, he kissed her on the forehead. Not the way a father kisses a daughter, but the way boys have been kissing girls since kissing was invented—starting out with something small in hopes of turning it into something more.

The baby inside Glenna understood this. It was too young to kick but not too young to tingle.

"Watch them," she told the anthropologist. She pointed so he'd know exactly where to look.

Some of the local Indians walked toward the path leading to the broken pot then circled back like nervous dogs that needed to go outside.

"The baby in the jar." She pointed at the path, easy to see now that it was trampled into an indelible line through the jungle. Easy to follow, too, and the Indians followed it every day.

"How do you know what they want?" Fred Bennett and Glenna walked side by side out of the vicarage in long, matching steps like a bride and groom walking down the aisle.

How can you not know?

She kept that thought to herself as the crowd of Indians parted and let them find their way to the broken pot.

"The bones are gone," the anthropologist said, as if everyone didn't already know. Glenna stood beside him as he poked his hook at the barren ground where the skeleton used to be, proving to himself what his eyes had already told him.

"Carried away by animals?" He looked at the circle of Indians at the perimeter of the clearing. He looked at Creo and Conozco, who walked around him in slow circles like satellites orbiting the earth. He looked at Glenna, who stood by him as he knelt beside the rectangle of shards he'd built around the baby bones.

"Looks like they got them all." He didn't notice there were no tracks. No drag marks. Nothing to indicate animal involvement. "A wild boar. Maybe a jaguar."

Didn't he see the ceramic shards had been removed in one section of his rectangle? Removed and carefully stacked—not scattered—making a perfect ceremonial gate for the removal of a baby-size spirit.

When Glenna pointed to the opening with her toe, the anthropologist said, "Perhaps a monkey."

"Or a preacher." She waited for the anthropologist to explain everything away with Latin words, but he said nothing.

Thunder rumbled in the west. The local Indians passed rumors among themselves in tones that were almost indistinguishable from the wind.

"Preacher," Glenna said again, far too loud. She tried to erase the word by whispering it but knew that would never work. She heard the sound of large clumsy feet dragging through the forest toward the clearing. The preacher was still hidden by the trees. Long before Glenna saw him, she knew he had arrived.

"Junior Johnson," she said.

He stepped into the clearing, pointing his nickel-plated revolver at

Fred Bennett. It sparkled in the sunlight for a few slow seconds until clouds drifted over the clearing from the west.

"Feelin' a bit more religious, mister anthropologist?" The preacher sneered and pulled back the hammer.

Glenna watched the cylinder turn, watched the polished silver slugs move in a counterclockwise circle like seats on a Ferris wheel.

The pistol bobbed up and down as the preacher held it at arm's length. His nails were broken. Ribbons of grime followed the creases around his neck and wrists, mostly oily black but with a distinctly green tone. The preacher was skeletally thin from his days eating low-hanging fruit and drinking from duckweed-covered pools. He held onto his bullet belt with his gun-free hand to keep it from sliding down his hips.

His skin had tightened around his veins so they bulged and contracted with every irregular beat of his heart. Glenna tried to count them—at least one hundred every minute.

"*Tachycardia.*" She repeated one of the words from the vocabulary calendar. It meant the preacher's heart was racing to the finish line. Still, he looked more alive than ever. He lived in the moment in his thin, haggard, refugee fashion, even though the moment he lived in wasn't very good.

Glenna turned her attention to the fragments of the burial pot, away from Junior Johnson because she knew he wanted her to watch his triumph over the anthropologist.

She sorted through pictures of lightning bolts and power spirals.

The pot had broken cleanly around the pictures. Every painted image remained whole. She wondered if Fred Bennett had a Latin explanation for that.

"There." She found exactly what she needed. A picture commissioned by the spirit world a thousand years ago, put into a supernatural account so she could make a withdrawal at exactly the right moment.

She stepped in front of the pistol and held a pottery shard so Junior Johnson could see the caricature of himself.

It was hard to read the expression on a bearded face with almost no muscle covering the bones, but the preacher's eyes opened wide.

Glenna looked into his eyes and saw the reflection of the bearded skeleton on the pottery fragment. Not a perfect match with Junior Johnson's face, but close enough so even he could see it.

"Miracle," Glenna told him. More than faith healing, storms that wouldn't cross the Argentine border, or a sparkplug girl who stopped Rolex watches with her touches. Junior Johnson had been preaching miracles for thirty years. Now he saw a real one, and it didn't suit him.

"Move aside, girl." He motioned with his revolver. "There are accounts to be settled." Junior Johnson tried to pull the hammer on his pistol a little further back. The polished slugs rocked in the cylinder. Each silver bullet held a distorted reflection of the world.

Fred Bennett scrambled in front of her. He slipped and fell, caught his weight on his hook-hand, burying it up to the wrist in the soft forest floor. It took him several clumsy seconds to pull it free. "Put the gun away, Johnson." His voice was full of authority, but his prosthesis looked impotent, covered with moldy leaves and root fiber. He spoiled the moment further by taking time to pick it clean.

The local Indians stepped into the trees, ready to disappear when the shooting started, still watching, still waiting to see which white man came out on top.

Creo and Conozco stood on opposite sides of the clearing, pulled apart by their loyalty to two masters. One twin drifted toward the preacher. The other drifted toward Fred Bennett.

Lightning flashed overhead as the preacher closed one eye and sighted down the gun barrel. No chance of missing at that distance. The anthropologist placed his hook hand over his heart as if he were about to swear an oath.

That might have been enough for the preacher if one of the twins hadn't stepped into the line of fire. He faced Junior Johnson but looked over the preacher's head as if he saw something hiding in the canopy more interesting than his death. Creo or Conozco? Glenna couldn't tell. So much alike, maybe there wasn't any difference. One human spirit split in two identical pieces like double vision after a blow to the head.

The Guarani was shorter than Fred Bennett, so the preacher adjusted his aim.

".38 special," Junior Johnson said. "Bullet will fit into an anthropologist's eye real easy." He pointed the pistol lower. "Extra heavy load. Maybe it'll even go through an ugly Indian." A distant thunderclap punctuated his threat.

He'd been holding his bullet belt up with his left hand, casually so it looked like an affectation. But when the time came for some serious shooting, he released the belt and assumed a two-handed grip. "If you want to save that Injun, Doc, it's time to step out from behind him."

Fred Bennett looked like he might do it but, instead, he stooped a little lower. "This is crazy, Johnson," He looked over the Guarani's shoulder. "We can work things out."

Having the upper hand usually put the preacher in the mood to talk. Glenna thought he might take a moment to gloat. Something that would give the anthropologist time to make a plan. But the preacher's bullet belt and his pants slipped enough to show the elastic band of his boxer shorts, and Glenna knew that would cut the conversation short.

Clouds drifted overhead, thick and growing thicker. Thunder hid the jungle sounds. The local Indians had disappeared, but Glenna knew they were still watching. The preacher knew it too. That was one of the reasons he'd have to pull the trigger.

The Guarani in front of Fred Bennett chanted. It was the first time Glenna had heard him speak. The stream of words was a continuous whisper that didn't stop when he inhaled—difficult to hear even in the silent gaps between the thunder.

"Death song," the preacher said. "He knows there'll be a killing. Only things not settled are the whos and how-manys."

The other twin joined in the chant, words and tones so perfectly matched it sounded like a single voice. Glenna stepped away so she could watch them both at the same time. Identical facial expressions. Identical Guarani twins, each as ugly as the other. Naturally they'd share a death song.

"Gonna count to four," the preacher said. His belt slid past the widest part of his hips and picked up speed. His boxer shorts were riddled with holes and covered in stains Glenna didn't want to think about. How would the local Indians work the preacher's ruined underwear into the oral history of this murder? The western storm lurched across the Argentina border, full of thunder and lightning, building momentum with every second.

"One." The preacher canted his hip, trying to block the steady slide of the bullet belt. But gravity would not be denied. He clamped his knees together, wiggled his hips like a clumsy hula dancer, tried to get the belt to slide past his pants, but it was clear everything would be south of his knees before his count was finished.

"Two, three." He switched to a single-handed shooter's stance and groped for his pants with his free hand, but they had moved beyond his reach.

"Wait, Johnson." The anthropologist sidestepped into the open, away from the Guarani. "We can—"

Glenna knew there had never been anything they could do. She saw it in the preacher's eyes as he struggled to hold up his pants with one hand and kill a man with the other. She saw the exact moment he increased pressure on the trigger. She heard it in the stereophonic death chants coming from Creo and Conozco, louder, perfectly synchronized guttural words.

"Four," the preacher said—at exactly the same time a Guarani twin stepped in front of him.

Any sensible words the anthropologist had were lost in the explosion and muzzle flash.

The smell of blood and gun smoke filled the clearing.

27

Just Electricity

GLENNA STOOD STILL, as did the rest of the group, the way people do when disaster strikes. The preacher's gun belt and pants puddled around his ankles as he watched the saucer shaped red splotch grow across the Guarani's chest. His lips shaped silent words too fast for Glenna to decipher. A prayer? A confession? An apology?

The Indian showed no reaction to the gunshot wound—no signs of pain or fear. The implacable expression on his face never wavered. He chanted his death song without a change of tone or rhythm.

Glenna tried to work out exactly who was shot. The Guarani, definitely, but Fred Bennett's face and chest were covered with a bloody spray. His hook-hand—the only thing he seemed interested in at the moment—had been shattered by the preacher's bullet.

Irregular, bloody circles spread like mushroom rings around thumb-size holes in the front and back of the Guarani's shirt. Through and through. Glenna wasn't sure where she'd heard that term, but it described the situation perfectly.

The Indian's pupils dilated so much they swallowed his eyes. His lips turned blue but continued moving, chanting his death song, perfectly synchronized with the uninjured twin's vermillion lips. One incomprehensible word followed the next. They interlocked like strands in a rope suitable for a soul to climb to wherever spirits go when they can't stay in this world any longer.

Thick, dark clouds, full of lightning and rain, dropped so low they seem to touch the canopy. The wounded Guarani dropped lower too. His knees folded together, and he sat on the grass in the middle of a pool of blood slightly smaller than his shadow. He lowered himself further, still chanting, until he lay flat. His exit wound pressed against a circle of blood that had already expanded past his shoulders.

Glenna knew the circle would be red if she could see it in bright sunlight, but now, in the filtered shadows of the coming storm, it was solid black.

The uninjured twin kneeled at his brother's side, their breathing and their chanting still perfectly matched.

"One soul," Glenna said. "One soul. Two people." She stepped into the circle of blood, held a hand over the dying man's impassive face, felt specks of blood splatter onto her fingers as he breathed his last. She lowered them closer to his lips until a spark jumped the gap.

Thunder rolled over the jungle like an avalanche. The chanting stopped. Glenna stepped back as he exhaled a fog of microscopic blood droplets.

"Done," she said.

Fred Bennett searched for a pulse in the Guarani's neck with his human hand, but it was clear he wouldn't find one. Although no explanation was called for, he told Glenna, "It was just electricity." He looked at her bloody fingers. "The spark, I mean. Nothing mystical. Nothing supernatural." He waited for her to agree with him and when she didn't, he turned his attention to the shattered metal hook-hand that used to frighten everyone but now only frightened him. "Static electricity. That's all it was."

The uninjured Guarani followed Glenna as she walked the few paces between his dead brother and the preacher, her blood-spattered hand extended.

"Just electricity," she told Junior Johnson, reaching for him, wiggling her fingers. "Nothing mystical. Nothing supernatural." Repeating the anthropologist's reasonable words that clearly didn't describe the situation. Her hair puffed out around her head, fully charged with power looking for a place to go.

The local Indians stepped out of the trees so they could be closer to the magic when it happened. The *pombero* boy was nowhere to be seen, but Glenna smelled fermented mangos, sweet and full of alcohol—enough to make a girl's head spin.

She reached for the pistol in the preacher's hand, slow enough so he could pull the weapon away if he dared defy her. He dropped it when her spark jumped the gap. She caught it before it hit the ground.

"Just electricity." It didn't really matter what Glenna said. Ordinary words, biblical words, vocabulary calendar words.... No words could convince the local Indians or Junior Johnson that what had happened was anything but magic.

The preacher stepped out of his pants and ran into the trees. Lightning flashes illuminated his progress.

"Stroboscopic." A vocabulary calendar word that served Glenna's purpose. She picked up the gun belt and fastened it around her while the local Indians, the remaining Guarani assistant, and the anthropologist watched.

"Maybe I should take the pistol." Fred Bennett reached for the gun with his hook-hand, stared at the shattered remains of his prosthesis, then reached with his human hand. At the last second, he pulled back because it seemed he was no longer sure Glenna's sparks were just electricity.

She slipped the pistol into its holster and walked toward the compound. The anthropologist and the Indians lined up behind her.

A storm was no time to use the radio, but Glenna couldn't talk Fred Bennett out of it. "Perilous, hazardous, precarious." No vocabulary calendar word was adequate. She caught his attention with a spark to his nose, but nothing would dissuade him.

The Asuncion police had English-speakers but didn't like to waste them on calls from the jungle after rainy season had begun. Glenna heard them laughing in the background, calling Fred Bennett names that would sound offensive in English but sounded like poetry in Spanish.

The anthropologist put his high school Spanish into high gear. "*Asesinato, homicido, matar, ejecución.*" Finally he broke down and told them, "Murder." He admitted, "*No hablo Español,*" in case they hadn't guessed. Lightning strikes punctuated his attempts to report the murder with snaps and static bursts.

Inconsequential. Glenna finally hit on a vocabulary word that registered with Fred Bennett. The murder of an Indian so far from Asuncion would not get the attention of the police. Indians died every day. No one reported them. No one investigated. No one cared. Indians would take care of things without the help of the police, the way they always had.

The radio speakers screeched a high-pitched burst of static the way a pet cat warns its owner play time is over.

Fred Bennett rolled his chair away from the microphone just as lightning struck the antenna and turned the radio into a fireworks display. Communication was as dead as the man Junior Johnson shot.

"Now what will we do?" The anthropologist knew the answers to a lot of questions but not to the only one that mattered. He slipped the remains of his prosthesis off his amputation stump and dropped it into the trash. "Useless."

Glenna kissed him on the cheek, the way he kissed her not so long ago. The way someone with all the power kisses someone who has none. She stroked the stubble on his face with the back of her hand

and watched his eyes respond and walked out the front door of the vicarage, moving in a way she knew would make Fred Bennett follow her. A way that took his mind off the fact that he was following a simpleminded girl who wore a pistol and made all the decisions.

Glenna looked at him over her shoulder, gave him a smile that pulled him along the way the moon pulls the tides. The compound smelled of rain falling in the jungle. Lightning flashes turned the clouds into an old-time lava lamp.

A congress of capuchin monkeys waited among the cemetery pots. Their eyes reflected the lightning strikes. They showed their needle-pointed teeth. One of them hopped onto Glenna's shoulder. He put a golden effigy into her left hand and accepted a spark of electricity in return.

The capuchin picked through Glenna's hair, looking for lice but found only more electricity. She carried the monkey to the Elizabeth pot in the middle of the compound.

Junior Johnson stepped out of the jungle. No pants, but the elastic on his boxers still worked. "Stay away. Leave Elizabeth in peace."

He carried a stick sharpened on one end, too crooked to be a proper spear but capable of taking a life. He turned the pointed end toward Glenna, held it the way a role player in a medieval fair would hold a lance. Junior Johnson drew a breath and charged her. He leaned into his assault. Every step was turned into a black-and-white still photograph by perfectly timed lightning flashes.

The preacher was much faster than she expected. His face was frozen into an expression identical to the one on the broken solitary pot. She reached for the monkey on her shoulder, grabbed him by the tail and tossed him into Junior Johnson's face.

It didn't take the preacher long to throw the monkey off, but by the time he did, Glenna had her pistol out.

Fred Bennett stood five paces away stringing every peaceful word he knew into a meaningless sentence.

She pointed the pistol at the Elizabeth pot, pulled back the hammer back and fired a shot. Not as loud as she expected. Hardly more than a firecracker pop. Not enough to scare the capuchins that had gathered in the compound yard, but plenty to shatter the pot.

The monkeys rushed the bones, collecting ribs and vertebrae, long bones and the skull. They scattered into the trees carrying bits and pieces of Elizabeth so far and wide there was no way she could ever be collected and imprisoned again.

Glenna handed the golden effigy to the anthropologist. For once he had nothing to say.

One by one, she tipped over the cemetery pots, spilling piles of bioluminescent bones. Monkeys moved out of the forest and collected them. In minutes, the canopy was full of bone sparks moving through the trees.

"Shiners," Glenna told Fred Bennett. The preacher wasn't one of them yet, but it wouldn't take long.

Local Indians filed out of the forest, men—as usual—but women, too. Wives, mothers, and grandmothers joined the men because the situation had changed since the jungle gods sorted things out. Now that Glenna was the one who wore the pistol.

They formed a circle around her and the scientist, talking things over in their asthmatic language, waiting to see what would happen next, the way they'd been waiting for millennia.

An old woman walked out of the circle, as slow and steady as the arrow of time that carried the tribe from the distant past to the present. She matched her steps with lightning flashes so she seemed to disappear in one place and reappear in another.

She extended her right hand slowly so no one could interpret the gesture as a threat. She held her fingers a few inches from Glenna's abdomen, and absorbed the sparks of static electricity that bridged the gap.

"Pombero." The old woman placed her palm on the baby bump.

Fred Bennett reached for Glenna with his hook-hand before he remembered it wasn't there.

"A Guarani word," he told her, as if she didn't know.

"It means magic," Glenna said. She put her arms around him and kissed him on the lips.

He didn't pull away from the sparks.

Epilogue
Now You Know

OLIVIA FUMBLED WITH her seatbelt for the fifth time since she and her manfriend had hired the chicken bus in Asuncion. "This won't fasten, Geoffrey." She looked to him for help but, when he ignored her, she gave up and knotted it around her waist.

The driver spoke to her over his shoulder as he maneuvered around washouts. *"Lo siento, señora. El camino no es liso."*

"He's speaking Spanish again," Geoffrey said. To show how much he disapproved, he pinched her leg hard enough to make her eyes water.

"He's apologizing for something." Olivia forced a smile. She turned it toward Geoffrey first then looked at the rearview mirror. The driver smiled back. Geoffrey didn't.

"No importa." She lapsed into Spanish without meaning to. "It doesn't matter." She translated the message so Geoffrey would know she wasn't keeping secrets.

She considered reminding him she didn't *really* speak the language. It was one of those weird things that popped into her head back when she was struck by lightning. Over the last two decades, it had mostly gone away, but had started coming back when she got the news Glenna was pregnant.

That had been part of what had made Olivia interesting to Dr. Geoffrey Butcher—at least in the beginning.

"It's annoying. I know." She made eye contact with him but only held it for a second before he pinched her again. She took his pinching hand in both of hers, raised it to her lips, and kissed it.

Olivia had learned a few words of Spanish since the lightning strike. It had been almost twenty years, after all. And when she couldn't work them out, she used the translation app on her iPad.

"Lightning and language. It doesn't make sense." Geoffrey pulled his hand away from her and wiped it on his shirt. He massaged his chest for a moment, concentrating on the scar where the doctors had saved his life five years ago and left him with a heart that couldn't keep in rhythm without the help of modern technology.

Olivia watched his lips move as he counted the beats.

"What are you staring at?" He showed her his angry face, the way he always did when he thought about his near-death experience—when his heart stopped for a full minute and he experienced things he didn't quite believe were real.

Olivia saw the driver's eyes watching them in his rearview mirror. He touched the crucifix mounted on his dashboard, crossed himself, and almost ran off the road.

"*Lo siento.*" The driver firmed his grip on the steering wheel and said something that probably meant they were almost there.

"It will all be fine, Geoffrey. You'll see."

Olivia's significant other was smart. He'd figure everything out once they got to Junior Johnson's compound—about the Spanish, about Glenna, about the strange photographs posted on the Glenna Anoli Facebook page.

Geoffrey looked like he wanted to pinch her again but he didn't. That was a start. He fished the iPad out of her backpack and reviewed the Glenna pictures for the thousandth time, trying to make sense of the glowing shapes that hovered in the background.

"This one looks human." He mumbled something about ectoplasm and spiritualism. "This one is a perfect sphere."

Dr. Geoffrey Butcher was a rational man who did not believe in ghosts. He'd told Olivia that a hundred times. But she knew he desperately wanted to believe. The auras in Glenna's pictures looked exactly like things he'd seen on his trip through the near-death tunnel that took him almost all the way to the other side.

He rubbed the scar on his chest as he scrolled through the images of Olivia's beautiful daughter posing with the Reverend Junior Johnson and the local Indians. Every picture had bright auras beside Glenna or behind her. Some of them looked like people. Most of them did not.

The preacher didn't appear in the recent photographs. A new man had taken his place. This one was a scientist like Dr. Geoffrey Butcher, but with an amputated left hand rather than a scar down the middle of his chest. Olivia recognized him from a dream she'd had almost twenty years ago. Another mystery that came with being struck by lightning.

"I need to make sure Glenna's all right, now that she's with child." She sighed. "Maybe bring her back home, if that's what she wants."

"Simpleminded girls don't get to choose, especially after they got themselves knocked up." Geoffrey inspected photos on the iPad—the way he always did—looking for distortions that would indicate they'd been Photoshopped.

"Knocked up." Olivia repeated the words several times, trying to make them sound pleasant. She put an arm around Geoffrey's shoulders and kissed him on the cheek. He wiped at the spot and did his best to ignore her.

"Men are always sweet in the beginning. But eventually all their sugar turns to vinegar." She would have gotten another pinch for that, but Geoffrey was still absorbed in his Glenna mysteries.

"Better not be fake." He rubbed at the spot where Olivia kissed him until his cheek turned red.

"*Es verdad.*" Her Spanish came back again. "It's true, I mean. Mysterious but true." She watched his pinching hand move toward her leg again, but before it made contact the chicken bus stopped.

"*Estamos aquí,*" the driver said.

"We're here," Olivia translated. "You can judge for yourself."

Glenna and her one-handed boyfriend led a parade of local Indians and elderly white North Americans across the compound. It was as crowded as a small Central American village on a festival day. Olivia had seen photos and videos of her daughter on Facebook. She knew Glenna was pregnant but hadn't expected her to be quite so far along.

"My Goodness, darlin', you're so...." She struggled to find a diplomatic word but before she could Geoffrey stepped between them, snapping photographs on her iPad.

A short, muscular, incredibly scary Indian pushed him aside.

"No, Creo. Leave them alone." Glenna spoke in perfect English flavored with a hint of Oklahoma. Not like when she had lived at home and was practically mute.

Olivia turned her attention to her daughter's beau. She recognized him right away as the tall, good-looking man from her twenty-year-old dream.

"My name's Doctor Fred Bennett." He extended his missing hand toward Geoffrey as if he'd temporarily forgotten it was gone.

Olivia's boyfriend looked like he might turn and run. She enjoyed watching him squirm. It looked like Fred Bennett enjoyed it, too.

"Uncle Billy's in a nursing home." She aimed the comment at her daughter. "Never was right after...." She decided to wait for a more suitable time to talk about Billy's condition. "Anyway, he sends his regards." The way Olivia sputtered through those words made it clear to everyone Billy did nothing of the kind. She forced a hug and a kiss on Glenna. Forced herself not to pull away when electric sparks stung her lips and nose. "See your charge is as strong as ever."

Olivia would have said more, but Geoffrey decided she'd wasted too much valuable time already. He shoved the iPad in front of Glenna and Fred Bennett. "Explain this. The auras. What's really happening here?"

The one-handed man turned his back on Geoffrey, which Olivia knew wouldn't make him very popular. He shouted orders at a group of Indians who were setting large ceramic pots in a row.

The ugly Indian Olivia had encountered earlier walked toward an open pot carrying a double armload of bones. A skull fell on the ground, bounced, then rolled over one of her feet.

"My goodness." It was the skull's front teeth that gave her a scare. One of them had an inlayed gold cross she recognized. "Reverend Junior Johnson."

Geoffrey wanted to know what she was talking about, but Olivia lapsed into Spanish and rattled off a couple of dozen words ending with, "El predicador es muerto."

Fred Bennett translated. "The preacher is dead." He picked up the skull and tossed it to the ugly Indian. "Put him in the jar, Creo."

Olivia tried to lean against Geoffrey, but he wasn't in a comforting mood. He shoved the iPad in front of Glenna again. "These glowing auras... tell me what they are."

Glenna looked Olivia's boyfriend in the eyes and said, "Old Carl," as if she were answering his question.

"What?" He shrugged and waited for an explanation.

"That was an old pervert," Olivia said. "Glenna had some dealings with him years ago." She didn't think Geoffrey would want to hear how things had worked out for Old Carl.

Glenna pointed at him and said, "Old Carl," again.

Fred Bennett turned away from Junior Johnson's final resting place. He gave Olivia's boyfriend a stern look but was too far away to stop him from grabbing Glenna by the wrist.

"Damn it!" Dr. Geoffrey Butcher jerked his hand away. Shook it. Blew on it as if he'd been burned. "Damn near electrocuted me."

Only then did he notice his watch had stopped. "That's a Jaeger-Lecoultre timepiece. Cost three thousand dollars."

"Consider that a warning shot," Fred Bennett said.

Geoffrey took off the watch. He shook it. He held it to his ear. "How'd you do it?" He leaned in close to Glenna.

Olivia knew it was too close.

Fred Bennett moved toward them, but Geoffrey's face was already three inches from Glenna's. He was in the middle of a diatribe about expensive watches and spoiled little girls who needed to be put in their place when a spark jumped between them and stopped him in midsentence.

"Maybe you should back off, Geoffrey," Olivia said. "This is no way to get the girl's cooperation."

He was in no mood for cooperation. He was in the mood to rant and pinch, and maybe to administer a slap or two, and no Indians or elderly North Americans or even a one-handed scientist was going to stop him.

The people in the compound formed a circle around Geoffrey, Olivia, and her daughter. Clearly, they were expecting something serious to happen and wanted front row seats. The Americans had their phones and cameras out, collecting new pictures and video to post on the Glenna Anoli Facebook Page when they got back to the good old U.S. of A.

"Geoffrey!" Olivia tried to sound forceful, but her voice was barely more than a squeak. "Things never go well for men who aggravate my Glenna. *Muy peligroso."* She managed to achieve an almost neutral tone. "Very dangerous, I mean."

Dr. Geoffrey Butcher stood as straight and tall as he could manage. He tossed the iPad on the ground and reached for Glenna with both hands.

"No lo haga, por favor." Olivia said. "Don't do it, please." No emotion in her voice this time because she knew it was too late to stop Geoffrey from doing what he always did to uncooperative women.

The North Americans and local Indians closed around Glenna, Geoffrey, and Olivia in a circle so tight Fred Bennett couldn't penetrate it. Phones and cameras documented every move.

"I *have* to know about the auras." Geoffrey clenched both hands into fists.

It was something Olivia had only seen him do a couple of times, but those were unforgettable occasions.

"I have to know!"

The circle of witnesses stepped back, repelled by the force of Geoffrey Butcher's shout.

"Okay." Glenna reached out with her right hand and touched him on the chest.

He jerked and fell to the ground. A seizure shook him violently.

"Now you know."

The crowd parted as she walked toward Fred Bennett, but the North American iPhones and cameras stayed pointed toward the man twitching in the dirt until several seconds after the convulsions stopped.

"We'll have to make another cemetery pot," she told Fred Bennett.

Olivia looked for the chicken bus, but it was gone. She tried not to react when the local Indians started chanting. They edged toward Glenna again as the crowd of North Americans backed further away. She put an arm around her daughter's shoulders, ignoring the jolt of electricity.

"It's okay, Mother." Glenna folded her hands across her belly. "I'm safer here than I've ever been before."

Olivia found that hard to believe. These Indians weren't anything like the Choctaw back home. They looked wilder, scarier, not even vaguely civilized, but no one else seemed worried. Fred Bennett and the stocky Indian man Glenna called Creo went back to stacking bones in a ceramic pot. The North Americans kept taking videos and photographs even as four local Indian men dressed in ragged jeans and rock-and-roll band T-shirts picked up Geoffrey's body and carried it toward the jungle.

The other Indian men and boys followed them, but the women moved even closer to Glenna. She touched them as they came within her reach. They didn't pull back from the sparks the way Olivia thought they would.

"Blessings," Glenna explained. "For their children yet to be born."

The women touched her belly one at a time—reverently and much more orderly than Olivia thought was possible from such a group.

"Pombero," each one said after her turn.

"Spirit boy," Glenna said, as if that explained everything.

The Indian women lowered their heads and backed away, leaving Olivia and her daughter in the center of a circle of North Americans watching everything through the screens of their smart phones.

An elderly man separated from the crowd. He showed Olivia his video of Dr. Geoffrey Butcher dying. A shining sphere separated from his body then drifted toward the jungle.

"First time anyone caught the exact moment." He looked at Glenna for a moment then turned back to Olivia. "You must be very proud."

"Yes," she said. "I knew my girl was special even before she was born. Of course, I *did* have some of the details wrong."

She put her hand on Glenna's pregnant belly. She could feel the life a few inches from her fingers—a head, a pair of hands, a pair of feet. And she could feel a pulse of electricity growing stronger with each passing moment. "What will happen now?"

"No one knows." Glenna put her hands over her unborn child. "But things seem to be following a plan."

Author's Note

JOHN T. BIGGS has always been a fan of cultural diversity. If you come from someplace far away and your people worship pagan gods who live on mountaintops, he wants to talk to you. If you're a member of an indigenous tribe, complete with heroic legends, ghosts, and magic spells, John will listen to everything you have to say. Any cult or eccentric minority that comes with traditional stories will do. But be warned, if they are good, he'll probably steal them. Names will be changed, and plots will be tweaked by the time they find their way to the printed page, but the touch of authenticity that comes from the heart of your culture will shine through.

Strange and interesting people have always populated John's world. His mother grew up in a spiritualist family, so he met people who were strongly invested in ghosts. His father ran a junkyard in a small Southern Illinois town where John met a variety of characters who turn up in his fiction. Copper thieves, and unemployed coal miners frequented Biggs Iron and Metal Works. So did alcoholics, and drug addicts, and people with PTSD before it had a name. Normal customers probably came there too, but John can't seem to remember a single one of them.

It was no surprise when he started writing fiction it came out weird. His genre is hard to place. It's not exactly horror and not exactly mainstream but incorporates a bit of both.

Everything John T. Biggs writes is so full of Oklahoma that once you read it, you'll never get the red dirt stains washed out of your mind. The tribes play a significant role. No authentic discussion of the state is possible without them. Traditional Native American legends are reworked and set in the modern era, the way oral historians always intended.

One of John's stories, "Boy Witch" took grand prize in the 80th annual Writer's Digest Competition in 2011. Another won third prize in the 2011 Lorian Hemingway short story contest. Sixty of his short stories have been published in one form or another, along with several of his novels—*Owl Dreams, Cherokee Ice, The Owl of Death Row, Sacred Alarm Clock,* and *Clementine: A Song for the End of the World.*

Facebook: John T. Biggs
Twitter: @biggspirit

www.johnbiggsoklahomawriter.com